NONE SO BLIND

NONE SO BLIND

XENON

Copyright © 2019 Xenon

The moral right of the author has been asserted.

Apart from any fair dealing for the purposes of research or private study, or criticism or review, as permitted under the Copyright, Designs and Patents Act 1988, this publication may only be reproduced, stored or transmitted, in any form or by any means, with the prior permission in writing of the publishers, or in the case of reprographic reproduction in accordance with the terms of licences issued by the Copyright Licensing Agency. Enquiries concerning reproduction outside those terms should be sent to the publishers.

This is a work of fiction. Names, characters, businesses, places, events and incidents are either the products of the author's imagination or used in a fictitious manner. Any resemblance to actual persons, living or dead, or actual events is purely coincidental.

Matador
9 Priory Business Park,
Wistow Road, Kibworth Beauchamp,
Leicestershire. LE8 0RX
Tel: 0116 279 2299
Email: books@troubador.co.uk
Web: www.troubador.co.uk/matador
Twitter: @matadorbooks

ISBN 978 1789018 363

British Library Cataloguing in Publication Data.
A catalogue record for this book is available from the British Library.

Typeset in 11pt Adobe Garamond Pro by Troubador Publishing Ltd, Leicester, UK

Matador is an imprint of Troubador Publishing Ltd

*For my beloved Jenny, that she might live again in these pages.
And for Gypsy, who set my pen to paper.*

PREFACE

NONE SO BLIND is the first in a series of ten novels that cover a period of about seventy-five years. Each stands alone, though with references to events in earlier books, and some characters appear in more than one.

The series is set in an imaginary world based loosely on a Classical Greek milieu, though transported to a northern temperate zone and with women playing a much more independent role than in Classical antiquity. The military side is largely based on Alexandrian and Macedonian Successor models.

The land of Gea is largely an ethnic, linguistic and cultural unity, though not a political one. Its history has been one of intermittent warfare between its fifteen independent states and with the surrounding countries. However, for the last quarter of a century, the inexorable rise of Troia has welded the states, now provinces, into a formidable empire. Insurrection, civil wars and foreign conflicts nevertheless remain common.

None So Blind is set in the year 499, when the new emperor, Aristogeiton, is proving a weak and vacillating leader.

The Geans are culturally and militarily advanced. Their strength is in the hoplite, a heavily armoured, close order infantryman, fighting in a disciplined line with shield and long thrusting spear.

Cavalry is relatively unimportant, generally used for scouting or pursuit of a defeated enemy.

Light javelin armed infantry, called peltastes, and missile troops, or psiloi, with bow and sling, play a supporting role.

The army has a complex command structure, based on ektatoi, equivalent to modern non-commissioned officers, of whom the most important is the feared hyperetes, best regarded as a sergeant-major. Above the ektatoi are line officers of various ranks, culminating in strategoi or generals.

Many cultural and military terms are left unexplained, as the context should suggest the basic meaning, and more is unnecessary.

At the end of the book, information can be found under the following headings:

Glossary	332
Major characters	344
Minor characters	346
Measurement	350
Ranks in the Gean Army	352
Map of the Provinces of Gea	354
Map of the Sea of Grass	355

Other maps are available at http://www.harpalycus.com.
The Chronicles of Gea   356

THE SMALL SCRIBE laid down his reed pen with his usual meticulous care, then knuckled his eyes savagely. It was tiring work, especially in the ever-shifting light of two torches. He stretched and kneaded his gnarled and ink-stained fingers with his other hand, before picking up his pen again. He would not sleep yet. He had a tale to tell.

ONE

17th day of Metageitrion. Year 499. Gla.

DIOMEDES CANTED HIS heavy aspis shield back, with the rim on his shoulder so that it bore most of the weight, and took a firm grip of his lead-weighted wooden practice sword. He moved slowly around the sandy arena, trying to manoeuvre Gelon into facing the late afternoon sun.

A spatter of household troops had gathered on the edges of the sparring ground to watch their swordmaster. No-one was taking bets on the outcome. Gelon was a big man. Very big, and with strength to match. Moreover, he was surprisingly fast for his size. But they knew Diomedes.

Gelon crouched low behind his battered shield, the sigil of a cockerel almost obliterated by countless blows. He wore a Korinthian helmet, and all that could be seen of him were malevolent eyes glittering behind the narrow slits.

A buffet of shields, and both drew back. The bigger man made a half-hearted feint, which Diomedes simply ignored, but then Gelon tried a full-blooded rush, relying on brute strength. Diomedes, spare of frame but stronger than he looked, deflected him neatly with an angled shield, his sword licking out like a snake's tongue. Gelon just managed to twist out of the way before hastily retiring.

There was silence as they cautiously circled one another, until a sharp voice shattered it. 'Swordmaster!'

Diomedes' shield dropped slightly, and he glanced to his right, whence the call had come. Gelon instantly saw his chance, and his sword whirled out towards his opponent's exposed head. Exactly as anticipated. The swordmaster had already thrust his aspis upwards, catching hand and sword and stretching them up with the momentum. A heartbeat later, he had dropped to one knee and swept his sword round to hammer with numbing force against the exposed greaved leg.

'Ouch,' cried Gelon, which, considering the force of the blow, was commendably restrained of him, and collapsed in a tumble of bronze.

Diomedes pushed his sword into the sand, slid off his shield, rested it against his hip, and gratefully removed his helmet and leather skull cap. He scrubbed his hand through his short, damp hair.

'Bastard,' said Gelon, thrusting his aspis from him and sitting up, glowering. 'You arranged that.'

'Sorry,' said Diomedes as he unlaced his cuirass. 'Not at all. But the instant I heard it, I knew what you'd do if I offered the bait. Never refuse an opportunity.' He gestured to one of the watching hoplites to take his equipment and turned to the young man who had called out. 'You should know better, Patroclus,' he said mildly.

'I beg your pardon, Swordmaster.' Patroclus's tone was that of a man who could not care less. 'My Lord Miltiades wishes a word with you at once.'

Diomedes nodded. He glanced down at Gelon, who was gingerly removing his bronze greave to reveal an already spreading bruise. 'Better get some cold water on that,' he said and strode off across the courtyard towards the citadel.

The spectators drifted away as Gelon hauled his big frame to his feet. He pulled his helmet off, revealing long, oiled, red hair caught back in a ponytail. He glared after Diomedes with real venom. 'Bastard,' he said again.

TWO

MILTIADES WAS SITTING at his work table reading a scroll, when Diomedes opened the door. To one side, his secretary, Adrastus, was busily copying something from a wax tablet.

Miltiades was the holder of Gla, a rugged fortress that, as one of the Five Fetters of the Empire, blocked the southeastern approaches to Gea, holding the border against the restless barbarian tribes that ranged the lawless lands beyond. Standing near the Great East Road that ran from Ilios to Leuctra, it thrust out of the endless, undulating grasslands of the Vale of Tempe like a fist bursting from dark chasms below.

Generally affable and well liked, despite an explosive temper, Miltiades was a tall, handsome man with a fine head of obsidian-black hair. He continued to read as Diomedes entered, vaguely gesturing towards the wine amphora. The swordmaster gratefully poured himself a third of a kylix and topped it up with spring water. It was hot work sparring under a blazing late summer sun.

'Some water?' he asked.

Miltiades had stopped drinking wine several moontides ago as it gave him fire in the gut. The holder shook his head absentmindedly. Diomedes stood and waited patiently, sipping his drink.

Eventually, Miltiades sighed and put down the scroll. 'Sorry, Dio. Have a seat.'

Diomedes did so. Miltiades scrutinised him. He saw a tall, wiry man in his late forties, his short hair beginning to grey. His angular face was marred by a pair of long, puckered scars, one that ran from his left ear to the corner of his mouth, another emblazoned across his forehead. The skin was tanned, and his eyes lay within a web of wrinkles spun by years of screwing them up against the sun.

'I was watching you. Should you still be sparring? Isn't it time that you left the training to some of the younger lions?'

Diomedes shrugged. 'When they start beating me.'

'Even you have to admit that the years are taking their toll. None of us is getting any younger.' He spread his hands out in a gesture of resignation. 'I know. I know. The usual platitudes. But they happen to be true.'

'Platitudes frequently are. I trust that this is not a veiled invitation to yield gracefully to a younger man, complete with fanciful descriptions of spending the evening of my years dozing peacefully in the sun.'

Miltiades grunted and shook his head. 'I've probably got the best swordmaster and military advisor in the Empire. I'm not letting you go that easily. I'm afraid that snoozing in the sun is not going to be an option for some time. However, and not suggesting anything by it, shouldn't you be training up someone?'

'I am. Ilus.'

Miltiades was slightly surprised. 'Not Gelon?'

'Most definitely not Gelon. He's a bully. And he hasn't got the nous.'

'Ah, bullying is not part of the job, then? But doesn't hanging recruits upside down from the ramparts constitute bullying?' Miltiades struggled to suppress a grin.

'I did not hang him upside down from the ramparts,' protested Dio resignedly. He knew that the story was going to ignore his denials. 'I merely showed him that it was a long way down, and informed him if I caught him dozing on guard duty again, he could measure it for himself. The tale has vastly improved with the telling.'

'Such tales generally do. It will all add to the legend. I might embellish it a little myself.' He smiled at the expression on Dio's face. 'You're stuck with it.' He passed across the scroll. 'Latest news. Read that.' He rubbed his chin. Dio still couldn't get used to him without his beard. Why he had shaved it off was a mystery.

Dio scanned the scroll and looked up. 'I'm not surprised. This pot's been ready to boil over for some time.'

There had been a significant border clash between Laomedon, warden of the Debateable Lands, and Lycidas, the satrap of Thessalia, over Laomedon's 'pacification' of the marsh people known as the Stymphalians. From what Dio had heard, Laomedon's brutal response to their initial dogged resistance amounted to genocide, and the terrified population were now fleeing wholesale for the safety offered by the tolerant Lycidas. It seemed that Laomedon had pursued them into Lycidas's neighbouring province, and it had come to the spear clash in a full-blooded battle.

Miltiades kneaded the bridge of his nose. 'So, what do you think?'

Dio considered. 'Neither wants conflict. There's no real advantage to be gained. Laomedon simply overreached himself. He made the bad mistake of meeting Thessalian cavalry in open country and paid the price. He assumed that he could bully Lycidas, but I know the man, and there's iron there. That insolent bastard's been taught a serious lesson. He may not be the brightest, but Laomedon has some good advisors and does occasionally listen to them. There will be a bit of posturing, a lot of outrageous lies, the bigger the better, perhaps even a minor skirmish or two, then it will all die down.'

'So, what do you suppose the emperor will do about it?'

'Aristogeiton will do nothing. As usual. He probably thinks a bit of bickering between his satraps keeps them occupied.'

'My opinions exactly,' declared Miltiades.

Always are, thought Dio. He would undoubtedly hear them, almost verbatim, at the next staff briefing.

Miltiades got up and stretched before walking over to the window. The sun streamed in, and dust motes whirled and sparkled. 'How's the new intake coming along? When they're the right way up, of course.'

'Highly amusing. Not bad. They're getting there. I've weeded out four no-hopers, but there's a couple of promising lads.'

Miltiades looked over his shoulder. 'Don't forget that symposium this Selenes. I know you and your scroll of a hundred excuses to get out of going to symposia. It's an order from on high.'

That meant Kal. Dio felt somewhat gratified.

Miltiades returned to his table, taking back the proffered scroll as he did so. 'By the way, what were you planning for tomorrow morning?'

'Thought I might take the new recruits for a stroll.'

Miltiades rolled his eyes. 'Meaning a sixty-stadia half-and-half jog, cross-country, under full armour.'

'Not at all,' said Dio mildly. 'I was looking at a hundred.'

Miltiades laughed. 'You do know that your official title is not swordmaster, but "that bastard swordmaster"?'

Dio remained unconcerned. 'Wouldn't be doing my job if it wasn't.'

'Well, their little stroll will have to wait. Kal wants to go on a rove in the morning. She says she's bored, and she's giving me substantial earache. Do me a favour and take her.'

Dio pulled a face. 'So that my delicate ears will take the beating instead. Thank you so much.'

Miltiades waved a dismissive hand. 'Don't start looking for sympathy. You give as good as you get, and you know it.'

'I wish,' muttered Dio, getting up to leave.

As the door closed behind him, Adrastus placed a scroll before Miltiades for signing. The holder penned his neat signature, then sat back with folded arms.

'Have you done it?'

'I have,' said Adrastus, with a self-satisfied smile, 'and subtly done too, if I may say so myself. No-one will guess its source.'

'They had better not.' There was a touch of tetchiness in Miltiades' tone. He rose and walked over to the window again to look down on the sparring ground. It was deserted.

'Have you considered Gelon?'

'I have. He's not suitable. But he may be useful in a peripheral role. Merely promise him the position.'

The holder swung round to fix Adrastus with a javelin glare. 'I will need it in writing, you understand.'

'Naturally,' said the secretary imperturbably and began to gather up his writing materials.

Miltiades turned back to gaze at the Sea of Grass and across to the purple peaks of the distant Rhodopians. 'Endings and beginnings,' he murmured. 'Endings and beginnings.'

THREE

They walked along a low grassy ridge, bows in hand, quivers slung on their hips. Kalliste was Miltiades' wife and a striking woman, handsome rather than beautiful, but with a strength of character and innate confidence that gave her natural dominance in any company. She was of medium height, graceful and shapely. Her oval face had strong features and a long, full-lipped mouth that was made for smiling. Her dark brown eyes were large and expressive, and her light brown hair, still showing no tinge of grey, was piled up in a complex structure of coils and ringlets, two braids falling to frame her face.

As usual, she was laughing, pleased that she had won the last round, a handbreadth nearer the prominent thistle for which they had been aiming. Consequently, it was her choice of target.

'That stump, sixty paces.' She pointed.

He nodded, checked his arrow shaft and nocked it to the string. He estimated the distance as accurately as he could, gauged the strength of the breeze on his left cheek, and relaxed into his shooting stance. He preferred the modern draw to the jaw rather than to the chin. He took up the tension, sighted, waited until he was still, and gently rolled his fingers from the string. The arrow traced its graceful arc across the vast blue of the sky, but drifted left and missed the stump by a good two handbreadths to bury itself in the grass beyond.

'Bad luck,' she said, with manifest insincerity.

'The breeze shifted,' he complained.

'Excuses plant no barley.' She lifted her bow and sighted. The arrow flew true and thumped into the stump with a satisfying thwack. 'I win again. That makes it seven-five to me. Perhaps I should take over your duties.'

'I'm a swordmaster, not a bowmaster,' he grumbled.

They walked toward the stump to retrieve their arrows. 'You're coming to the symposium, of course. I told Milt to make it an order. Otherwise, you would probably stay in your room reading a scroll. Or wandering the walls terrorising poor little recruits.'

'Ah. You heard about that, then.'

'Certainly did. I'm told the poor lad nearly died of fright.'

'If I'd been an Aggie, he would have been genuinely dead. It was a lesson he won't forget for a while.'

'Nor will the rest of his intake, from what I hear.' She stopped and pointed down into the hollow to their left. 'Small thorn bush and the rocky outcrop. The exact midpoint between the two.'

He raised his eyebrows. It was a very long shot. 'You're first this time.'

She took her stance, then lowered her bow again. 'You didn't really dangle him by his ankles?'

'No, I didn't. I just showed him it was a long drop and mildly intimated that he was not keeping a thorough watch.'

She nodded. 'I told them that you wouldn't dangle him by the ankles.' She looked slyly at him from the corner of her eyes. 'Not by the ankles.'

Dio felt an embarrassed flush warm his cheeks. He never knew how to respond to Kal's occasional innuendos. 'I can't think what you mean.'

'Don't worry your head about it. You'll get one of your headaches.' Kal lifted her bow and took careful aim, angling high for distance. The arrow described its perfect parabola and landed well short and left. 'Dyaus damn that wind.' She glared at him. 'Any sentence containing the words barley and excuses will precipitate immediate physical violence.' Her eyes glinted dangerously.

'Never said a word.'

'Don't. And that pathetic look of mock innocence could be removed to your advantage.'

He grinned and took his shot. It wasn't brilliant but fell undoubtedly closer to the designated spot. 'Seven-six,' he said. 'Not so triumphant now.'

'I've got to be careful not to cause too much damage to your fragile ego. It's a delicate balance. I've been walking it for nigh on twenty-five years.' She suddenly smiled. 'I remember meeting you for the first time. I thought you terribly correct and forbidding. I was convinced that you didn't like me at all. I even wondered if you were resentful of me coming between you and Milt.'

'You thought I was forbidding? I was terrified of you. You were so self-assured and confident. I think that I would rather have faced a mob of extremely irritated Dryops. And you haven't changed all that much either.'

She laughed. 'You'd better believe it. Your choice of target.'

FOUR

THE SYMPOSIUM HAD finished. Miltiades had sensibly embraced the new fashion that allowed men and women to partake collectively in the feast, but nevertheless insisted that the men should remain for the traditional wine and conversation after the meal, while the women withdrew to 'gossip as much as they wished'. Kalliste had returned to bid their guests a good night, especially the bumbling strategos in whose honour the evening had been held. Miltiades had certainly raised a clear enough signal banner by yawning mightily and muttering about a long day on the morrow before withdrawing to his private rooms with almost impolite haste. Dio did not bother rising from his couch. It had become customary that he remain behind to talk to Kal for a while. She returned from seeing the last of the guests out and flopped down wearily onto the couch alongside his.

'Some wine?' he asked.

'Please.' She lay back and closed her eyes.

He signalled to the two slaves who stood unobtrusively either side of the main door, and the lad brought him an amphora of Rhodian red and a silver kylix, the older man a pitcher of water. Dio mixed it one third wine to two of water and handed it to her.

She sipped the wine gratefully. 'I had a scroll from Aglaia. She sends her love.'

'How's Pyrrhus?'

She could not keep the fond smile from her face. 'He's well. She was telling him about her Uncle Dio, and now he wants to be a swordmaster when he grows up. He has a fine wooden sword, and Aglaia says he has killed lots of yarrows.'

'Wait until he has to face nettles.'

'So, how did it go in here?' Kal asked. 'It was certainly dour work in there. Why can't I stay and talk about important things instead of listening to Iocaste grumble on about the cost of fabrics, and Aella almost popping out of her chiton to tell me that Icarion has a mistress. As if I didn't know already, and as if I cared an obol's worth.'

Dio laughed. 'It couldn't have been more boring than it was in here. Apollophanes must be the most tedious man I've ever met. How he got to be a strategos, I'll never know. Still, he'll be on his way to Leuctra tomorrow, thank Dyaus.'

'So, what did this tediosity talk about?'

'The best way to train horses, his unbelievably close relationship with the emperor, and the scandalous price of slaves.'

She glanced at him sharply. 'Don't you dare tell me that you didn't discuss other things.'

'Attic goat's cheese?'

She threw a cushion at him. It was her usual response to his teasing. 'Behave. It's the only reason I let you stay. Because you talk to me properly instead of assuming that I'm a silly woman with nothing in my head but the babbling of babies and the drone of idle gossip.'

'Let me stay?' He feigned astonishment. '*Let* me stay? All I wanted to do was to get to my bed. Milt managed it with expert subtlety. I'm not so lucky.'

'Are you telling me that you do not want to stay and tell me all that was going on? That you would cheerfully leave me in a state of total ignorance?' She smiled happily at him.

Dio spread his hands. 'I should know better,' he said simply.

'You certainly should. Years of training and you're still not there. Most would give up on you as a hopeless case. I am made of sterner stuff, however. Now tell me what you were really talking about.'

'Horse training and the price of slaves. Oh, and attic cheese.'

She sighed. 'I've never been one for violence. But when it is richly deserved, I'm prepared to make an exception.'

'And the political situation,' he added. 'But you wouldn't be interested in that. Not a baby within babbling distance.'

She glared icily at him. 'Exactly what about the political situation?'

Dio pulled a face. 'It's a bloody mess, not to hone too fine an edge on it. Aristogeiton is losing his grip, if he ever had one. And someone is going to put on the sphairai.' The reference was to the bands of ox hide worn round the hands of boxers.

'And who would that be?'

He made an exaggerated shrug. 'Your guess will be as close to the wand as mine.'

'Is this a game I can play too?' She pretended to consider the question deeply, and then cocked her head to one side. 'Laomedon? At a venture.'

She was no fool. Dio tilted his head. 'That's where I would put my drachma.'

'This battle between him and Lycidas. Has Aristogeiton intervened? He can't really allow his satraps to go for each other's throats, can he?'

Dio frowned. 'Perhaps he might this time. It may be the final cut that shocks him into action. His response could be swift and merciless. He might even deliver a gentle rebuke.'

Kal looked distressed. 'That would be dreadful! Could he not limit himself to a gesture of mild disapproval?'

'An imperial tut, perhaps,' he offered. 'Though obviously not too loud.'

'The almost imperceptible rise of an eyebrow,' she countered.

He grinned. 'I can't beat that.'

'I win again!' She suddenly regarded him suspiciously. 'You don't let me win, do you?'

'How else could you possibly manage it?' he said cheerfully.

'Lying toad.' Another cushion flew at his head. 'So, what caused it all?'

'Laomedon's attempt to pacify the Stymphalians.'

'I hear it's difficult.'

'It is indeed.' The Stymphalians were an indigenous people who now occupied only the Marsh, a large, desolate area of isolated islands, reaches of treacherous swamp, open lakes and a labyrinthine network of secret tracks, many hidden below water level and defended by submerged, sharpened stakes. This almost impenetrable fastness lay between Laomedon's domain and Thessalia.

'But I thought he was doing a good job?'

Dio pursed his lips. 'It depends upon what you consider good. There are some very unpleasant tales coming out about his methods.'

'I've heard some of them. Probably exaggerated. Besides which, you can't tame a place like that without breaking a few heads.'

'Children's heads? Babies' heads?'

Her eyes widened in horror. 'You're not serious.'

'I'm afraid I am.' He paused. 'There are times when men lose control, but this is policy. Carried out in cold blood and covered by a cloak. Choosing his men. Destroying the evidence. But I've spoken to those who've been there. There's no doubt.'

'What did the others think?'

'They mostly thought that it was what the Stymphalians deserved. Serves them right response. Much the same as you.'

'I'm sorry,' she said, white-faced. 'I didn't realise.'

'All except Rad.' Radamanthus was Miltiades' deuteros, and Dio liked him. He could think for himself and was prepared to say what he thought.

'Did Milt agree with all this?'

'He said that it was regrettable, but that Laomedon was getting the job done. In the long voyage, it was *sadly* necessary.' He shook his head, then added quietly, 'It may be worse.'

She looked up sharply.

'Laomedon is building up a large and seasoned force, talking to a lot of satraps and gaining a reputation as a man of decision and action. Aristogeiton is doing nothing. There are rumours.' He shrugged. 'It may be nothing. Fevered imagination, but…'

'Do you really think he's aiming for the throne?'

He nodded. 'He's a member of the Imperial Family with an inflated sense of his own importance.'

She glanced across at the two slaves who were standing against the farther wall. She leaned forward conspiratorially and whispered, 'Listen, Dio. I need to talk to you about Milt. I'm concerned about him.'

He shushed her and looked at the slaves, making a circular motion with his index finger. Stone-faced, they about-turned and faced the wall. She looked back at him, clearly puzzled.

'They can probably lip-read.'

'They can what?'

'Lip-read. It's a fascinating skill many slaves have developed. They watch the shape of your mouth, and work out what you're saying from it, even when they can't hear you.'

'They can do that?'

'Some of them extremely well.'

Her eyes flicked around as she considered the revelation.

He added, very quietly, 'Under the circumstances, best we don't talk here. I suggest we go riding tomorrow. Officers' Call tomorrow, so how about the fifth dekate? Then we can talk freely.'

She nodded, then put her hand in front of her open mouth and widened her eyes in mock horror. 'So they will have heard,' she paused and frowned slightly. 'Seen, rather, everything that we said in there?'

'I thought you merely babbled of babies and complained incessantly of the price of cloth.' He was no longer whispering.

'Oh, we talk of far more,' she said severely. 'Of husbands and… and men and things.'

'All very discrete and proper, I'm sure.' He was enjoying himself.

She treated him to a withering look. 'It's not funny. The ladies can be a little direct at times.' She giggled. 'I've just remembered what Dorithea told us about her husband.'

'Oooh. Do tell.'

'Not a chance. Ask one of the slaves.'

'I might do that.'

'As if! You would be turned to stone with boredom.' She looked slyly at him. 'Might not though, if you knew that you were the major topic of conversation. After Icarion and his mistress, of course.'

'Me?' He was scandalised. 'I've done nothing that throws me into that arena.'

'Oh, you don't need to have *done* anything, my dear. In fact, it's the *not* doing anything that's the problem, if you understand what I mean.' Her eyes were bright with mischief.

'Well, whatever it was, I don't want to know.'

'Of course you do. Don't be silly.'

He considered. He sighed. 'Very well, what were they saying, then?'

She smiled triumphantly. 'Why you have no woman. They know that you aren't a man lover.'

He rolled his eyes.

'They have decided, therefore, you must have a secret mistress.' She looked around her, then said in a stage whisper, 'And they know who it is.'

He stared at her. For a heartbeat, he was bereft of speech, and, when he spoke, his voice sounded almost strangled. 'Who?'

She laughed delightedly. 'Why, me, of course. Surely you'd guessed.'

He was horrified. 'You! They didn't say that?'

'Of course not. They wouldn't dare. But I can hear hints that have all the subtlety and restraint of dumping a pile of bell cuirasses into a stone storage pit.'

'You corrected their misapprehension, I hope.'

'I most certainly did not. I just smiled serenely. Much more fun.'

'Dyaus Pitar,' he groaned. 'What am I going to do with you? What will Milt think, for Athen's sake?'

'Milt's too engrossed in other things. Besides which, he knows you. None better.' She waved her hand dismissively. 'He'll ignore it as the ridiculous nonsense it is.'

Dio frowned. 'I wouldn't be so sure. Rumour and calumny can overpower truth.'

'That sounds very profound. I might even agree with it, if I knew what it meant.'

'You know perfectly well. No matter what Milt believes, the fact that such a rumour is circulating will require him to act.'

'Herakla save us! He's the one that suggested you escort me to Ilios for the Dionysian theatre. He goes off to his bed and leaves us arguing all night. As I said, he knows you. We've all been friends for twenty years.' Her tone was suddenly fierce. 'No empty-headed gossip or rancid old woman is going to break that friendship.'

'Nevertheless, I really think that it's time I went. You do realise that every one of the ladies will be up at their windows to check when I leave.'

'Well, slip out through the stable block, then. That'll teach the nosey bitches. They'll be up all night.'

'Don't make it worse.' He looked seriously at her. 'This could cause difficulties.'

She held up a hand. 'Pooh. It means nothing. It's a poor joke. You, of all people, should appreciate it, with your execrable taste in humour.'

'I wish I was as unconcerned.' He rose to go. 'You sleep well, Kal.'

'You too, Dio. And don't fret about such silliness, for Dyaus's sake.'

FIVE

Dio stood on the walkway of the inner wall and looked out across the two concentric lower walls to the Sea of Grass beyond. It was a mysterious and monochrome place of racing shadows as ragged clouds tumbled across the full moon. It seemed almost a new and alien landscape. He was in a meditative mood. Kal's revelations had disturbed him. These silly rumours, no matter how dismissive she was of them, could create problems. And it made him face the normally repressed fact that he was closer to Kal than he ought to be for his comfort. He did not love her, dream of her or lust after her, but she was important to him. More important than he cared to admit, though he wasn't sure in exactly what way.

He had always had a strange response to women—wary, intimidated, even fearful. Not of them, but of the dangers of any serious relationship. He could socialise well enough, but was fearful of any suggestion of intimacy. He told himself that it was a sensible concern about becoming ensnared, trapped in a world beyond his own iron control, but there was a deeper fear. His almost visceral reaction to the slightest physical touch was evidence enough. He kept all women at arm's length, both metaphorically and literally. Only strength of will kept him from flinching from even the most innocuous contact.

However, Kal had never been a menace. She was safe, happily married, a doting mother and a natural homemaker. She had never seemed to threaten his carefully constructed defences. They were happy and at ease in each other's company, but nothing more. Friends. Just friends. But he now had an uneasy suspicion that she had somehow crept through his guard. As all too often, there was no certainty, no firm ground beneath his feet. The world seemed to him a reflection on water, a false picture, inverted, disturbed by ripples of unease; yet he dared not raise his eyes to the uncompromising solidity of its reality.

He knew full well that he was a coil of contradictions. A man with real talent, but ever doubting it. A man who lacked self-confidence to an uneasy degree, yet could show the face of self-assurance with such apparent ease that no-one recognised it as a mask. A man who could speak with confidence and skill, erudite and articulate, able to address armies and fire their souls, yet with stops and barriers that sometimes held words in his mouth, words that should be said, and that he yearned to say. A man well-liked and respected, able to socialise, regarded by many as a friend, but ultimately knowing it all to be hypocrisy. He was, at heart, a loner.

Nevertheless, beneath this choppy surface of dissonance and paradox ran a deeper and barely discernible current. A long-suppressed ache and need he refused to acknowledge, save for the dread of its rise like the kraken from the depths.

He wore his persona like his armour, impressive, impenetrable, a gilded show; but the soft and snivelling organism within mewed with terror that this armour might fail. He could find no answers.

It was dark now; the moon obscured by thickening cloud. He could see nothing beyond the walls of the fortress. He could hear movement below, murmurs of conversation, a sudden burst of laughter, the creak of leather and ring of metal. The guard was changing. Everything was changing.

SIX

'AND THAT'S IT,' summed up Miltiades. 'A bit of posturing and a lot of noise.'

Antenor, a long-time eilarches at Gla, caught Dio's eye and winked. He knew where the briefing had come from. Dio pulled a wry face.

'So, the emperor's taking no action,' said Radamanthus. A statement, not a question.

'Not as far as I know.'

'Never bloody does.' There was a murmur of agreement from around the large table.

'Apollos hasn't pulled his strings this morning,' said Antenor. There were several chuckles. The seemingly complete domination of the emperor by the leader of the Imperial Council was well known and widely resented.

'Let's get back to business,' said Miltiades curtly.

Twenty-five senior officers were gathered at the large

table in the briefing hall of the citadel, with Miltiades at the head, Radamanthus to his right and Dio to his left. Behind Miltiades, at his graphotrapeza, a tall writing table, sat Adrastus, Miltiades' secretary for two years now.

Dio did not like him. Not at all. A tall, spare, balding Phthian, what was left of his hair worn long and tied back in a ponytail with a rather silly bit of red ribbon, he had an angular hooked nose and a prominent throat apple. He was urbane and efficient, with a superficial servility that could not hide the arrogance beneath, like silk showing through a beggar's betattered tunic. He had the air of a vulture waiting for something to die.

Icarion, a bull-necked, bald syntagmarches, and the one with the new mistress according to Kal, held up a hand. 'Could I ask about this Aggie raid on those steadings towards Choraea? Are we looking to a response?'

Agrianians, the bane of the life of the eastern steaders, regularly snuck out of their mountain fastnesses to rustle cattle, and were not above rape, murder or pillage. Every so often, an expedition would be mounted from Gla. It would march into the mountains, the Aggies would disappear, and the army would burn towns and villages in retaliation. It kept things more or less under control, though woe betide any Gean detachment that got separated from the main force.

Miltiades glanced at Dio for the reply.

'Dressed like Aggies, but masked and speaking Gean. Didn't smell like Aggies either.' There was a ripple of laughter. 'Local lads up to no good. Not our responsibility. Passed on to Raxamenes.'

'The Aggies have been relatively quiet for two years now,'

said Miltiades, 'and I don't propose launching the trireme unless we have real cause.'

'I would have thought being an Aggie was sufficient cause in itself,' someone at the far end of the table muttered.

Miltiades glared down the table, his fist clenched and his face suddenly white with fury. He relaxed with a visible effort. 'There will be no response,' he said curtly.

Dio rested his chin on his hand. Miltiades' already volatile temper was shortening, reacting too easily to the slightest provocation. Just a weak joke in bad taste. Kal was right to be concerned. There was something darker about him, like the first shadows of winter.

Antenor lifted a languid hand. 'Anyone know anything about this Monce preacher and his little flock who've appeared in the town? It's caused trouble elsewhere. Three or four have been lynched, and there was a full-blown riot in Ascania.'

Dio glanced across at Theagenes, an elderly syntagmarches, who was known to be a Monist. His long face was dark and glowering like a storm about to break. This new and growing cult of the 'One', to the deprecation of the rest of the Gods, was causing real unrest. People, fearing that the Gods would respond badly to such disrespect, tended to react violently.

Miltiades looked at Theagenes as well. 'You must know what's going on. Get the message across that we don't want any public display. I don't want any bloody riots here.' His voice was sharp and irritated. Theagenes nodded briefly. Miltiades glanced around. 'Well, that's it. Thank you.'

There was a murmur of voices and a scrape of chairs.

SEVEN

Kal, already mounted on a fine, spirited bay, was waiting for him when he arrived at the stable block. 'Good afternoon, Dio,' she called. 'Here's a philosophical conundrum for you. Who watches the watchers?'

'And one for you. Can you step into the same argument twice?'

She laughed. 'A philosophical duel to the death, then. No unattributed misquotations, and the first to cite Aristobulos loses.' She was dressed in the manner of the Western Thracians, with loose baggy leggings and a short, belted tunic. It was a beautiful sunny day, and her cloak was rolled across the saddle cloth behind her.

He looked up at her with the familiar lift in spirits that he felt whenever he saw her. There was an odd sense of almost proprietorial pride which he chose not to analyse.

A groom was patiently waiting with his horse, Blackwing, and Dio stroked her muzzle affectionately before swinging himself up onto the thick saddlecloth.

'Should we take a turn round the courtyard first?' she asked, tossing her head. 'I would hate to disappoint Helena.'

'Stop it, Kal,' he growled. 'It isn't amusing. I was awake half the night worrying about it.'

'Oh Dio, don't be a bore. It's just gossip. It comes and goes, and nobody takes any notice of it. Believe me. It's the sea in which we swim. What little waves do break simply subside again, and all is as smooth and calm as before.'

They walked their horses through the serpentine route that twisted and turned from the central courtyard, through the two offset gates, to the main gatehouse. Dio acknowledged the sentries' salutes as he and Kal left the fortress and passed through the huddle of houses and shops beyond.

'All very poetical,' he said at last. 'But what has it to do with the real issue? If it becomes general belief, then Milt will be forced to do something about it. He has a status to uphold, whatever his personal views.'

'Everybody goes through the rumour press sooner or later. If you have no dark secrets, they'll invent them. And who asked you to go for a rove with me a se'ennight ago, for Herakla's sake?' She pursed her lips. 'And who, for that matter, complained about his delicate ears taking a beating?'

He looked at her, all innocence. 'I've no idea. Who was it?'

Her extravagant snort of derision was impressive. 'Look, if Milt is happy enough to send us off on a rove together, he's not exactly worrying about his reputation, is he? So you can stop worrying too. It's a lot of fuss over nothing. Wish I'd never told you.' They pulled up their horses to allow a couple of young men to cross the churned-up street. They had red blankets draped over their shoulders and carried walking staffs. Their god guards were large and brazen letter mus set in a circle. They must be part of that group of Monists mentioned by Antenor.

'Anyway, why are you so dismissive of poetry?' asked Kal as they rode on. 'You're always saying that much of our thinking seems beyond our control. That it appears without authorship was, as I recall, the phrase you actually used. You even claim that you don't know how you are going to finish a sentence when you start it. Yet you manage to. So, if your much-vaunted rationality is fashioned in some mysterious way that is beyond your control, how do you know that it holds any more truth than other modes of expression, such as poetry?'

'Because poetry doesn't even pretend to relay practical insight or positive answers to problems. Its truth, if that's what it is, is vacuous. Essentially meaningless. Or so trite and banal as to be disregarded.'

'And what determines this banality? Your rationality? Perhaps poetry is equally dismissive of logic.'

They passed beyond the final tumbledown houses and into the surrounding countryside of the Vale of Tempe, the Sea of Grass. All that could be seen was a seemingly neverending vista of rolling grassland pocked with just a few stunted trees struggling to survive in the poor soil. That, and the almost cloudless sky from which the sun blazed down remorselessly. Only occasionally, a distant cluster of rude buildings would come into view that constituted a steading, where tough individualists wrested a harsh living from the land's sparse resources.

They pushed their horses into a canter, and skylarks and meadow pipits rose in alarm before their hooves. 'A fanciful thought,' said Dio. 'And the day a strategos wins a battle by writing a poem, I might give it some consideration.'

She furrowed her brow for a few heartbeats, then gleefully intoned, 'Go, put the horses on the left, where foes are of support bereft. And place the archers on the right, to where the shieldless flank's in sight.' She bowed mockingly as they slowed their horses to a walk.

'That would actually need to be on the left, oh great military genius, which makes my point for me. Because you are giving rational orders, but just put in rhyme.'

'But you never made that a qualification. You implied that a strategos could not win a battle by writing a poem. And he could!'

At one of the few streams in the arid landscape, its course marked by the occasional rowan, they stopped to allow the horses to drink.

'The qualification was in the context. We were discussing the relative merits of poetry and rationality, not some weird hybrid of the two.'

'You're the one always pontificating about precise and exact language. Suddenly we have to assume a context. And who decides this context? You, I suppose.'

'Well, in this case, it happens to be manifestly obvious.'

'Pish. In *your* opinion. I suppose that now, whenever an argument is going against me...' She frowned momentarily. 'I think it happened once in Gamelion, in eighty-six; I wasn't well that moontide. Anyway, I can now simply change the context, and the ground will shift under your argument quicker than Poteidan could get angry. This I like.'

They splashed through the rivulet and cantered up the gentle slope beyond. It was a fine day with just a few fair-weather cumulus clouds idling across the sky.

He could see the awful possibilities only too clearly. 'All right. All right. I yield the point.'

'Yes!' she cried, so loudly that a roe deer started from behind a clump of thorny bushes and bounded away, its white rump brilliant in the sun. 'First blood to me, Swordmaster.'

'Can't help it if I'm in an inordinately generous mood.'

'Pish. Well beaten and you know it.' This was what had brought them together, a shared delight in argument for its own sake. The subject was immaterial. They pulled their horses back to a walk and rode on in companionable silence. They could squabble like two dyspeptic coots, as Miltiades had once inelegantly described it, or simply be in one another's company without needing to say anything at all.

A blue-grey bird sped by on scythe-like wings, low over the shivering grass. Dio pulled up his horse to watch it go. She stopped too. 'What was it?' She was only being polite. She had as much interest in wildlife as he had in poetry.

'A merlin.'

She nodded mechanically. But her mind was elsewhere. She looked directly at him. 'Dio, how is it that you always know so much about what's going on? Milt says that you're always one step in front of the phalanx.'

He made a dismissive wave of his hand. 'It's my job,' he replied. 'I have to know what could be a threat to Milt before it is one.'

'It's the slaves, isn't it?'

'Sometimes,' he admitted. 'But largely I make sure that I know, and am on good terms with, those who survive by knowing; the wanderers, merchants and bards, jugglers and thieves. And I listen a lot. But I'm not that good. Consider your spear thrust of last night.'

She chuckled. 'That's because you don't listen to women. If you did, you really would learn some things.'

'I'm not at all sure that I would like to. I think I would rather remain in sublime ignorance.'

Both horses had begun to graze the sparse grass. A rare cloud passed in front of the sun, and it immediately felt cool. She slid gracefully down. 'Come and sit. We need to talk.'

'I thought we were.'

'Talk properly.' A couple of rounded, erratic boulders provided the seating. The horses continued to graze. The cloud passed, and the sun pulsed back into warmth. He waited. She was looking away.

She sighed and looked back at him. 'What's wrong with Milt?' She was unconsciously rubbing the golden pomegranate of Herakla that hung round her neck. When she turned to the comfort of her god guard it was a sure sign that she was seriously troubled.

'Wrong?'

'I've never known him to be so distracted or uncommunicative in all the time we've been together. Even in the worst days of the Thracian War. It worries me.' She was thoughtful for a few heartbeats. 'Milt has changed,' she said. 'His temper is worse. He's lost all sense of fun. He seems preoccupied with something, more distant, more secretive.

He's no longer the man I knew. He's hiding something, and I don't know what. And it frightens me. He's so far from me now, and he doesn't seem to trust me anymore. But he trusts that long, thin, supercilious prig.'

He had to smile. She undoubtedly meant Adrastus.

'That man has no sense of humour,' she continued moodily. 'He rarely smiles, and when he does it's yellow teeth and nothing else.' She shuddered. 'His eyes are as dead as a codfish at Soli market. I've never heard him laugh. Have you?'

He shook his head.

She grimaced and returned to her original question. 'I don't suppose you know what it is?'

'I don't. I wish I did. But I must admit I've felt the same thing. Milt did have a meet with a furtive visitor about ten days ago. But he's never seen fit to mention it to me.'

'I saw the man arrive, hooded, in the middle of the night. I asked Milt about him, but he told me it was official business. I overheard mention of the Emperor. And Laomedon.' She paused, then said carefully, 'Do you really think Laomedon is planning a move against Aristogeiton?'

'I do.'

'And Aristogeiton is a waste of space and Apollos is nothing but a reed shield?'

'As chief councillor, Apollos has the power, but neither the ability nor the inclination. And the satraps wouldn't exactly jump to his commands. When the head is weak, the arm lacks strength.'

She nodded as though that settled the matter beyond all possible conjecture. 'It will come to civil war,' she whispered. 'And Milt will have to choose sides.'

Dio did not want to say what was in his mind. It felt like betrayal.

'He's chosen already, hasn't he?' The question was blurted out, forcing itself past the block of her mind as a great gate crumbles to the ram. She looked slightly surprised at herself.

Dio did not immediately reply. When he did, he was careful with his words. 'I don't know. I have no reason to think so.'

'But?' said Kal bleakly. 'And there is a *but*, isn't there, spoken or not.'

Dio shook his head wearily. 'I suspect that you're right. I'm sorry.'

'There was that mysterious visitor. He's never spoken about him to either of us, so it must be something.'

'He's never been one to emblazon his thoughts on his shield.'

She gave him a wan smile. 'There's the wolf accusing the lion of savagery, if ever I heard it.'

'I'm not the one in question.'

She made no response, staring out over the Sea of Grass, her face set hard and her eyes as distant as the hazy line of the Rhodopians to the north. There was silence for several heartbeats. 'What's he getting into?' Her tone was flat, but he could hear an undercurrent of despair. 'I thought I knew him, Dio. I know that he's ambitious, but...' Her voice trailed away. She seemed close to tears.

'We still don't know. Perhaps we're seeing things that aren't there, making too much of it all. There may be other explanations.'

'We're not. I know. I feel it. I know it.'

He was silent. He was as sure as she was. She looked at him again, catching his eyes. He shifted uncomfortably. He rarely made eye contact with Kal, careful not to look at her beyond the briefest of glances. Now he felt vulnerable, as though she could see through his ever-present guard to some shadowed truth lurking beneath.

'Laomedon and you,' she said. 'You have a history.'

'We do.'

'You've never told me about it. I've heard rumours. Some rather more imaginative than others.'

He thought back. 'When Milt was seconded to Kerakos, four years ago, you remember?'

She nodded.

'Laomedon had just been made warden. Puffed up like a toad with his own self-importance. He's an arrogant son of a bitch, unpleasant and cruel, not exactly your jovial symposium companion. He took to sparring every morning. He's strong, fast and quite skilled, but it was obvious that his opponents were making damn sure that they lost. Even Zeuxis only managed a draw, which was farcical.'

'Who's Zeuxis?'

'The Imperial swordmaster. Anyway, the bastard was swaggering around as though he was Achilleus. Then he decided that he was going to don a plumed helmet by going one better and actually beating a swordmaster. I declined. He baited me until I had to agree or be seen as a coward. I was advised to lose. You know me. That wasn't an option. I should have been more circumspect, though, but he had seriously pissed me off.'

He was back in the training ground in Krak, a dank, misty morning, a revolving ring of intent faces as he moved round, his bare feet digging into the cold, damp sand. Before him, a bear of a man, wide chested, powerful arms and legs, his face hidden by his helmet. Only the porcine eyes peering through the narrow slits and the condensation from his breath hanging in the air told of the man within an envelopment of bronze.

Laomedon charging, swinging his lead-weighted wooden sword with full intent, not holding back as the training ground demanded, but grunting with the effort. Dio parrying and stepping neatly aside, again and again, not availing himself of the frequent opportunities for the riposte and 'killing' stroke.

Dio shook his head slightly, then picked out the bones of the story for Kal. How Laomedon had tried to goad him with insults, to make him lose his temper, but he had kept control. Until the Krak swordmaster, acting as marshal, had called for a halt. Dio had removed his helmet for comfort, whereupon Laomedon had surged forward and taken a wild swing at his unprotected head. He had instinctively ducked beneath the blow, which would otherwise have probably killed him; then, blood boiling, he had gone for the bastard. A flurry of fast strikes had knocked Laomedon's sword aside and bypassed his wildly waving shield with practised ease, landing blow after blow on his cuirass and helmet until the panicked man had lost his balance in his hasty retreat. Dio had hooked his foot around the anchor leg and then contemptuously pushed him back, so he hit the ground like a falling tree. He had put his sword to Laomedon's throat, before raising it in ironic salute and walking away through a grim silence.

'So, I gave him a lesson. Humiliated him, not to hone too sharp an edge to it. It was stupid. Unforgivable.

Unprofessional. He swore revenge. Milt was furious. He hurled me back to Gla quicker than a slingshot. That's why I returned two se'ennights before him.' He became thoughtful. 'I wonder if it could be that Milt and he came to some sort of understanding at that time. He never mentioned my behaviour on his return.'

'You never told me of this.'

'I didn't think it was the kind of thing you'd want to know. Besides, I was ashamed of myself. I should have had more sense, more control.' He shrugged. 'But what's done is done. You can't unwring a chicken's neck. There's no way that I could ever support that pig-headed whoreson. If Milt declares for him, I shall have to leave.'

She opened her mouth as if to say something, then gave a weak shake of her hand. 'Who shall I argue with then, for Herakla's sake?'

'I won't have a choice, Kal. That bastard's an unforgiving dog turd with a long memory. I'll be marked down. Not on his priority list at the moment, but the time will come. A man's misdeeds will seek him out. I run, or I fight. The one thing I can't do is stand still and wait for the javelin to strike.'

She said nothing.

He sighed. 'Let's just hope that we have read it wrongly.'

Overhead, skylarks rose in a cascade of song. In the distance, three corvids were mobbing an obviously irritated buzzard. They sat in silence, lost in their thoughts.

EIGHT

Dio stood in the shadow of the main gate and watched the man ride away until lost in the oncoming tide of night. He was a big man, gaunt-faced and balding, his long jaw disfigured by a large wart. Dio wondered why he didn't grow a beard to hide it. He certainly seemed to be disguising his receding hairline with a red headband. Three times in recent se'ennights, he had ridden in to speak to Miltiades and Adrastus, and had been closeted in the holder's office for the whole day, arriving and leaving in the dark. But never a word from Miltiades about it. It was troubling.

'Who is that creepy bastard?' The distinctive voice came from behind his left shoulder.

'Wish I knew, Rad. He has the smell of trouble about him.'

'Don't even know his bloody name.'

'Pheidon. Seemingly one of Raxamenes' men.'

Raxamenes was the satrap of the Thebeaid. Although Gla was in his territory, as one of the Five Fetters it was under direct Imperial command, and he had no authority there. But he certainly had influence.

Dio sighed. 'But that's all I can find out. Just down as a messenger and says less than a tortoise with lockjaw. Outside of Milt's office that is. I just hope to Dyaus that Milt knows what he's doing and isn't getting into murky waters.' He turned, and the two walked back towards the central courtyard, following the tortuous route that threaded its way through the two inner offset gates.

Radamanthus was a stocky man, with thin greying hair, rather protuberant ears and a gravelly voice. Dio got on well with him. He was a no-nonsense professional who knew his job and was a natural leader of men. He made up his own mind and wasn't afraid to speak it. Which is why, despite his real ability, wealth of experience and a combat record second to none, he remained a mere telarches, while well-born and well-connected but useless imbeciles, like Apollophanes, were strategoi.

'Raxamenes hunts with Laomedon,' Radamanthus said.

'I know.'

'And I keep hearing disturbing whispers about that particular pungent pile of pigshit.'

'So do I.'

Radamanthus stopped and turned to face Dio. 'Do you suppose that there's anything in them?' He wasn't the sort to use the slaves' entrance when there was a front door.

'Dyaus forbid. But my instincts say yes.'

'Well, I hope they're wrong this time. Just for a bloody change.'

'They're either always right or always wrong. And my instinct is to say they're always wrong,' said Dio with a straight face.

Radamanthus wore a look of perplexity as he struggled with the conundrum, then gave up. 'You're too subtle for a simple soldier boy like me. I'm off duty. How about a drop of decent red at Fat Delia's?'

They retraced their steps to the main gate and emerged into the squalid and makeshift sprawl of Glapolis, the town that had grown up round the fortress, catering to the garrison and passing trade on the Great East Road.

A hundred paces or so beyond, a small crowd had gathered. A short, gnome-faced man, wearing a long, black gown with a pointed, red-lined hood, had climbed onto a small cart to address a group of belligerent-looking locals. Behind him crushed five followers; four young men, all clean-shaven, and a girl. They wore prominent god guards and carried red blanket rolls slung over their shoulders, with staves in one hand and blazing torches in the other.

The leader had a thin and reedy voice, but was not lacking in enthusiasm. 'The Monos is the all, the One. Praise be to the Monos. Come the Great Awakening and only those who have heeded His call will rise to a new and better life. Those who ignore His holy words will have their names erased from the Book of Life as though they had never been.'

'You can start with my wife,' yelled someone, and there was a bawl of laughter.

'Bloody Monces,' muttered Radamanthus. 'Must be that preacher chap.'

The preacher had made the mistake of positioning himself near an overflowing trough. A man at the back of the unimpressed crowd bent, scooped up a handful of mud and hurled it at the Monist. It missed and splattered full in the face of the girl standing behind him, who shrieked and clawed at the mess. There were howls of mirth and derision from the spectators. Several stooped to follow suit. Dio made a quick signal to the gate guard, and a dilochagos with eight hoplites came down the street at the ram.

The first assailant was just gathering his second handful, when he was hauled upright by a grip of iron on his collar, and an authoritative voice demanded that they all stand very, very still. They all did. In heartbeats they were surrounded by a ring of wicked-looking spearheads. There was the quiet slop of mud balls dropped surreptitiously to the earth.

'If you would be so kind as to take these young enthusiasts into protective custody,' said Dio to the guard commander. He raised his voice. 'The rest will disappear. Very quickly.' The crowd sensibly did not debate the issue, and made themselves scarce with impressive dispatch.

'Bring that Monce priest to me,' said Dio. The dilochagos grabbed the small man by the shoulder and thrust him before Diomedes. He was pale and visibly shaking.

'Now,' said Dio, amiably enough, 'you can talk about your beliefs to whom you like, if they're prepared to listen of course, but not at the top of your voice in the street. It causes trouble, and I don't like trouble. I catch you playing this damn fool game again, and I will have you in a cell so fast that you will pass a very surprised Pegasus.' He glared at the man, whose eyes dropped. 'Do you understand?'

'I do, sir.' His tone sounded meek enough.

'Very well. Dilocho, take this bunch to the gatehouse lockup, and release them in a dekate.' The dilochagos saluted and began to usher them away.

'Stop wriggling,' demanded Dio. The slightly built man in his grip subsided into immobility. Dio swung him round to face him, studied him carefully for several heartbeats, then nodded slightly. 'As for you, I ever see you within a hundred paces of a Monce, and you and I will discuss it on a one-to-one basis, if you take my meaning.' The man did, and nodded furiously. Dio released his grip on his shoulders. 'Now, bugger off.' The man duly buggered off with some alacrity.

Radamanthus was grinning. 'Well, I wouldn't recognise such a scruffy nonentity again, but I bet he believes that you would, and that's all that matters.'

'Green-flecked eyes and a scar on his left earlobe where he lost an earring. No problem.'

They strolled on down the churned-up street. 'So, what's that business of blankets over their shoulders all about?'

Dio laughed. 'I asked Theagenes. The Book of Truth says that every true believer must rest their heads at night beneath a roof, so they always carry the makings of a small tent just in case. As usual, some have found a way round it. Never let religion come between you and your comfort. Two short rods in a scabbard and a small square of fine material. They often wear it as a red neckerchief. They can then construct a little lean-to shelter just for their heads if needs be. That remains within the word of the law.'

'I'd say you were feeding me donkey carrots if I hadn't noticed Theagenes' scabbard. I did wonder. Mind you, I heard that they keep their women in order, so they can't be all bad.' He thought for a moment. 'But didn't someone tell me they don't marry?'

'Marriage is frowned on, but accepted, though the religious leaders can't marry. That's why divorce is so easy amongst them. For the man. Naturally, the woman has no such right. Nor any right to challenge it. And divorcés can't marry again. Or, at least, only if their previous spouse has died.'

'Who in Hades would want to get married twice? Once you've disturbed a hornet's nest, you make damned certain not to disturb another one.'

Dio raised an eyebrow. 'Surely it's not that bad.'

'How would you know? You've never had the displeasure.' He looked back up the street to where the last of the sectarians was being ushered into the guardhouse. 'They going to be a headache?' he asked.

'Don't think so. They're just enthusiasts. It'll pass.'

'I'm not so sure. I've even heard rumours of army units made up solely of Monces. In Mykerenos.'

'So have I, but why on Dyaus's Earth should anyone want to raise such a unit? They would stop fighting to chant a hymn or something. Last thing I would want is a Monce watching my back.'

Radamanthus chuckled. 'He would probably be picking his spot for the knife thrust.'

They continued to a rather shabby drinking establishment that lurked beneath the faded sign of a bunch of grapes. Night had fallen, but it was still quiet. In the flicker of oil lamps, a couple of locals were lounging in a corner, a group of hoplites were getting down to some serious drinking, and Gelon was sitting by himself, nursing a kylix of wine, his huge hands almost engulfing it. He glanced up, looked stone-facedly at Dio, took a final drink and left without saying a word.

They watched him go. Radamanthus spoke. 'I'm told you're training up young Ilus.'

'He has the makings.'

Fat Delia rolled across, true to her name, and put down two kylixes of wine on the greasy and stained table before them. 'We don't usually see such august visitors here this time of night.' Her breath was short, and she wheezed her words. She smelt unpleasantly of sweat.

Dio glanced at the two local lads in the corner. 'Look just like civilians to me.'

Fat Delia shrieked with laughter, which rapidly degenerated into a fit of coughing. 'You do make me laugh,' she managed to get out once she had gained control of her larynx.

'So it would appear,' said Dio, and Delia wobbled off back to her stool, still chuckling. 'Tell me again why you come here?' asked Dio.

'Wine's good, and Fat Delia will laugh at anything. Makes some men imagine they are wits.'

'That worked for you, then?' enquired Dio innocently.

'See what I mean?' Radamanthus chortled in a self-satisfied sort of way then addressed himself to the wine. It wasn't bad at all. 'You know that Gelon and his sycophantic crew have been giving Ilus a hard time?' he said after a while.

'I know.'

'He wants the position of swordmaster.'

'I know that too. But Milt gave me the choice.'

'Aren't you going to intervene? Keep the evil bugger off Ilus's back?'

'No. He has to deal with it himself. If he can't, he won't get the job anyway.'

'You're a hard man.'

'Had a hard teacher.'

'Who did teach you? There aren't that many swordmasters around these days.'

Dio put his kylix down and leaned back. 'Pandarus of Ithome.'

Radamanthus choked and nearly sprayed wine out with surprise. He gaped at Dio. 'He was the finest swordmaster ever.'

'So they say. I've certainly never seen a better.'

'How did you get him as a master?'

'Do you want the long version, or the short?'

'Short'll do.'

Dio shrugged. 'Saw me fight. Took me on.'

'On second thoughts, the longer version might be preferable.'

Dio grinned. He wouldn't give the full version, though. How he had been born a bastard and his mother had never spoken of his father. He knew nothing of him. He had loved his mother, the one person in his life with whom he had never had to pretend, with whom he could talk openly and feel comfortable and safe. She had been vivacious and gregarious, with a bubbly sense of humour and a kind and generous nature. Rather like Kal, in fact. She had suddenly died when he was in his early teens, and he had been left with his grandfather Perimedes, a cold and distant man who had as little to do with him as possible.

Perimedes had been a wealthy merchant and not beyond a little usury on the side, so the family was not popular. Together with Dio's bastardy, this led to a difficult childhood amongst his peers, and he had learned two things which seemed contradictory on the surface. The first was to fight and fight well, so few cared to cause him trouble; but he had also developed a superficial affability, the knack of accommodation and the use of humour to defuse tension.

He didn't think Radamanthus would appreciate such a preamble, so he began in the middle.

'For various reasons, I had to learn to look after myself and got pretty good. Or, at least, I thought I was. Thought I was the Golden Gryphon, in fact. With my reputation, some were tempted to try me. Make a name. One lad came at me in the agora, with a knife. Broke his arm and walked away without breaking sweat. There was an elderly man watching, holding a staff. Bald as a vulture but straight as a lance, and looking as though he had been carved in granite. He said, "You're good. But you'll be dead within the year." I laughed at the old fool.

'He whipped his staff across, flicked me off my feet, and had the end of it pressing against my throat before I knew what was happening. He just glanced down and said, "Let that be a lesson, boy. No matter how good you are, you will always, sooner or later, meet someone better."

'Then he looked at me as though seeing me for the first time. "Three pieces of advice," he said. "For free." Well, he had my full attention, as you might imagine. He could have crushed my windpipe just by leaning forwards.

'"Always expect the unexpected. Because it's going to happen.

'"Knowledge is life. Learn everything you can about every person, every place, every situation you encounter. You never know when it could save your life.

'"And always plan ahead, consider every possibility. Then take every advantage you can, fairly or not. Forget honour. Weight the knucklebones in your favour whenever possible. Then, with luck, you might make eighteen more moontides."

'He removed the staff and walked away. Well, I jumped up and ran after him. I said, "I know a fourth." I still cringe when I think how callow I must have sounded. He stopped, though he never looked round at me at all. "What might that be?" he asked. "Find the master who can teach you such things," I said. Well, at the time I thought it clever. Perhaps it was, because he finally turned and looked at me. "You'll do," he said. "Come along, boy," and strode off without another look and me following.

'And that was that. Moved into his school the next day. My grandfather was unconcerned, so there was no problem.'

Dio became thoughtful. 'Pandarus was getting old and had never had any children. I think he wanted to pass on all his skills as a kind of bequest. He became the father I never had. He worked me hard, and there were plenty of times when I cursed him for it, but he knew his business. I've been grateful for his training and advice more times than I have hairs on my head. And don't even think of making the obvious comment.'

Radamanthus spread his hands out in a gesture of wounded innocence.

Dio drank some wine and stared into the distance, seeing something more than Fat Delia overspilling her stool. 'He died of the coughing sickness, the year Idomeneus I came to the throne.'

'That would be four seventy-one,' said Radamanthus.

Dio nodded. 'I've only ever cried twice. Once for my mother. And the other time for a pitiless old man who never called me anything but boy, and who never gave me a word of praise. Strange, that.'

'It's a strange world,' said Radamanthus sententiously, and took a long drink of his wine. 'So, this planning ahead business. People talk about these scuttle bags of yours. Is that what they're all about?'

'Certainly is. Dry clothes and weapons, boustria and cheese, full water flask, rope, flint and kindling, some basic medicinal herbs like feverfew and willow bark and so forth. Wrapped up in greased fleece. Grab one and you have what you need to survive. Been very useful on occasion.'

Radamanthus looked interested. 'You'll have to give me a list.'

'Glad to.'

There was a comfortable silence as they concentrated on the wine. Fat Delia came over, rolling mightily from side to side, to enquire if it was to their taste.

'Certainly is,' said Radamanthus cheerfully. 'Long, red and fills a hole as though it were made for it, as the temple virgin said to the high priest.' Dio winced. Fat Delia howled with laughter.

'You!' she said. 'You do make me laugh.'

'See what I mean?' chuckled Radamanthus as she waddled off. Dio cast his eyes heavenwards. Radamanthus changed the subject. 'Why didn't you join the army? Dyaus, you could have been a strategos by now.'

'Can't take orders, especially stupid orders given by such mindless imbeciles as that old goat, Apollophanes.'

Radamanthus grunted. 'Tell me about it.'

But that wasn't really the truth, reflected Dio. It was true as far as it went, but much more important was his well-hidden fear of responsibility. He could advise Miltiades what to do, knowing that he would almost certainly follow his advice, but the thought of ordering men into battle himself, of being personally responsible for their deaths, terrified him. Which was strange. Because, when necessary, he had found that he was the one who stepped forward and took the hard decisions, seeing both the problem and the answer, whilst others waffled and panicked. He could do it when he had to, but the abstract thought of doing it unmanned him. A swordmaster who does not like killing, but who kills without hesitation. A leader who fears responsibility, but who takes it. A soldier who hates war, but who lives by it. A man who craves love, but who desperately avoids it. A thing of contradiction and paradox. He looked over at Radamanthus, drinking his wine, secure in himself, more or less at peace with his world. Why could he not be like him?

NINE

It was more than a moontide since the symposium, and Dio had not seen Kal in all that time. Not that this was unusual. Gla was a huge fortress, and Kal spent much of her time in the holder's rooms near the top of the citadel, while Dio was busy with the training of the new intake of recruits. He had also needed to liaise with Aristandros, in Leuctra, over increasing incursions by the Thracians across the Athos, and that had taken him away from Gla several times.

He was working the intake hard because he was worried. An increasingly strong current of discontent, with swirls and eddies of growing factionalism, was sweeping throughout the Empire. Famine and food riots in Thalassa, a slave revolt on the Argenusae, and the pirates based round Rhodope taking a worrying toll of shipping. There was the ongoing friction between Laomedon and Lycidas that could burst into flame again at any time. And the Eretrians, old and implacable enemies of the Geans, were flexing their muscles once more. The holder of the Akrochalcis, the great fortress that guarded the strategic Chalcis Pass, was screaming for reinforcements and getting none.

All the signs were that the Empire was losing control. How long before it burst asunder in civil war was unpredictable, but that it would seemed more certain every day. Miltiades, for once, did not seem to be listening to him, downplaying the problems, decrying the risks, proving a positive little optimist. Kal had been right. He had changed. What was behind the change was what worried Dio above all. At least, with the browning of autumn, the campaigning season was coming to an end. They had the cold and gloom of winter to survive, and there would almost certainly be no open civil strife until spring. But spring would come.

TEN

I T WAS EVENING and Dio was reading a scroll on the life of Antisthenes by the shifting flame of an oil lamp when there was a tap on the door. A slim, young slave girl, dark-haired and doe-eyed, entered, her eyes demurely fixed to the floor. He recognised her as one of Kal's girls.

'Swordmaster.' She had a very soft, small voice, almost a whisper. 'My mistress asks that you receive her. She needs to speak to you. Unless there is any objection, she will come in a dekate.'

Dio was surprised. Kal rarely came to his rooms, and then just to call, in passing, for a quick word. 'Of course. Please tell her that I look forward to seeing her.'

The girl looked embarrassed and coloured slightly. 'I was told to say that the dekate was to give you time to tidy up your tip of a room. I'm sorry, Swordmaster.'

Dio smiled. Typical Kal. 'Tell your mistress that I am

grateful, and that I will sorely need every hekate, but I'll do my paltry best.' The girl looked around, clearly puzzled, then bowed her head and slid back quietly through the door.

Dio glanced around his small room, seeing it with her eyes. He had the meticulous tidiness of an old campaigner, and his room was fit for inspection by the most exacting hyperetes at any time. It was cosy, with a decent fire in the hearth and the cold of a dull autumnal day kept at bay by a thick leather cover over the window opposite.

It was frugally furnished, though on either side of the hearth were alcoves, one partially shelved and holding his precious collection of scrolls, the other containing bow stands, arrow boxes, and a rack of his swords. In the corner on the opposite side of the door, his armour was hung on a wooden crow, his shields on the walls behind.

Mounted on the wall above the hearth were his three treasures. There was a Thracian rhomphaia, a vicious scythe-like weapon, with a superb, intricately-carved bone handle, and a sword from the Ch'n of the distant east that could be sharpened to such an edge that it would cut silk. Finally, a simple, functional, but beautifully balanced kopis, with its elegant curved edge. It had belonged to Pandarus and had been the old man's final bequest to his protégé.

He got up and closed the door to his bedroom, checked that he had ample wine, and sat down again. He could not imagine what Kal needed to speak to him about, especially in such an unusual manner, and with such short warning. The children? Miltiades? Something about himself? Was she in some sort of trouble? He had no idea.

He threw some more wood on the fire, and it crackled and spat in annoyance. Time seemed to hang in the air like a cloying mist. The wait was endless, until it all suddenly clicked back into place with a sharp scratch on the door. Kal entered, huddled tightly within a hooded cloak. He rose to help her take it off.

'Thank you.'

Even in the poor light of the oil lamp and the flickering gleam of the fire, she looked weary and wasted. Her face was almost gaunt, and there were dark shadows beneath her dull eyes, which held none of her usual laughter and mischief. 'Kal,' he said, shocked. 'Whatever is the matter?'

She made a vague gesture, a slight lift of her hand that might have meant anything, and went and sat down on one of the couches.

'Sit down, would you, Dio?'

He did so. She sat on the couch across from the fire and stared at its cheerful blaze.

'Kal,' he said softly. She did not respond. 'Kal. What is it?'

For several heartbeats, he thought she was going to remain silent. Then, her voice toneless, she abruptly said, 'Milt is going to divorce me.'

The words he could understand. But their content eluded him. It just made no sense. He stared at her. Bereft of speech. She continued to gaze into the fire.

Eventually, he managed to speak. 'Why?'

'I don't know. He says that *he* doesn't really know why. It's something he needs to do. In some way, he needs to be free of me.'

He asked the obvious. 'Is there someone else?' He belatedly recognised its ambiguity, but Kal, usually the first to pounce on sloppy language, seemed not to notice it.

She shook her head. 'There are slave girls. But they're not meaningful. He changes them as easily as I change my chiton.'

Dio could still not fully grasp it. Miltiades and Kal had been a constant for most of his adult life. He regarded both as his friends. It was inconceivable that it could just end. Like this. A disturbing thought suddenly struck him. 'It's not… rumours, is it?'

She finally looked at him. 'No. I actually asked him if it was that. He laughed. He said he had heard the talk, but the idea was just too silly. He knew us both too well. When I said I needed to talk to someone, it was he who suggested I come and see you. Though that was what I intended anyway. But he said that you were my best friend. You had been his friend, and still were, but he knew that I had become closer to you over the years. That I needed your friendship more than he did.'

There was a pleading note in her voice. A need for confirmation. For reassurance. She looked so lost. But the words wouldn't come. Something stopped him.

'What can I do?' he asked helplessly.

She smiled for the first time. It was a poor effort. 'What you are doing, Dio. Listening to me. I really needed to talk to someone who would not immediately assume that I'm to blame. Not paint me in scarlet and studded sandals. You know what will be said.' Her voice suddenly held pain. 'But you won't believe it of me?' Her eyes caught at his. 'You won't assume that I'm a whore, will you, Dio?'

The emotion in her voice told him that it was a serious question. Divorce was not taken lightly, and this was the automatic presumption of many when it happened. 'Oh, Kal. Of course not. How could you even think it?'

'Because people will. You know they will.'

And he knew they would. Dyaus's balls, but this was a mess.

She looked back into the heart of the fire. 'Why is he doing it? I thought that, being a man yourself, you might understand Milt, and explain to me what's going on in his mind.'

'I'm sorry. I've no idea. He must have said something to you.'

There were tears in her eyes, reflecting the ruddy gleam of the fire. 'He did. He said that he just doesn't find me attractive anymore.'

Dio definitely should have said something then. He knew exactly what he should have said, but he couldn't. He said nothing.

She looked back at the fire. 'We've not been intimate for many years. We've slept apart for a long time. But I still thought Milt was my friend, my husband. I knew he was changing. I didn't like to think of it. I think I deliberately refused to face it.' She paused. 'It was the twentieth anniversary of our wedding last year. We celebrated it. You remember. That night I made a special effort to look good and went to his room. He just said that he was tired and rolled over away from me.'

'Do you still love him?' He found it difficult to say. His voice sounded unnaturally thick.

'I thought I did, but now I think it was nothing but a lazy habit of mind. I don't feel anything for him now. Just lost and abandoned.' The tears began to flow again.

Dio sat still and silent. Trapped by his wards and guards. A bug in amber. He knew that he was failing her and could do nothing about it. Eventually, he forced himself to speak. 'Do you think that it's really over?'

She nodded miserably.

'When did he tell you this?'

'A se'ennight ago. I've hardly slept since.'

'What will happen? Have you spoken of it?'

Her head dropped, and she sat for a few heartbeats, regaining control. Then she spoke haltingly, the strain sounding in her voice, 'He's promised to make sure that I'm comfortable. He suggested that I take over the country house at Leuctra, or go to live with Aglaia. But I want to stay at Gla.' She glanced up, her eyes beseeching. 'My life is here.'

He wondered if he was hearing more than she was saying. The thought disturbed him. 'What does he say to that?'

'He says, if that is my wish, he can find a suite of rooms sufficient for my needs. But it would be on the understanding that I stay well away from him. I don't understand why he's so deliberately hurtful.'

'People sometimes are when they feel guilty. They shift the blame onto the other.' He had the uneasy suspicion that he merely sounded pompous.

'I've been a good wife to him, borne his children and brought them up well, supported him and advised him, run his household, organised his social functions and massaged his ego. What have I done wrong?'

'Nothing,' he said decisively. 'Don't start blaming yourself.'

'It must be me. I've failed him in some way.'

'Why is it not that Milt has failed you?' he asked gently.

She did not answer. 'Why the disgrace of a divorce?' she asked, after a while. 'We were effectively living separate lives anyway. Surely I'm not that hideous?'

The iron bit curbed his tongue. As always. 'I don't understand it. I'm sorry. I'm not being a great deal of help to you. Do you want me to speak to Milt? He might talk to me.'

'Would you, Dio? I would be grateful. You're his friend as well as mine. But you will stay my friend, won't you?' Her voice was pleading.

'Of course I will. How could I not?'

She smiled gratefully at him. 'Thank you. I got a scroll from Aglaia yesterday. How am I going to tell her?'

Dio was silent. He had no answer.

She looked at him imploringly. 'Will you write to her and tell her? I don't think I can.'

'If that's what you want, of course I will.'

She nodded sombrely.

'What about Antinous?' he asked. Aglaia and Antinous were Kal's two children, now adults. He dreaded what this news might do to them.

'Antinous worries me most. He has the trappings of a man, and a soldier at that, but he's far more sensitive than most people realise. It will hurt him. And he won't be able to show it. It could twist him. Milt doesn't see these things.'

A log shifted and a flare of orange-yellow light threw a soft glow across her face. He looked away.

'No,' she decided, 'I'll write to Antinous. But I cannot tell Aglaia. She loves her father. I fear that she'll fall between the wolves and the lion. Tell her gently, Dio. You know her.'

He nodded. 'Do you want me to say that the scroll is at your request?'

'Yes,' she said instantly. Then, after a pause, 'But try and explain.'

'I will,' he promised. They sat in uncomfortable silence. Eventually, he broke it. 'Kal. I'm sorry. I don't know what to say.'

'What is there to say?' she replied listlessly. 'I'll go now. Come and see me, please, when you've spoken to Milt.'

'Of course I will. Is there anything else I can do?'

'I don't think so.'

'If there is anything at all, you know where I am.'

She rose and smiled at him. But her eyes remained bleak. 'Thank you. I needed a friend.' He helped her on with her cloak and opened the door. She turned on the threshold, opened her mouth as if to speak, then shook her head and hurried off. He watched her go, feeling abject. She had left with precious little to comfort her. He returned to the couch, sat down and brooded.

He had given her nothing. He should have held her, told her that she was still beautiful, that any man who could not see her as such was wilfully blind. She had needed such reassurance, and he had failed her. He just could not. It was beyond rationality. He was totally unable to show any overt sign of interest in a woman; no admiring looks, flirtatious comments or even genuine compliments. To do so was to drop his guard, to leave himself open to the possibility of rejection, shame and hurt. He knew how ridiculous it was, but he could do no other.

On rare occasions, he had tried, sternly instructing himself in what to say. Just a meaningless remark about her appearance. Part of the small coin of everyday social exchange. Implying nothing. But when the moment came, he was never able to do it. As soon as the words formed in his mind, they curdled on his tongue, tasting false and artificial. They had to be spontaneous, and he could not be spontaneous.

She had never minded his singular lack of gallantry. She joked about how she could bleach her hair, stain her skin and stick a large raisin on her nose in lieu of a wart, and he would not notice. But she had never needed it before. And now, when she did, he had proved helpless and hopeless.

What could he do about the rift between her and Miltiades? A rational part of his mind examined prospects and found little cause for optimism. A selfish part complained of the disturbance that this would cause to his settled life. A frightened part shied away from unsettling thoughts and possibilities. But instinctively he knew that she was going to need whatever support he could provide, and he was determined not to let her down. Which was somewhat ridiculous after his pathetic failure that night.

ELEVEN

Dio and Miltiades walked slowly round the outer walls. The sentries saw them coming and stared out with ostentatious diligence. Miltiades had taken recently to wearing his red officer's sash, and it gave the men good warning of their approach. He smiled. 'Dangling the odd chap over the walls seems to work. I'll have it written into the new training schedule.'

Dio groaned. 'Am I never going to escape that sorry tale?'

'Not a chance.'

It was a dismal day overlain with a blanket of dull nimbus cloud. It would rain soon. The chill of winter was already settling on the land, and Dio pulled his cloak tighter about him.

'I see that you've got that Monist preacher in a cell,' observed Miltiades after a while.

'I warned him. But you know what they're like. Bloody fanatics. Just can't shut them up.'

'Was there trouble?'

'Very nearly. Most really don't like this religion. It's effectively atheism. Denies the Gods, and folk are scared to death the Gods will take umbrage. And a God with umbrage is not to be taken lightly.'

Miltiades glanced at him. 'You're a bloody atheist, yourself. You never even wear a god guard.'

Dio shrugged. 'But I don't shout about it.'

Miltiades rubbed his shaven chin in what was becoming a characteristic gesture. 'I'll send him to Raxamenes. He can deal with him.'

He didn't seem to be himself. He would normally be doing a bit of mindless stomping about and telling Dio to run the little toad out of town. Dio could guess what was preoccupying him.

Dio stopped and leaned on the parapet, looking out across the vast swathes of rolling grassland. Miltiades joined him. 'So ask,' he said.

Dio glanced at him. 'Why, Milt? Kal just wants to know why.'

Miltiades sighed and seemed to study the distant hazy horizon for a while, then said, 'I just don't know. I know Kal's done nothing wrong. She's been a good wife, and friend, to me. We have different interests and find little to talk about these days, but that isn't it. I just feel stifled. Trapped. And before you lay into me, I know full well that I'm not. That I can live my life, and Kal can live hers. But then what's the point? All I know is that, when I made the decision, it was as though something heavy was lifted from me.' He turned to Dio. 'I'll make sure that she lacks for nothing. I've told her that. But now I've made up my mind, I can't go back.'

'But what's the difference between her living in your apartments or living in a different set of rooms in the same fortress? It just doesn't make sense to me. And what difference does having a wife, in name only, make to you? It will make a tremendous difference to her. A divorced woman is assumed to have committed some heinous sin. You know that.'

'I would prefer her to live elsewhere. And it would be easier for her. But I'll go along with her wishes. And I'll tell everyone that it is my doing, and that Kal bears no blame.' He spread his hands. 'What more can I do?'

Dio regarded him closely. 'Is it that you wish to marry someone else? That's the only explanation I can come up with.'

'Who? Who else would I want to marry?' His answer sounded defensive to Dio's ears. 'It's no good, Dio. I've questioned myself endlessly. To no avail. I don't know why I feel this way. I just do. And I can do no other.'

Dio felt defeated. He was getting nowhere.

'But you will be her friend?' asked Miltiades, 'You'll stand by her? She needs you.'

'Of course I will,' said Dio. But Miltiades' insistence brought a distinct feeling of unease in its wake. He was beginning to wonder if Miltiades had perhaps been playing a long game. Encouraging Kal and Dio's friendship, feeding them opportunities, pushing them together in the hope that something would happen to provide him with a useful excuse. Nothing was clear any more.

In the distance, thunderheads were gathering over the Rhodopians.

TWELVE

'Come in, Dio.' He was met by Kal with a brilliant smile. Two moontides on, the haggard look had gone, and she had regained much of her old spirit, though still subject to occasional bouts of depression. She was dressed in her favourite 'comfable' clothes, a long Thracian tunic belted at the waist, and her hair was no longer a complex coil of ringlets but tumbled about her face in waves. He liked it like that. It suited her.

She was attempting to place a wall hanging, a vibrant Megaran embroidered rug, with the help of a slave girl. Her suite of seven rooms was much smaller and less opulent than her previous home, but she seemed to be getting great satisfaction from decorating and furnishing it herself. Miltiades had sworn that he would look after her but was scarcely abiding by his promise. She had but two slave women and a relatively small 'allowance'. Dio had always been aware of a rather mean side to Miltiades' nature, and now it showed up badly.

'I need your help. Dianthe isn't tall enough.'

Dianthe was the slight girl who had brought Kal's request to speak in his room that night. She moved quietly aside, averting her eyes, as he accepted the rug and held it in place.

Kal stepped back and considered it, putting her head to one side, and then moved to the other corner of the room and considered it again. 'A little to your left, I think.' He obliged. She considered. 'Can you lift it a couple of fingers?' Dio did so with an uncomfortable stretch. She considered.

'A man could lose the use of his arms after a day or so,' he grumbled.

'Stop moaning.' She brought over a stool and stood on it to mark the position with a piece of charcoal. She had to lean across him to do so, and her breast momentarily brushed his cheek.

As always, he was ludicrously conscious of touch, but this time, to his surprise and shame, the ridiculous idea that it might have been deliberate caught sudden fire in the dark recesses of his mind, throwing wavering and uncertain shadows across his consciousness.

He hastily dismissed the notion. Kal was not like that. This disruption to his comfortable and settled world was making him delusional. He was seeing a kitten as a full-maned lion.

Touch did seem more frequent of late, though innocent and fleeting enough. But it was a vague impression only, and easily explained by the increasing time he was spending with Kal, coupled with her natural inclination to be tactile.

Perhaps he was simply more aware of it. He had even wondered if she might be deliberately desensitising him, knowing his inhibitions as she did and suitably dismissive of them. If so, it seemed to be working. He no longer jumped when she laid her hand on his arm momentarily or flicked his legs in retribution for some sally at her expense. But it was no more than that.

Whatever the reasons, he was creating cities in the air from the passing clouds. These silly and baseless thoughts concerned him. They were springing up like dandelions in a well-tended garden, and it was time to uproot them before they seeded.

She used his shoulder as support as she clambered down from the stool. It meant nothing, he told himself. Nothing.

She rolled the rug up and laid it in a corner. 'I'll have to sew on a couple of loops. Can you put me up a couple of hanging hooks later, where I have marked the wall?'

'Just call me hammermaster.'

'I wish!' she cried. 'The last two you put up were decidedly crooked.'

'They looked fine to me.'

'You haven't got my discriminating eye. You're a man, after all. Dianthe agrees with me. They were definitely crooked, were they not? I had to resew the loops.'

The little slave girl looked worried.

'It's all right, Dianthe,' said Dio sympathetically. 'I accept the reproof.'

A look of relief spread over her features.

'Fetch Dio some wine, would you?' The girl disappeared. Kal looked after her, musingly. 'You do realise that she really likes you, don't you?'

'Kal!' He was shocked. 'You know my opinion about slavery.'

'That doesn't stop her liking you,' she said reasonably. 'After all, you consider that slaves should have the right to express their feelings as much as free men.'

'But not to be abused, taken advantage of.'

'I don't think that she would regard it as abuse.' She made a slight gesture of warning. The girl returned with two kylixes of watered wine. He felt embarrassed as he thanked her, and could not help but notice Kal's sly smile.

'Thank you, Dianthe. You may leave us now.' The girl bowed her head, gave Dio a quick sidelong glance through her long eyelashes, and slipped gracefully from the room.

They both sat. 'See?' exclaimed Kal triumphantly.

'See what?'

'All men have poor vision, but you're just plain stone blind.'

'Dyaus, I'm old enough to be her grandfather.'

'What's that got to do with it? She's definitely smitten. I overheard her telling Melissa.' That was Kal's second slave, a staid and matronly woman.

He was suddenly and inexplicably aware of the swell of Kal's breasts beneath the loose top of the tunic. He quickly averted his gaze. It disturbed him. He had never felt his eyes drawn to them before. He had never, as far as he could recall, even consciously thought of them. He felt embarrassed and ashamed and spoke quickly to cover his confusion. 'You've an overactive imagination. Why would a woman look at a grizzled, scarred old reprobate like me?'

'Because everyone knows you're a kind, considerate and lovely man.'

'That's the prevailing view among this year's intake, I take it?'

'All right,' she conceded. 'Some recognise you as that. Dianthe won't be the first. There have certainly been ladies interested in you.'

'How many?' He was incredulous.

'Lots,' she responded without hesitation.

'Name three,' he challenged.

She smiled triumphantly. 'I could too. For a start, there's Zenobia. She would dance naked on the rooftops if she thought it would get your attention. Though it probably wouldn't.'

'I think it might,' said Dio wryly.

'Then there was Sophronia. You can't deny Sophronia. They almost had to prise her off you with a mattock handle.'

He pulled a wry face. 'All right. I'll grant you Sophronia.'

'And Merope. I had hopes of Merope.' Her tone was wistful. 'I really thought you might get together.'

'She was a nice girl, but you know I'm happy as I am.' He remembered Merope well. Kal had always been inviting her along whenever he was there. Deep within, something was wondering.

'Are you listening to me?'

He was jolted out of his reverie. She had been saying something but he knew not what. 'Of course.'

'Then what was the last thing I said?'

'Are you listening to me?'

She rolled her eyes heavenwards, then regarded him seriously. 'You really find women difficult, don't you Dio?'

'I suppose I do,' he admitted. Then he added, with the feeling of walking across a thinly frozen river, 'But I get along well enough with you, don't I?'

She laughed. 'That's because I'm an honorary chap and treated as such. If I'd ever preened or pouted or fluttered my eyelashes at you, you'd have been gone with the mountain hare. And it took a long time before you really allowed me to get to know you.'

'I'm sorry. I'm just a very insular person. I don't make friends easily—real friends, that is.'

'It was worth the wait.'

He should have returned the compliment but, as always, it clogged in his mouth. She put her wine down and rose to bring out another wall rug. She shook it out to show him. It was unusual. Geometric designs in muted natural browns.

'You like?'

'I do. Where's it from?'

'Eretrian work. You can help me hang this one as well.' She went over to the farther wall and laid it down. 'By the way, the next decent day we get, will you take me out riding? I'm beginning to think my world has shrunk to these few rooms.'

'Of course. Which brings me neatly to why I called in. Would you like to go for a meal at Theopompus's tonight?'

She clapped her hands with delight. 'I would love it.' She stifled a laugh. 'So long as they don't show us to the "romantic" corner like last time. Your face was a thing of wonder.' Then she stiffened. 'Milt won't be there, will he? It's his favourite place to eat.'

'No. I checked with him.'

A shadow seemed to pass over her face, then she forced a smile. 'Will you hold it for me?'

He went over and stretched the brown rug against the wall. She indicated for him to move it up and left.

'When we go riding, would you mind if Thais comes along? She so rarely gets the chance to ride. To the right a little.' Thais was a friend of Kal, married to Antenor. A small, delicate blonde, intelligent and strong minded, but somewhat serious and lacking in humour.

'That's no problem. Just let me know when.'

'That's perfect.' She came and marked the position. 'Antenor and Thais came for a meal two nights ago. Do you know what Thais said to me? When Antenor wasn't there, of course.'

'I just haven't kept up with the mind reading. Sorry.'

She stuck her tongue out at him and went for a third rug from the adjacent room. She called back from it. 'She said that I should get myself a young stud. Now that I'm officially alone. She said there were plenty available.'

There were times when he felt physically shaken. Uncertain. Unsure either as to the implications or his own response. It was a reaction that worried him. 'I'm sure there are. But I somehow doubt that you will avail yourself.'

She returned and laid the rug by the wall. 'Heavenly Herakla, I should think not.' She stood silently for a moment. Then said, very seriously, 'I'm not going to share my life with another man. Not after Milt. How could I trust anyone again?'

He was astonished by the surge of disappointment that overcame him. She must have seen something in his face because she stepped forward and laid her hand lightly on his arm. 'I don't include you, Dio. I trust you. Of course I do.'

He smiled weakly. 'That seems somewhat inconsistent.'

'I don't do consistency,' she said brightly. 'It's my most consistent attribute.'

He spread his hands helplessly. 'There are times when you mangle my mind.'

'I shall magnanimously refrain from the obvious cheap jibes.'

'You're too kind.'

'I am,' she agreed.

THIRTEEN

There was frost on the ground, and a chill westerly wind poked and prodded at every bit of exposed skin it could find. That did not stop training. On the broad drilling ground just outside the fortress, the new intake was practising a Tyrrhenian shuffle. A flank march to the left exposed the unshielded side and was to be avoided when under missile fire. Instead, a small phalanx of twenty-six recruits, in three lines, was moving slowly but surely, simply stepping to their left to the rhythmic chant of the dilochagos, their shields high and to the front, spears at overhand thrust, presenting a mobile bronze wall of helmets, shields and greaves.

A lochagos ran forward and touched a lad in the first row with his vine stick. The youth immediately fell to the ground. The recruit in the second line stepped smartly forward and took his place, and the crab-like progress continued, each man in turn warning the man to his right of the obstacle by yelling, 'Ware,' as he stepped over the casualty.

Dio nodded in satisfaction. 'Well done,' he said, as two of the lad's half-file helped him to his feet and brushed him down. 'As a reward, four laps of the field. That'll warm you up nicely.' They knew better than to complain and set off, running in full armour.

Dio leaned back against the stone column that marked that corner of the field. He could trust the dilochagos to keep them going, and, as always now, his mind immediately reverted to the situation between himself and Kal, worrying at it like a wolf at the kill.

Events were making him seriously reassess Kal's place in his life. What she meant to him. Suddenly he was seeing her in a romantic light, a mindset that he had assumed had long since evaporated from his life. Of late, his thoughts turned incessantly to his relationship with her and how it had developed. He had honestly regarded her as a friend—well, he certainly *hoped* it had been honestly. He had never harboured any overtly erotic thoughts about her, though he could not deny, in retrospect, that there had been a slight underlying sexual frisson. He had always looked forward to seeing her and suffered from an obscure feeling of disappointment afterward as he wended his way back to his empty room. He had occasionally wondered what he would do if anything happened to Miltiades, but had come to the rather ignoble conclusion that he would immediately distance himself from her. Which, by itself, was evidence enough for an undercurrent of attraction.

He looked up as the clatter of metal approached and the troop ran past. Philon was dropping behind again. He caught the dilocho's eye and nodded at the recruit. The drillmaster immediately moved forward until alongside the lad and politely invited him to move a little faster, in the time-honoured manner of dilochos. Dio returned to his bleak thoughts.

It was his response that day, to a mere glimpse of the sweep and curve of her breasts, that really disturbed him. He just did not think of Kal in a sexual way. He never had done. But he recalled how once, when they had gone to the Great Dionysia in Ilios, they had had problems finding rooms. Kal had jokingly said that, if necessary, they could share one, and rig up a curtain between them to accommodate the social niceties. He had not known how to respond, and they had luckily found two rooms shortly thereafter. But since that time, he had had a gentle fantasy of sleeping in the same room as Kal and simply hearing her quiet breathing in the dark. That was all. 'There's none so blind as those who will not look,' Pandarus had told him. He could not pretend that he hadn't been warned.

The intake went by again, running well. Even Philon had caught up.

So he looked. Finally. He returned to every action of hers that could be considered even slightly flirtatious, suggestive or meaningful. Every word. Every touch. Did throwing a cushion at him portend anything more than natural playfulness? Had that barely perceptible brush of her breast been deliberate or a simple accident? Was all her talk about Dianthe and Merope having feelings for him a coded message? He looked, but he remained as blind as ever.

Things that seemed unambiguous and transparent when they happened became nebulous and opaque on further consideration. Every action that seemed to point in one direction was negated by some counterpoint. Her talk of his attractiveness to females followed by an explicit declaration that she would not involve herself with anyone again. Her seemingly clear desire to be with him, suggesting things they could do together, negated by the heedless way that she invited others along. Every suggestive comment really a joke. Every compliment nothing but social graces. Every seductive-looking pose simply a comfortable position.

He looked up as the intake approached, now red-faced and sweating, for the third time. 'Sprint!' he roared. 'Extra guard duty for the last three.' They would have groaned, if they had had the breath.

Pandarus had once drawn a fascinating open cube in the sand of the sparring arena. 'Which way round is it?' he had asked. And the cube had suddenly shifted from one view to another and back again before Dio's amazed eyes. 'There are two interpretations to everything,' Pandarus had said. 'Always remember that, boy.'

Dio could not escape the suspicion that he was relentlessly reading into her actions what he wanted to be there and what he feared to be there, only to dismiss his conclusions as unwarranted and irrational, before starting the whole sad unending cycle again. Shifting endlessly from one perspective to another, never reaching a definitive outcome.

The recruits came straggling in, panting and shining with sweat. Philon was last, of course. The laboured breathing quietened down.

'Enemy sighted to the northwest,' he said quietly. Only one or two heard him, but immediately yelled to the others, and within heartbeats a phalanx had formed, shields locked together and a line of wicked-looking spear heads to the fore. The ektatoi walked along the line, tapping spears and shields that were not properly aligned. The dilochagos gave Dio a speculative look as he passed.

It was not only Kal. It was himself as well. He was truly ambivalent about his own feelings—torn and frightened. Part of him feared any possible entanglement, arguing fiercely that his freedom was at risk, that, at his age, his ability to cope with the day in, day out requirements of a relationship was beyond him, that he was trapping himself in a stifling quagmire of his own making. His fear of responsibility and commitment loomed large, as did his even greater fear of rejection and embarrassment. Nevertheless, part of him was lost in a strange surge of inarticulate excitement and longing, emotions that had almost been forgotten through the long, lean years. A scarcely to be enunciated wish for something he had years ago set aside as unattainable.

He sighed. 'Take them home, dilocho.'

He was still lost in the thick fog of uncertainty as he watched them go.

FOURTEEN

THE SE'ENNIGHTLY OFFICERS' Call had just finished, and the assembled officers were drifting away, chatting to each other. Miltiades, having a brief word with Antenor, gestured to Dio to stay, so he sat down again. Antenor left, giving Dio his characteristic wink, and Miltiades walked across to the window to unhook the leather cover. A blast of cold air surged through the room. He looked out across the windswept grey wastes. In the distance, thick rain clouds were gathering. Nowhere looked as bleak as the Vale of Tempe in winter. As the last brace of officers left the room, he turned. 'How is she?'

'Fine,' said Dio. 'She does request that she can use the library. She wants to do some serious philosophy.'

'Of course she can. Anything. Anything at all.'

Dio had many years ago decided that Miltiades was far more motivated by concern for the impression that he made than by any real generosity of spirit. Recently, he had suggested it to Kal, but she had refused to be drawn, saying it seemed disloyal to discuss it.

'I hear she has a dog.'

Dio couldn't help smiling. 'The biggest, nastiest-looking brute you've ever seen and the softest lump imaginable. Frightened of a mouse. He adores her.'

Miltiades shuddered. 'Don't like dogs. Bitten when I was a youngster.'

Dio knew of his phobia. It had been Dio's idea that Kal should get herself a dog now that she could. 'She's also learning Thracian, believe it or not. She's fascinated by their culture.'

'I suppose because she *is* Thracian. Technically. Her maternal grandmother was pureblood Thrakoi, and they count descent only through the female.'

'The Maidean clan, she tells me.'

'I believe so.'

They still spoke as friends, but there was an underlying tension between them now. The old camaraderie had gone. And it was glaringly obvious that Miltiades was no longer listening to Dio. Someone else was sounding the salpinx. The spindly and gawky Adrastus slipped silently into the room, bowed his head gravely to Dio and began to gather up the scatter of scrolls and wax tablets. It wasn't difficult to guess who.

'Won't be that long before it's spring,' said Dio, almost to himself, 'and that's likely to bring more than swallows and may blossom.'

'You really think there will be war?'

Dio had the distinct feeling that Adrastus was listening attentively but pretending not to. 'I'd put a year's pay on it. And I'm not a gambling man. Laomedon won't wait forever.'

'You still think he's aiming high?'

'Don't you?' Dio was deliberately baiting Miltiades, and Adrastus for that matter, looking for any confirmation of his suspicions that they were firmly in Laomedon's camp already.

'No, I'm not sure I do. It's a risky thing to move against an emperor, even one as inept as Aristogeiton.'

'And what do you think, Adrastus?' asked Dio suddenly.

'Oh, I'm not employed to think, merely to do my Lord's bidding to the best of my limited abilities.' He was urbanity itself.

Dio was suddenly angry. 'Well, you don't listen to what I think, Milt, and Adrastus apparently doesn't think at all, so you'll have to do the thinking all by yourself.' He got up and walked out.

FIFTEEN

'You said that?' exclaimed Kal, seating herself on the couch opposite Dio. She sounded half horrified and half delighted.

Dio nodded. He scratched the ear of Kerberos, a massive brindled mastiff with a head twice the size of Dio's. He stopped, and the dog put up a huge paw and hooked it over his arm until he started again.

'If I don't scratch him, he'll eat me,' he explained to Kal.

'He'll only do that on the command 'lunch'. Distract him with that rag. He likes tugging games.'

'Dyaus! He nearly pulled my arm out of its socket.'

'Don't be such a feeble girl. He's only a puppy.'

'Athen aid us when he grows up.'

'So, what did Milt say?'

Dio shrugged. 'Nothing.'

'You should be careful. Milt has great respect for you, but he does not take kindly to being confronted. He keeps it well under control, but he can be seriously vindictive. You could find yourself without a job.'

'If he is where I think he is, I'll jump into the river before I'm thrown. I've enough money. I'll simply move on.'

She stiffened. 'Move on?' she repeated, as though trying to come to come to grips with the words. 'To where?'

'I've no real idea. Probably Ilios initially. And then see what the situation is.'

She was biting her lip. Kerberos whined, went across and laid his huge head on her lap. She scratched his ears, then looked up, worried but determined. 'I'm sorry, Dio. I'm thinking only of myself. I just don't know that I could have managed without you. But it's time I fended for myself. You've no option. But not before you have to. Please.'

'I promise,' he said. Kerberos returned and carefully placed the sopping wet rag on his foot before stepping back, wagging his tail. 'Doesn't this thing ever sleep?'

'Only when he's had a good meal.' She grinned mischievously. 'Lunch!' she suddenly commanded. Kerberos put his head on one side and looked at her. 'Needs a bit more training, I expect.'

'Please don't bother on my account,' said Dio hastily.

She looked down. 'You do know what they are saying?'

'Considering the rumours beforehand, it's predictable.' He almost said that he had warned her, but refrained.

'Many of the ladies won't talk to me,' she said sadly.

'Surely that's no great loss. Those that won't talk weren't true friends. Your genuine friends, like Thais and Philomena, have walked every step of the way with you.'

'Has anyone said anything to you?'

He smiled grimly. 'They wouldn't dare. But I know things are said, and it has undermined my authority to some extent. Sour bastards like Gelon are stirring the pot with enthusiasm. But it's not enough to worry about. And those that know me, like Radamanthus and Antenor and Eurybiades, know better. It's a storm that will pass.'

'I'm sorry,' she said. 'I've brought this down on you.'

'No, it's Milt's doing. You blame yourself too readily and without cause.'

'Perhaps. Perhaps not.' She picked at a dog hair on her tunic. 'I've been thinking,' she said after a pause. 'Perhaps I should move to Leuctra.'

His heart lurched. 'You should go where you will be happiest.'

'Happiest?' Her tone was wistful. 'I don't think I will see happy again.'

He did not know what to say. Kerberos rolled over and presented his tummy to be tickled. 'You great mummy's boy,' Dio exclaimed in disgust.

Kal laughed, but her eyes were raw.

SIXTEEN

ANTENOR HAD TAKEN advantage of a brief spell of good weather to take his eile out on exercise, though the ground remained frozen hard, and had invited Dio along to observe. Antenor had wanted to give his new deuteros a trial run and was not impressed. But there were other things on his mind, and he was waiting for the moment to sound the salpinx. Strict instructions from his wife were not to be ignored.

'How could that stupid bastard manage to get himself lost?' he grumbled. 'He couldn't find his way from the bedroom to the privy.' He was a tall, well-made man with a handsome, if angular, face, naturally dour by nature, and married to Thais, Kal's friend.

'He did have the sense to listen to his hyperetes,' pointed out Dio mildly.

'That won't protect his delicate sensibilities when I debrief the idiot.'

'Can I come and listen?' Dio grinned. 'I'm always anxious to extend my vocabulary.'

'You won't need to. If you're within ten stadia of Gla, you'll hear it well enough.' Antenor decided that the time had come and pulled up his horse. Dio did the same and looked questioningly at him. 'Dio, we're friends, aren't we?'

'I certainly hope so.' He had a distinct premonition as to what was coming, but pretended otherwise. 'Have you some sort of problem?'

'No, you have.'

'Aah. That would be Kal, I take it?'

'Look. I know it's none of my business, so as soon as you've had enough of my pontificating, just tell me to bar the gates and I will.'

Dio gazed into the distance. 'Go on.'

'You know what they are saying about you two?'

'I know, but it's not true.'

'Dyaus's balls, do you think I don't know that? I've known you for ten years, and I've never known a straighter man. If you and Kal had had a relationship, you would have confronted Miltiades with it. Not gone behind his back. Those that know you all say the same. But some are stirring it.'

'Gelon, for example.'

Antenor nodded.

'Well, I can't do anything about the gossip press, I'm afraid.'

Antenor hesitated, then plunged in. 'But you can about what you're doing now. You're always seeing her. It's the fuel that's feeding the fire.'

'She needs support. What can I do?'

'I know. Thais tells me how good you are to her. But is it good *for* her? Her reputation is suffering.'

'Milt said that he would make it clear that the divorce was not based on any suspicion of Kal's behaviour.'

'Oh, he is doing, but either he's awfully bad at it, or he's playing a very clever game. Because he has everybody convinced that he's lying, for purely noble motives of course, to protect the soiled reputation of the woman he really still loves. It's nauseating. Half the women in the post have got him down as a chivalrous Troilus to a false Cressid. He's a bloody romantic hero.'

'Yes, I had picked up on that, surprisingly enough.'

Antenor looked him straight in the eye. 'Can I ask you something? You obviously don't have to answer it if you don't want to.'

'But then you will draw the obvious conclusions.' He could not keep the bitterness from his voice. Antenor looked surprised. The swordmaster and emotion were sorry bedfellows. Dio sighed. 'My apologies. I'm just getting very cynical over all this. Take your aim.'

'Have you bedded Kal?' He was nothing if not direct.

'No.'

Antenor nodded, 'But are you planning to have a relationship?'

That caught Dio on the hip. His first instinct was to deny it as confidently as before. But something stayed him. He suddenly had the urge to discuss his feelings with someone. They had been submerged for too long, too long desperately ignored or rationalised away. 'I don't know. I've never been in this place before. It's new territory, and I'm not at all sure where I am.' There was a long, rather awkward silence, then Dio looked down. 'But I don't think so. I don't want involvement. Nor does Kal. She has made it quite clear that she doesn't want another man in her life. Milt hurt her greatly.' He stared down at his hands on the reins as if he had never seen them before.

'And?' said Antenor quietly, surprisingly gently for such a gruff individual.

Dio looked up. 'I can't pretend that I don't like Kal, and sometimes I wonder.' He shook his head. 'But I think the answer has still got to be no. It would be a jump into the unknown, and unwanted for both of us.' Not much by way of a full and heartfelt opening up of his emotions, he thought, but the best he could do. He felt the armour buckling around his mind.

'Well, you have to make your own decisions, and, knowing you, they will not be rash or poorly thought out ones. But I have to suggest one thing. You have obviously considered the slurs on her name and believe that her need for your support is greater than any harm it might do.' He shrugged. 'You're probably right. The very fact of divorce did the real damage. But have you considered something else? You're committed to remaining alone. But is Kal? Are you giving her the impression that there is a future for the two of you? Is she beginning to hope? And then is she going to be disappointed again? Is that fair on her?'

Dio was shocked. He had never thought about it like that. 'Is that how Thais sees it?'

'She thinks it might be a possibility,' said Antenor cautiously.

Dio felt two tides of hope and fear meet and break into a tumble of confusion. 'Thanks, Antenor. You have given me much to think on.'

SEVENTEEN

It was a fine, sunny day despite the bitter cold, the grass white with frost and scarred with the elongated, twisted shadows of bare trees cast by the low sun. Well wrapped in fur-lined cloaks, Dio and Kal cantered out through the main gate, conscious of the mutterings and sidelong glances. Both pretended to be unaware of the attention that they were attracting, and neither mentioned it.

'It seems ages since we last rode,' said Kal, 'but it's a pleasant day.' Everything was as sharp as a needle, the distant Rhodopians looking crystal clear, as though they were nearby hills situated just over the horizon. The sky was cloudless, and the only thing that moved was a lumbering heron flying across before them. 'He'll be lucky to find anything but ice.'

'It's a bad time. If we don't have a thaw soon, there'll be a lot of dead birds and animals.'

'It's a cruel time,' she agreed sadly.

He knew she was not referring to the weather. He was nervous and tense, and his stomach yawned with emptiness. He felt more apprehensive than he ever did before a fight. He had already tried, several times these last few days, to say something to her, but each time he had failed, never able to bring himself to the shield line, allowing the opportunities to drift helplessly away. This time, he looked at the abyss at his feet, as deep and black as Tartarus, and plunged.

'Kal, we need to talk.'

She immediately pulled her horse to a halt and stared at him, wide-eyed, wary. Her cheeks were flushed with the cold, and he could not help but think her beautiful. He forced the thought away.

'What they are saying. It must be very hurtful for you.' His delivery was hesitant.

'Actually, no,' she replied, with more than a tinge of sarcasm. 'I'm finding it all perfectly delightful.'

'I'm sorry. That was a stupid thing to say.'

She sighed and laid her hand gently on his. 'No, I'm sorry, Dio. I can see that this isn't easy for you.' Her facial expression became taut and unreadable. 'Tell me what you want to say.'

'My seeing so much of you. It's convincing people that their inane suppositions are correct.'

'Milt said that he would make it clear that it was his doing and no fault of mine.' Her voice was sharp and strained.

'Milt is either cleverer than I thought, or he is being advised by someone. He has said just that, but in such a way that everyone thinks that he is being noble and protecting you. He is coming out of this with his reputation greatly enhanced. I heard the other day that he said, "If it helps Kalliste for me to be regarded as the wrongdoer, I am happy to fulfil the role." Your noble protector? The unctuous bastard. He knows exactly what he's doing.'

She was watching him. He saw pain in her eyes. 'So, you feel that you should be seeing less of me.' She looked away. 'Yes, that's a good idea, Dio. Perhaps things will calm down.' There were tears in her eyes. She moved to urge the horse on, but this time his hand fell on hers. He simply acted instinctively.

'Kal, no, you misunderstand. It's not that I want to see less of you. I wondered if *you* might think it a good idea.'

'You salve your conscience by forcing me to make the decision.' She had never been bitter with him before.

He spoke slowly and with intensity. For once the words came easily and unforced. 'If you want me to be there twenty dekates a day, I will be. If staying away will help, I'll stay away. I just don't want to hurt you in any way. I'm not suggesting anything other than that you consider what's best for yourself.'

She sat for a moment, her face unreadable, then suddenly smiled. 'I'm sorry. Again. I seem to be giving you a hard time. There is no question. I want my friends around me. The gossips and bad-mouthers can go to Hades.' She looked across at him. 'Forgive me.'

'There's nothing to forgive, but there is something else. And it is difficult.'

She had visibly relaxed, but now she stiffened again. A figure of ice in a frozen landscape. 'Go on,' she whispered.

He didn't know how to. But now he was committed. 'I was told by a friend,' he began slowly. Her eyes never left his. 'He said…' He closed his eyes and said in a rush, 'That it might be unfair on you if I was giving you the impression that…' He ground to a halt again. 'I might be…' His voice faltered into an embarrassed silence. 'You know what I mean,' he lamely concluded, in total desperation.

She laughed. 'Poor Dio. Face a man with a sword and you have no fear. Try to tell a girl that you don't want to get emotionally involved, and you can't even form a coherent sentence.'

He gave her a sickly smile. 'Look Kal, I'm more than fond of you, but I've lived on my own for far too long. I know it's presumptuous to even imagine that you might have thought about me other than as a friend, but I was afraid that, if you had, you might be hurt. And I don't want to hurt you.'

She looked at him affectionately. 'If ever I'd wanted more than a friend, I'd have found none better. But I know you're a man content with your life and needing nobody else. I know you find relationships difficult and worrying. And I know how much it's cost you to say what you have.' She chuckled. 'Albeit in an almost incomprehensible splutter.'

He smiled sheepishly.

Kal continued quietly. 'I'm grateful for all that you've done for me. But I don't want anybody in my life. I've been hurt enough. I couldn't risk it again. So, you can put your mind at rest. But, Dio, I still need you as my friend. Never forget that.'

All was still for a moment, then he nodded and gestured that they should ride on. Neither spoke, but the space between them swarmed with unsaid words.

He stifled a sigh. He had said it. He rather wished he hadn't.

EIGHTEEN

Dio RAN UP the steps. Dianthe was waiting with the door half-open, a look of dismay on her face. Her eyes were red. He pushed past her without a word. In the small entry hall lay the body of Kerberos, collapsed in a pool of urine, a spew of vomit by his mouth. Kal was in the reception room, sitting, staring at the empty fireplace.

She immediately rose and came towards him. Her hair was awry, her eyes puffed and red, the rivulets of tears still glistening on her pale face. She held out her arms, and he found himself holding her in a tight embrace. For once, he did not feel the usual surge of embarrassment. He just wanted to take the hurt from her.

She burst again into tears and tried to tell him what had happened, but she was sobbing so wretchedly he could make little sense of it. He stroked her hair and murmured helpless words of sympathy. Eventually, she calmed down a little and pulled away, still sniffling. He experienced an unexpected reluctance to release her, and he felt ashamed of such a response at a time like this. He should have been thinking of her needs, not the warm solidity of her body within his arms.

'He had some sort of fit,' she said, 'when he was eating his dinner. Suddenly started jerking and frothing and then was sick. I couldn't do anything. It was terrible.'

'I've heard of dogs having fits like that,' he lied. 'There was nothing that you could have done.'

There was a tap on the door, and Dianthe entered. 'The hyperetes of the guard is here, my Lady.' Kal looked surprised.

'I sent for him,' explained Dio.

A craggy veteran came in, rubbing his short-cropped hair in perplexity. 'I'm sorry, my Lady, it looks like—'

'Could you get a couple of men to clean the place up, Icarius?' interrupted Dio, giving him a fearsome warning glance. 'And bury the dog with respect.'

'Could you bury him by the hawthorn tree on the track to Antimelos, about twenty stadia out from the town?' whispered Kal, her voice tremulous.

Icarius looked uncertain. 'I'm not sure where…'

'I can show the officer the place,' said Dianthe promptly.

'Then I'll make sure he's buried properly, my Lady, and we'll raise a cairn for him.'

'Thank you.' She gave him a grateful smile. He withdrew with Dianthe.

'Just need a word with Icarius,' said Dio. 'Won't be a heartbeat.' He followed them into the entry hall, closing the door of the reception room behind him. The hyperetes turned back, about to speak. Dio forestalled him. 'I know what you were going to say, Icarius, but I want you to forget it, and make sure that your men forget it as well.'

'I understand, sir.'

Dianthe was looking on with wide eyes. He turned to her and asked her to get him a cloth. He hooked out some of the meat from Kerberos's dish with his knife and wrapped it in the rag. 'Get someone to catch you a live rat, Icarius—I'm sure one of the urchins from the town will oblige—and feed it this. Let me know what happens. But not a word to anyone. And I will have a debt to pay.'

'No sir, you won't. I haven't forgotten the Aggie you skewered that day on the Kyme. Saved my sorry arse. It's the least that I can do.'

Dianthe was looking horrified. The implications of what Dio had said had finally registered.

Dio locked eyes with her. 'She mustn't suspect, Dianthe. Do you understand?'

'I do, my Lord.' And there was a look of determination on her small face.

NINETEEN

'Thank you, sir,' said Icarius, seated primly on the small stool as befitted his relatively lowly rank, and accepting a kylix of wine from Dio. He felt slightly out of place, but determined to do what he could. Radamanthus lounged idly on one of the two couches, savouring his drink.

The third visitor sprawled on the other, a chubby, jolly-faced man with a ring of grey hair around a shiny bald patch: Eurybiades, the major-domo, in charge of all the civilian infrastructure, the cooks, grooms, cleaners and, most importantly, the clerks in the secretarial bureau. He had been at Gla since long before Dio had arrived, and there was little he did not know about the sprawling fortress. He and Dio had been friends for many years now. He had a wicked sense of humour and a natural contempt for officers, with but few honourable exceptions, and was unashamedly scatologically irreverent about his superiors. He looked up at Dio. 'So? To what do we owe the honour of being invited to this charming little symposium?'

Dio pulled a face. 'Not much honour in it, I'm afraid. I asked you here because you are three men I can trust. I've spoken to Rad and yourself about my concerns before, and Icarius had the misfortune of being dragged into it because of the other day.'

'The dog,' grunted Radamanthus.

Dio nodded. 'It was definitely and deliberately poisoned.' He glanced at Icarius for confirmation.

'The rat handed in his discharge papers the instant he ate some of the food. Same symptoms.'

'Rad and I have been turning over some stones. The meat was delivered from the town. The lad gave it to a man who had some tale about wanting to see the slave girl, and who dropped him a couple of obols. It happened just outside Fat Delia's, so we asked within, gave the man's description, and soon had him targeted as a local thug called Stratios. I paid him a visit that night. He was hired to do it by a balding man with a wart on his chin.'

'Pheidon! The greasy, tight-arsed little shit who runs between that donkey turd Raxamenes and fucking Miltiades.'

'Described to perfection, Eury.' Dio had to smile. 'Obviously, the trail stops there, but it's far enough. The order must have originated from either Miltiades or Adrastus. Or both.'

'Probably that long streak of horse piss,' muttered Eurybiades. 'He's the one who sounds the salpinx, despite all his humble posturings. And that's a bloody mystery in itself.'

'What about this Stratios character?' asked Radamanthus.

'I expressed my disapproval. When he came to, I suggested that he looked a bit peaky and could do with a holiday. He left at first light.'

'So would I,' said Radamanthus simply. 'Do you think Kal is at risk?'

'Directly and immediately? No. I think it was a bit of unpleasant pressure. To get her to move to Leuctra. Miltiades wants her out of his sight. If he had wanted her dead, then he wouldn't have warned her by poisoning the dog.'

'Perhaps he wanted her to know what was coming?' suggested Eurybiades.

'I don't think so. I have my quarrels with Miltiades, but he isn't that kind of sadist.'

'Do we ever really know?' asked Eurybiades.

He had a point, thought Dio. Was he really so sure that Miltiades was incapable of such malice?

Radamanthus looked at Dio pointedly. 'So, what are we going to do about it?'

'There's not a lot we can do. I just want you three to be aware of what's going on. Two reasons. First, and most importantly, if anything happens to me, I want you to do your best to get Kal to safety. There's a scroll in my room for Rad giving details of a man in Leuctra who will be able to get her out of the country. Everything I have is left to Kal. Details of that are in there too.'

'Don't worry,' said Radamanthus gruffly. 'We'll make sure that she gets out.' Eurybiades nodded.

'Thank you. Second, I may need some help in the future.' He noted the uneasy look on Icarius's face. 'Don't worry. Under no circumstances will I ask you to do anything that will be contrary to military discipline or direct commands. But I may want you to show a little less interest in my doings than another officer might; be not quite so inquisitive at certain times, if you understand me. And I would be grateful for any information you come across that might be of use.'

'Whatever you need, you know that,' said Icarius stolidly.

'You can rest on me,' added Radamanthus, and Eurybiades agreed.

'What about others?' asked Radamanthus. 'There's plenty here would stand by their swordmaster. Ilus of course. Antenor certainly would.'

'Tithonius,' chimed in Eurybiades.

Dio held up a hand, stemming the litany before it became a flood. 'No. Just you three. At the moment, I've simply asked three friends to help because I feared Kal's dog had been poisoned. And the more people are involved, the far greater the chance of it getting caught in the light. I don't want this to become a conspiracy. That's a very different matter. We'll leave it as it is. Not a word to anybody else.'

'So, no blood on the briefing room rugs, then?' said Radamanthus. 'Saves you a job, Eury.'

'Shit,' complained Eurybiades. 'You mean I can't kick that sorry Phthian bastard's sick arse from here to Thera? Some fucking useless conspiracy this is.'

TWENTY

KAL GLARED AT him as he entered the room. 'Why didn't you tell me?' She had been waiting too long, and the anger had welled up within her.

Dio sighed. 'I didn't want you worried.'

'And didn't it occur to you that I damn well ought to be worried? If they can poison poor Kerberos, they can sure as Hades poison me. Didn't you think that I ought to be aware of this unimportant little fact about my own life? So I can make my own silly decisions? Like being careful over what I eat, for example.' Her face was flushed, and her voice shook with anger. He winced at her ferocity.

'If they had wanted to poison you, they wouldn't alert you to the danger by poisoning your dog first.'

'Perhaps. Perhaps not. Whatever the case, shouldn't I have the right to know and to decide for myself? Or am I just a stupid woman without the intelligence to make a rational decision? So helpless that I need a man to make them for me? Well, here's a bone for you to gnaw on: I don't need a man to run my life. I don't want a man to run my life. In fact, I don't want a bloody man in my life at all!' Her voice had risen to a definite shout.

He was uncomfortably aware that the two slaves in the other room would hear every word, and the thought of there possibly being others outside, listening avidly and grinning at each other, brought embarrassment boiling to his cheeks. And with it irritation. He knew she was right, but he was responding emotionally, and he could feel rage rising within him. The inescapable twist and bias of self-justification warped her anger into unnecessary petulance, her legitimate complaint into ingratitude, her upset into rejection. His terrors came upon him.

'I'd better go,' he said, instinctively raising the shield behind which he had hidden for so long. She was facing away from him and said nothing. She was not going to back down now. He was about to turn and march out, seething with righteous indignation and crafting some hurtful Scythian shot to fire as he left, when her head dropped slightly, and her shoulders slumped. Her hair fell forward, revealing the nape of her neck.

And suddenly he could not go. He could not leave her. The anger drained away. Why this sight of her had that signal effect upon him, he had no idea. He stood for a moment, unsure what to do, and then said softly, 'Kal.' She did not respond. 'Kal. I'm sorry. I was wrong.' Her head lifted slightly. 'Please, Kal.'

She turned and looked at him, her grave eyes searching his face. Then she suddenly sat down on the couch. 'I'm sorry too, Dio. You didn't deserve that.' She smiled wanly. 'How could I be so ungrateful? But you should have told me. You really should.' The sadness and disappointment in her voice hurt him far more than the anger. 'And you lied to me. I thought that I could trust *you*, at least.'

'I thought I was doing the right thing. That's no excuse. I should have thought it through better.'

'And I shouldn't have lost my temper and said such stupid things. After all that you've done for me. And you were trying to protect me. I know that.' She looked across to the door that led to the slaves' quarters. 'You can stop listening at the door and come in now, Dianthe,' she said quietly.

There was a pause, then the door opened and a sheepish-looking Dianthe, her head submissively lowered, came slowly into the room.

'This little thing,' she said to Dio, 'denied absolutely that you had said anything about poison.'

'I told her to say nothing. She was trying to help. It's my responsibility.'

'I'm sorry, my Lady,' said the girl in a small voice.

'We'll say no more about it. Would you fetch some wine for the swordmaster?' Dianthe glanced up shyly at Dio and fled.

'I did tell you,' said Kal, 'but do you ever listen?'

'Sorry, did you say something?' he said, attempting to lift the still rather fraught atmosphere.

Kal smiled a perfunctory smile.

'How did you know?'

'Philomena. She burst in here asking who had poisoned Kerberos. Apparently, everyone knew, or assumed, that it had been poison. I felt like a complete fool.'

'I should have realised that others would draw the obvious conclusion.'

'That's not the point,' she said severely.

Dianthe returned with a kylix of wine. Dio looked up at her. 'I'm sorry,' he said as he took it. The little slave girl smiled at him and slipped out again.

'And that will be quite enough of that,' said Kal firmly. At least, it was a momentary and welcome touch of lightness. A brief ray of sun through the leaden clouds. 'Who did it?'

'Some bully boy by the name of Stratios.'

'But why?'

'We can't ask him now. He was seen decamping from the place early morning.' It wasn't technically a lie, he told himself, but he could not pretend that it wasn't equivocation. He was still deceiving her. But how could he face her with the truth? He didn't need to.

'It was Milt, wasn't it?'

He was silent for a while, then reluctantly agreed. 'At least, that's the most likely explanation.'

'But why would he?'

'He probably wants to persuade you to move away.'

'Then perhaps I ought to. Perhaps he will hurt Dianthe next. Or you. How could I have lived with someone for so many years and not know him? Remind me,' she added fiercely, 'if ever I look as though I am getting involved with a man again, about this day.'

That hurt. It surprised him how much.

TWENTY-ONE

THE POCK-MARKED, LITTLE scribe stood in front of Eurybiades and literally shook. His long face was a ghastly pallor and sheened with sweat. Eurybiades looked him up and down.

'Fuck me, Xen, what in the name of Hades is wrong with you?'

He was only a young man, barely out of his apprenticeship, and was plainly panic-stricken. He stammered and stumbled and trembled violently. His account was so broken and muddled that it took Eurybiades some time, and not a little effort, to grasp the problem. Apparently, Adrastus had given the lad a pile of scrolls for copying. In sorting them out, he had found one, evidently gathered up with the others by accident, which contained something he knew he should never have seen, but he would not say what. Whatever it was had terrified him.

'Calm yourself, you idiot!' bellowed Eurybiades.

The scribe closed his pale eyes and tried to control his breathing.

Eurybiades endeavoured to be calm himself. 'Now, first, did Adrastus go through that waste of space Charope, or did he just dump them on you?'

'He just gave them t-to me. I think… I think he did.' The youth swallowed convulsively. 'He… he usually does. I… Mine's the f-first in there. The first office. In the bureau. First one. He just gives them… to me.' He looked around fearfully, as though there might be a spy secreted in Eurybiades' small office. 'Charope's at the far end. Adrastus doesn't bother with him.' He took several tremulous breaths. Now that he had told someone, he seemed to be calming down a little.

'Good,' muttered Eurybiades, still thinking furiously. 'Now, were you working on anything that your useless arsehole of a superior would be checking?'

'No. Routine copying. The duty book.' His voice still shook, but at least he was making coherent sense.

'Excellent. He's an idle bastard, so I doubt he'll bother with you. Finally, did anyone see you coming here?'

'I don't think so.' He screwed his unusually pale eyes shut with concentration. 'No. No-one did.'

'Right. Straight back, then.'

The lad's knees visibly wobbled, and Eurybiades came around from behind his desk and gave him a substantial push to get him started. They hurried back to the bureau. No-one was in evidence, and they slipped into the cell. On the clerk's angled graphotrapeza lay a pile of parchment scrolls and the codex upon which he had been working.

'Now, stick your fingers down your throat and make yourself sick.'

The little scribe goggled at him.

Eurybiades shrugged. 'Do it, or take the scroll to Adrastus yourself.'

He hastily thrust his fingers down his throat and gagged.

'Farther, man, farther. Make yourself properly sick.'

He thrust farther and suddenly vomited.

Eurybiades scrutinised his efforts critically. 'It'll have to do. Now, listen, Xen. You never looked at the scrolls. I was passing and heard you throwing up. I sent you to your quarters. Have you food and wine there?'

'Not much.'

'You might have to go hungry. You stay in because you're ill. You don't go out for any reason. If anyone comes, take to your bed and bloody well make sure you look ill.' He regarded the clerk's pale and sweating face. 'Shouldn't be difficult. You do *not* recover until you hear from me.'

The youth mumbled something, turned and fled.

Eurybiades closed the door and rapidly scanned through the scrolls until he found the offending article. He whistled with surprise.

TWENTY-TWO

Dio called in as he had promised. Kal was sitting on the couch in the reception room. She smiled as he came in, but then looked down.

'How are you, Dio?' she enquired, almost formally.

'I'm fine. Had to give Gelon a torching.'

Dianthe came in quietly, took his cloak and left, closing the door behind her. Dio sat down.

'Why?' she asked. She seemed far away.

'He went way too far with one of the recruits. I suspect that I'm not going to be invited to his name day symposium now.'

She shuddered slightly. 'He's a nasty piece of work.'

'He is,' he agreed. 'How are you?'

'I'm not so bad. A bit miserable, if the truth be known, but I suppose that's to be expected.'

There was an uncomfortable silence. A distance still lay

between them, making them cautious and reserved, even withdrawn.

Kal was staring at the fire. 'I keep thinking of poor Kerberos,' she whispered. 'He had so little of life.'

'We cannot know what his life might have been. It might have been filled with pain and suffering. "Call no man's life happy until the funeral cakes are baked."'

'That's Chromius. Achilleus in Tartarus. We saw it together at Ilios. You told that awful joke to the man sitting next to you.'

'The chimera and the vulture? That's hardly awful—it's one of my best.'

'The two descriptions are not mutually exclusive. And you timed it so that you finished it just as the play started.'

'Always had an impeccable sense of timing.'

'And the idiot began to laugh.'

'As I recall, he was a man of exceptional taste and discernment,' he said stiffly.

'And everybody said shush. And you began to laugh. And everybody said shush louder. And I began to laugh, and we just couldn't stop.'

'I told you it was a good joke.'

'It had nothing whatsoever to do with what you are pleased to call a joke.' The familiar, easy and relaxed atmosphere was beginning to envelop them like a comfortable old cloak. 'That was the night we went to that Thracian eating house, and I was so sick afterwards.'

'I thought you were supposed to have Thracian blood. You should have been able to handle well-hung sand lizard in fermented goat's milk.'

'You said you thought it was rabbit in a cheese sauce.'

'My Thracian's never been that good, and the words for rabbit and lizard are very similar. A simple mistake anyone could make.'

'Anyway, I've just remembered. You said that the play was very humdrum stuff.'

'So it was.'

'So why are you quoting him?'

'Even Chromius can produce a good line. With a bit of straining.'

'I distinctly recall you saying that Chromius couldn't be deep unless he fell into a well.'

'Did I?' said Dio innocently. 'I must be one of those people who change their opinions with the winds. Extraordinary.'

'Really? I didn't believe such wretches existed. But I do now.' They laughed.

Then she cried. She stood up abruptly and said, 'Hold me, Dio. I desperately need a hug.'

He stood and took her in his arms, feeling decidedly uncomfortable. She clung to him, buried her face in his shoulder and sobbed. He could think of nothing to say and patted her back solicitously but ineffectually. The crying eased, then stopped. She pulled back slightly and regarded him with big, damp eyes.

'You don't mind? I know you have a thing about touch.'

'I'm fine,' he lied. 'You can have a hug whenever you want.'

'I sorely feel the need for one sometimes,' she said. 'I'll hold you to that.'

'So to speak,' he said. Dyaus, he thought, what have I done now? He could not suppress the memory of the press of her breasts to his chest or the rosewater smell of her hair.

TWENTY-THREE

'Quick thinking, Eury,' said Dio, leaning against the parapet of the outer wall and looking out across the untidy huddle of Glapolis. There were no guards within a hundred paces, so it was a safe place to talk. The wind was chill and moaned quietly to itself. 'You have described it all with impressive lucidity and in inordinate detail. Now what did the bloody thing say?'

'Gratitude,' lamented Eurybiades, 'is long gone from this world.'

'Patience might be but a step behind.'

'Well, to be honest, not a lot. They were all obviously code names. Apparently, the warthog is now in control, the wolf is concerned about the cockerel, and they have decided not even to approach the rhinoceros. Come to think of it, nor would I.'

'So, apart from confirming that somebody is talking to someone about something, it doesn't help us a great deal.'

'Ah, you forget the postscript.'

'How could I have forgotten it when you've never even mentioned it?' exclaimed Dio in exasperation.

'Written in another hand.' Eurybiades' eyes rolled upwards as he recalled the exact words. 'Tell M that Sofia sends her love and says that she cannot wait until their day of happiness is come.'

Dio stared at him as Eurybiades grinned in triumph. 'Dyaus's balls. That's got to be the Sofia who's the niece to Laomedon. He's marrying her to Miltiades.'

Eurybiades opened his hands wide in an expansive gesture. 'He's got three married sisters. He has nieces to spare.'

'But to Miltiades? He's not a satrap. What a move for him. Connected by marriage to the new Imperial Family. No wonder he dumped Kal. I take it the scrolls quickly disappeared?'

'Checked this morning. All gone. Surprised you didn't hear that pathetic piece of horseshit sigh with relief from here.'

'Thanks, Eury. You've done well.'

'Thought so myself, I modestly confess.'

TWENTY-FOUR

A STACK OF OLD wax tablets tumbled from a couch and crashed onto the already litter-strewn floor, raising a fine cloud of dust. They were in Radamanthus's office, which had clearly been ransacked by a gang of drunken burglars.

'Don't you ever tidy this place up?' asked Dio, somewhat superfluously.

'Nah,' said Radamanthus, moving a couple of wine-stained kylixes to one side and pushing away a dagger in a tooled leather scabbard. 'It only gets untidy again.' He unrolled a map of the Troian Empire, picked off a dead spider or two, and pored over it with Dio.

'I don't think,' speculated Dio, 'that Laomedon has that much support. The scroll Eurybiades found didn't sound as though he was having a lot of success. If he had, he would have moved by now. He's rash and impetuous by nature. But he has to be very careful about approaching the satraps, as most of them fear him. and would welcome the chance to rid themselves of such a threat.'

'But if they fear him, wouldn't that induce them to join him?'

'Only when he clearly has sufficient support to mount a credible challenge. It's a matter of momentum. It's a ravine he's got to jump. And at the moment I suspect he isn't sure he'll make it. He is chary of approaching the satraps for fear of them betraying his move because he lacks sufficient support, but without approaching them he can't gather the support. He's caught between the lion and the wolves. He may have built up a formidable army, but not enough to take on the rest of the Empire.'

He looked at the map again and stabbed his finger down. 'We know that he's already essentially at war with Thessalia to his north, and Lesser Troia to the east is Charmides' province. Like Laomedon, Charmides is a nephew to Aristogeiton, but by an elder sister, so he has a better claim to the throne. A victory for Laomedon would be an effective death sentence for Charmides, so he'll get no support there. The shitehawk's hemmed in. Whatever support he has gathered is going to be patchy and difficult to concentrate.'

Radamanthus scrubbed his face. 'And?'

'Antikles in Mykerenos hates the bastard, and Diodoros in Makedonia is Aristogeiton's oldest friend, so they'll be hostile. And Inachos in Lakadaemon, squeezed as he is between Diodoros and Charmides, is almost certainly going to stay quiet, especially as he's only just been made satrap.'

'So effectively the whole southeast would be anti, if it weren't for Raxamenes and Miltiades?'

Dio tapped the map. 'Not only that, but they're squeezed between Mykerenos and Makedonia. And, not to hone too fine an edge on it, Raxamenes is a cautious man.'

'Meaning he's a full-blown, white-livered, milk-blooded coward.'

'That too. I reckon that Raxamenes wouldn't dare move without Gla behind him.'

Radamanthus scratched his jaw. 'So, what you're saying is that Miltiades is more important to that big bastard than his command might seem to warrant?'

'Exactly. And don't forget that Ilios is much more vulnerable to a thrust from the Thebeaid than from the Debateable Lands. Gla could be the key to the whole enterprise. Hence the marriage alliance.'

'Couldn't Laomedon just quietly forget the whole thing, if not enough are marching to his flutes?'

'I very much doubt it. He's gone too far. It would all eventually break cover and then even the emperor would be forced to act. Laomedon's got to throw the knucklebones, and sooner rather than later.' Dio rolled up the map, glanced down and carefully picked up a dead mouse by its tail.

'Lunch,' said Radamanthus nonchalantly.

TWENTY-FIVE

DIO WAS JUST coming from the stable block when he was hailed by Patroclus. A tall, thin, patrician-looking man, he gave the impression of having some unpleasant smell under his nose. Dio had always claimed it was due to the tiny square-cut beard that he had affected. It had looked ridiculous, but someone must have told him, as it had recently disappeared. But not, apparently, the smell.

'Ah, there you are, swordmaster,' he called. His voice was cultured but light in tone, lacking authority, a failing of which he was uncomfortably aware. As Miltiades' personal aide, he regarded himself as a figure of some importance. Certainly when compared to the rough soldiery, of whom Diomedes was the prime example. There was no love lost between the two.

Dio looked across briefly as he walked by. 'Indeed, I am, Patroclus.'

'You must report to my Lord on the instant.' The tone was supercilious, even contemptuous.

Dio stopped, turned around and stared Patroclus straight in the face. The man's eyes immediately dropped.

'I think,' said Dio slowly and deliberately, 'that you might well consider rephrasing that.'

Patroclus paled. He seemed to be finding his red leather boots objects of fascination. Dio thought them silly.

'Swordmaster,' said Patroclus carefully, 'my Lord would be grateful if you could see him as soon as it may be convenient.'

Dio continued to stare at the increasingly uncomfortable man. After a while, he said, 'I will be there as soon as I can. You may go.'

The humiliated man at least had enough spirit to shoot a brief glance of pure venom in Dio's direction, and then scuttled away a little faster than dignity allowed.

There was a familiar laugh, and Radamanthus walked up. 'It's about time someone taught that popinjay some manners.'

'It was stupid and unnecessary. Pandarus would have had the skin from my back.' Then Dio grinned. 'But highly gratifying.' His face hardened, and he pulled Radamanthus to one side. He spoke quietly. 'Had a word with the despatch rider who just arrived. He's an old source. Aristogeiton has been assassinated.'

Radamanthus sucked his teeth sharply. 'Dyaus Pitar, so it starts.'

Dio nodded sombrely.

'How?'

'Three of his personal guard cut him down. They were immediately overpowered, but died in heartbeats from self-inflicted poison. Miltiades has sent for me. No doubt to express appropriate shock and horror. For the moment, not a word.' He strode away.

Radamanthus watched him go. 'It's going to be a long and bloody year,' he murmured. 'Here's to quick promotion.'

TWENTY-SIX

Dio scratched, then went straight in. Miltiades was standing by his desk reading a scroll, Adrastus sitting on his tall stool at his graphotrapeza in one corner of the office, assiduously writing and pretending not to be there. Miltiades looked Dio straight in the eye. Almost as if challenging him to say anything. 'The emperor has been assassinated.'

'I know. Suicidal fanatics.'

Miltiades stared at him with surprise, then shook his head. 'I don't know how you do it.'

He passed the scroll across to Dio, who skimmed through it. It contained nothing he did not already know.

'What do you make of it?' demanded Miltiades. They were back to pretending, then.

Dio stood for a moment, considering. He was seldom one to speak rashly. 'It's odd. Finding someone willing to die is not easy. Finding three?' He raised his eyebrows. 'Aristogeiton was too meek and mild for it to have been revenge, so it must have been a power play. But you don't assassinate an emperor then sit on your backside. You go in fast and hard. Yet there's no sign of any follow-up.'

Miltiades' window was open as usual. Dio glanced out at the pale and lifeless land scoured by an unforgiving wind. 'Besides, why now? It's too bloody early. It's the depths of winter. Ice. Mud. Lack of forage. Shortage of available food supplies. It doesn't make sense.' He shook his head in bewilderment. 'We'll know who was responsible when they make their move. Which has got to be soon.' He paused. 'But my gold's on Laomedon. As you well know.' He did not make it obvious, but he watched Miltiades for any telling reaction. And saw none.

Miltiades nodded. 'That means civil war.' A silence stretched between them. A thing of shadows. The holder's face was unreadable. 'I can do little until they break cover.'

So, they were going to play this game out to the bitter end.

Miltiades walked over to the window, his hands behind his back, and gazed out in that characteristic stance of his. 'I can look to strength in numbers. Put your armour on when you see the foe in his. Get the Thracians behind me. Talk to Zagos and Tereus in the Rhodopians. Dyaus, it might even be worthwhile approaching the Aggies. I can put the garrison on a war footing as of now, and even start some active recruiting.'

This was a totally different Miltiades. Normally he would have asked for Dio's opinion and recommendations, and then almost certainly have gone along with them. But not this time. It had the look of prearranged planning. Although the idea of approaching the Agrianians puzzled him.

'What about Antikles and Diodorus? Neither are friends to Laomedon.' Dio was almost enjoying this game. 'With Mykerenos and Makedonia in a shield line with you, if it is Laomedon, you would have the whole east as a solid bloc. A real position of strength.'

Miltiades pretended to consider, rubbing the bridge of his nose. 'I don't want to get dragged into conflict by allies with their own agendas, and both are too distant to provide immediate assistance anyway. I think I may make contact, but a hard alliance is probably not in our best interests.'

I'll bet it's not, thought Dio. He threw another discus for Miltiades to dodge. 'If you're going to actively recruit, what are you going to use for money?' He knew the answer as well as Miltiades. He just wanted him to say it.

Miltiades looked over his shoulder and raised his eyebrows. 'The regional treasury, of course.'

'The emperor would regard it as treason.'

'What emperor?' demanded Miltiades.

Now we come to it, thought Dio. 'Troilus, of course.'

There was no hesitation. He turned around to face Dio. 'Even weaker and more inept than his elder brother. Obviously not yet formally named by the Grand Council, let alone invested. And may well never be. I'm acting for the general good in an interregnum. If the man I eventually support becomes emperor, he'll be grateful.'

That was as close as a man could get to admitting treason without actually doing so. Dio caught the warning look from Adrastus, but Miltiades ignored it and seemed unconcerned.

'If he doesn't...' Miltiades shrugged. 'It will make no difference.' He returned to staring out of the window. 'There's Raxamenes in Kadmeia, of course.'

'Unless you've already decided to swing behind Laomedon, keep well to sea of that one. He's Laomedon's man.'

Miltiades spun round, looking surprised. 'You're certain of that?'

'I am.' As are you, he thought, and as obviously was Adrastus, who had stopped writing, but then quickly began again.

Miltiades returned to his chair and sat down, running a finger up and down the bridge of his nose. He glanced at Adrastus, who now seemed oblivious, then turned back to Dio. 'You're on surprisingly good terms with Neritos. He'd know if it would be worth approaching the Confederacy. He'd give you a hearing. His is the nearest tribal territory, and even an Agrianian pauses before he fouls his own threshold.'

'The Confederacy is a name. The Aggies spend their entire lives happily hacking each other to pieces. That hairy ape is only one of the Agrianian tribal leaders, and by no means the most influential. And,' he added, 'in my considerable experience, they are most definitely not beyond fouling their own threshold. In fact, it would be nice if they bothered to go that far.'

Miltiades blandly ignored the negative response to his suggestion. 'How risky would it be?'

'Speaking to him?' Dio pulled a wry face. 'Approaching the Agrianians is always a risk. They're as unpredictable as a bear with a headache.'

Miltiades looked thoughtful and rubbed his chin. He picked up the scroll again and read it once more. As though something might have changed in the meantime. 'Nevertheless, I'd be grateful if you could discover what Neritos is thinking. But leave it until after Officer's Call on Areos. You can brief them as to the possible military outcomes.'

'Agrianians and thinking?' muttered Dio sourly, and turned to go. He had a bad feeling about this. The Agrianians were not going to get involved beyond allowing some of their wild young men to be recruited. He could only assume that Miltiades wanted him out of the way for a while, and that worried him.

TWENTY-SEVEN

'How long will you be away for?' There was no denying the concern etched on her face and woven through her voice. He played the sad, old game of wondering what the true significance was. Was she merely unhappy that a useful support was not going to be around for some time, or did it portend more?

'I'll be leaving the day after tomorrow. Probably a se'ennight, possibly more.'

She sat primly, hands clasped in her lap, and stared into the fire. 'What's going to happen, now Aristogeiton's dead? Will it come to war?'

'It might.' The silence enveloped them. Only the crackling of the flames marked the passage of time.

'It's been eleven years since the last Thracian War. I was beginning to think that peace was the natural state of affairs.'

'Peace is just drawing breath between wars.' It was the wrong thing to say. He looked down and cleared his throat. 'Listen, Kal. Just in case. Should anything happen…' He hesitated. Her eyes were on him, large and round. 'Look to Rad. I trust him. He will ensure that you get any help you need.'

'You said there would be no problem with Neritos.'

'I'm sure there won't be. But you know me. I'm never satisfied unless I've planned for every eventuality, no matter how unlikely. I just… want to know that you'll be alright.'

Dyaus, he had nearly said *need*.

'I'm not the one visiting a homicidal barbarian,' she pointed out, a little acerbically.

'He's not that bad.'

He could feel the tension, the currents of concern, of unease. The halting speech. The long pauses. The slight edge. Neither were saying what they wanted to. He could not tell her of Sofia. It would only hurt her more. And he could not see how it would affect anything. After all, Kal was now divorced and unceremoniously thrust from the path of Miltiades' rise, so she was no obstacle. Merely a minor irritant.

But he didn't like this mission. It felt wrong. He could not see the threat, but it cast a long shadow. He had even considered refusing to go, but then Miltiades might use that as the excuse to push him aside. Drive him from Gla even. He did not want to face the implications of his almost panic-stricken reaction to the possibility.

There was a light tap on the door and Dianthe entered in her usual calm and unobtrusive way, with a herbal tisane for Kal. 'Would the swordmaster like one?' she asked quietly.

'No, I thank you.' He rose as the door shut behind the slave girl. 'I really must be on my way. Milt wants me to brief everyone tomorrow. That's a first.'

Kal looked up and gave him a tight smile. 'You will be careful, won't you? The Agrianians have a reputation for being untrustworthy.'

'You're telling me?' he asked incredulously.

'Well, someone has to,' she said, 'and I got the job, as usual.' She smiled again, though it could not mask the worry in her eyes.

TWENTY-EIGHT

D IO WRAPPED HIS cloak around him more tightly. The recent deep drifts of snow had largely melted, but the strong northerly carried ice in its maw, and the cold crumbled into his bones. He was following a good track that contoured across the foothills of the Panormus range, meandering in and out of thin, coniferous woodland. Beyond the near ridge of lower hills rose the sharper, more jagged mountains of Panormus proper, hazed blue with distance. Between the two lay the Kodros Valley, the territory of Neritos's people. The track Dio was on skirted a steep, conical hill ahead to drop into the fertile valley beyond, and thence through the main pass, known as the Skamandrian Gates. Unsurprisingly, it was always well guarded.

But for now, his attention was on the ridge to his right. He was studying the undulating ridgeline, looking for a particular pattern of rock formations. When he had visited

Neritos last, they had gone hunting for the elusive lynx in the high forests that cloaked the mountain slopes. He had become separated from the rest and stumbled upon an unsuspected narrow pass through the hills, one that led straight through and down towards the track that he was now following.

Dio had recognised at once that it was clearly a useful route for the raiding parties that occasionally harried the steadings in the grasslands below, bypassing the fort that overlooked the Skamandrian Gates. A gift of the Gods sent to supply Neritos the perfect alibi. The power of Gla was too great for him to ignore, but so long as he was circumspect and reasonably restrained, he could rustle a few cows now and then. With no verification from the fort, Miltiades would choose to believe the wide-eyed protestations of innocence.

Although unknown to the plains dwellers, it was clearly guarded. He had even spied, hunkered down below the col, a small stone hut for the pickets. From deep within the shadow of the trees, Dio had watched as the sentries changed, and had carefully committed its topography to memory, before turning to find the main party, who he fed a sorry tale of getting himself totally lost and mistaking Lake Asopus for the larger Lake Dyme. A tale of such self-effacing incompetence that there could be no suspicion of his discovery.

'A miser of information,' Kal had once called him, and it was true. Knowledge was never wasted but hoarded against its need. And now, that knowledge might be of inestimable use. The Agrianians were, to put it kindly, of uncertain temper. If he needed to get out quickly, this secret pass could be a lifesaver.

He grunted with satisfaction. Just round the flank of the rise to his right, he could make out the top of a distinctive pillar of rock. That was the place. He pulled his horse to a halt, the pack horse behind immediately stopping and beginning to graze. He would not be in view of their watch yet. He studied the ground. Just this side of the pass he could see a shallow, descending gulley that led across the top of an extensive scree slope, picked out by a broken line of residual snow still surviving in its hollow. Then, to his practised eye, from its end he could make out a rough track. It cut back down steeply to disappear into the fringe of trees that lined the road a stade ahead. He estimated distances and directions and scanned the surrounding foothills until the pattern was imprinted on his memory.

Finally, he looked around at his immediate environs and led his pack horse towards a large coppice of trees into which a stream meandered. Within he found what he had hoped to find. A good grassy clearing with the cold mountain stream to one side, bubbling and boiling over tumbled rocks. He unloaded the pack horse and carefully hid his scuttle bag in a hollow between two rocks, covering it with a layer of moss. He hobbled the horse and threw a blanket over it. There was little chance of it coming to any harm. He would collect it on his return. One way or another.

Then he returned to the track. He continued on his way, repeatedly checking for landmarks, aware that he might well be descending this hidden pass at night, but careful not to be too obvious. He would be under covert scrutiny—of that he had no doubt. But he was reasonably satisfied. He had not survived this long without ensuring that the knucklebones were as weighted in his favour as possible. Pandarus's lessons had put down deep and abiding roots.

TWENTY-NINE

He arrived at the small fortress as dusk began to wash out the colours of the landscape, making the rose and purple splash of the sunset even more vivid. The fort lay about twenty stadia below the Skamandrian Gates, built on a low rise to protect a tall stone watchtower, at the top of which, covered by thick, well-oiled cloth, lay a beacon bonfire, ready for lighting. Two repeater towers stood between it and Gla. If the Agrianians ever boiled out, intent on slaughter and rapine, the garrison would pray to every God they knew that they could hold long enough for Gla to send relief. It was not a popular posting.

Twice in Dio's time at Gla it had been overrun, and the garrison slaughtered. Thrice it had held. Each time, the Troians had stormed the Skamandrian Gates, wasting the poor fields and burning Neritos's 'capital', Amyklai, in grim retaliation. The Agrianians seemed to find lessons hard to learn, or had until recently. There had been no major incursions for six years.

The wooden gates, covered in hides to protect them from fire, were securely closed. A couple of well-muffled sentries on the walkway above watched his approach, before one recognised him and called down to open the gate. The commander of the post was waiting for him as he rode in, a short, stocky man with an unkempt red beard and a marked strabismus.

Dio dismounted from his tired horse and stretched his aching back. 'Theo,' he greeted. 'Still contaminating the place, you cross-eyed, old reprobate?'

'Dio,' responded Theophanes, 'still strutting around and doing bugger-all?' They grinned at one another. 'Not seen you in a long while.' He scrutinised Dio suspiciously with his disconcerting squint. 'So, what brings our esteemed swordmaster to the unmentionable nether regions of the Troian Empire? Not trouble?'

'No. Not yet, at least.'

'It's usually trouble when you appear,' said Theophanes gloomily. 'It'll be on its way, then.'

'We'll talk over dinner. I presume that you will be having dinner.'

'What passes for it in this forsaken piss hole.'

'You haven't changed, then. Still the same happy soul you always were.'

'I can't help it,' said Theophanes morosely. 'I'm just a natural fountain of glee. Ask Tenebros there.' He gestured at the hoplite taking Dio's horse.

'A veritable fountain, sir,' agreed the soldier stolidly. 'Keeps us laughing all day long, he does.'

'You see?' remarked Theophanes with some satisfaction. 'What did I tell you?' He signalled to a passing hoplite. 'Tell the cooks there will be a guest dining with me tonight. So, something special. Perhaps we could have mutton stew as a treat.'

The man smiled. 'Mutton stew, sir. For a change. Yes, sir.'

Theophanes led Dio to his living quarters, which consisted of a small two-room hut built against the wall of the watchtower. His quarters were cramped and spartan, a small table and a chest below the tiny window and a couple of couches, but a fire blazed in the hearth, and it was warm, if a little smoky. A guard roster was pinned up on the grimy whitewashed wall.

'I'll throw that sad bastard Linus out of his room, and you can have that. He's my deuteros, and he's not worth a gnat's fart. He can squeeze in with the ektatoi for one night.'

'I'll roll down with the ektatoi. Don't disturb your deuteros for me.'

'What, and ruin the only bit of pleasure I've had for six se'ennights? Do the lazy waste of mutton stew good. It will certainly brighten my day.' He gestured Dio to a couch and went to an amphora of wine and pitcher of water on the chest, together with a small collection of battered kylixes. 'Half and half?'

'Just a third,' said Dio.

Theophanes mixed the wine and water and handed him his kylix before sitting down opposite him. 'It's not Rhodian red, I'm afraid. Dog piss pink. And second-rate dog piss at that. But it's the best we get out here.'

'It's not bad,' said Dio, taking a cautious sip.

'Oh, it's not *bad*,' agreed Theophanes, taking a deep draught and pulling a face. 'It's only fucking awful. The water's not so bad, though.' He looked over at his visitor judiciously. 'So what are you up to? Something nefarious, no doubt, that will undoubtedly dump shitloads of mayhem on my weary shoulders.'

'Something along those lines,' agreed Dio cheerfully. 'I'm going to visit Neritos.'

'Just a social call, then? A bit like dropping in on a pride of lions for dinner?'

'Neritos isn't too intolerable. He's achieved a modicum of sense in his old age. It's finally dawned on him that, if you share a cave with a bear, don't prod it with a stick.'

'Humph. I know another one. Don't shove your head into a beehive to see what's inside.'

'Hey. This could be a good game. How long can you hold a conversation by only using metaphorical aphorisms?'

Theophanes scowled. 'Only as long as the other bugger uses words of one bloody syllable. You read too much. I'm just a simple soldier. Though any new game is welcome to fight the blasted tedium. A man could be bored to death out here. More wine?'

Dio shook his head.

Theophanes went and refilled his. The water was a perfunctory splash. Dio took a quiet mental note. He would speak to Miltiades on his return about getting Theo posted back to Gla.

Theophanes sat down again. 'So why are we talking to Neritos? He's been quiet for years, and there are no rumours of any trouble.' He paused, then added sombrely, 'Yet.'

'Just exploring some possibilities,' said Dio.

'I know. No-one ever tells me shit. Just watch the Skam, Theo, and light the fucking fire. That's all I ever get.'

'However, I would be grateful if you could send out a few patrols as often as you can over the next se'ennight or so, and warn them to look out for some poor sod running his horse into the ground and followed by a horde of bloodthirsty Aggies.'

'Will do. Lead a few myself. Do me good to get out more. Though it will leave the fort in the incompetent hands of that idle bugger Linus.' He looked at Dio shrewdly. 'The assassination, I presume?'

Dio shrugged.

'Laomedon?'

'That's where the clever money is going. Though he hasn't made a move yet, which is odd. These things need speed and momentum. Perhaps we're totally misreading it. It might have been personal rather than political.'

'It still leaves a bloody big hole to be filled. Someone's going to try. So, we're back to Laomedon. Could be worse. At least he's strong and decisive. They reckon he's done a good job of taming the Debateable Lands.'

By savagery and terror, but Dio wasn't going to get into an argument. Theophanes' view seemed a worryingly common one.

Theophanes looked thoughtful. 'It won't be good for you, Dio. They say you spanked him like a child at Kerakos. He won't forget or forgive.'

Dio grimaced. 'That's a river to ford when I come to it. For the moment, I've enough to worry about with that hairy bastard Neritos.'

'Rather you than me, I must say. Are you really anticipating trouble?'

'Always anticipate trouble when you're dealing with the Aggies. They're totally unpredictable—'

'Like any and all females between the ages of two and a hundred and two.'

'—prone to mindless violence—'

'Like all women.'

'—and without the faintest trace of rationality.'

Theophanes sighed heavily. 'As I said.'

Dio looked up. 'You've had some bad experiences with women, then?'

'Who hasn't?' he said gloomily. There was a rap on the door, and a hoplite entered bearing a rough wooden tray with two steaming bowls and hunks of bread. Theophanes brightened momentarily. 'Ah, the mutton stew.' Then his face reverted to its usual lugubrious set. 'Again.'

THIRTY

Neritos was squat and ugly. A button nose, pop eyes and hair sprouting luxuriantly from nostrils and ears. He was dressed in a dirty tunic, had filthy bare feet and smelt like an old goat. The only sign of his 'kingship' was a heavy gold chain around his neck from which dangled a finger bone. Reportedly, it was that of one of his brothers, whom he had slain in ritual combat for the kingship. Despite his unprepossessing appearance, it was obvious that everyone walked carefully around him.

Especially now that he was drunk, and bellowing out an incomprehensible drinking song with scant regard for the melody. A young lad with some panpipes was vainly trying to provide meaningful accompaniment. Some of Neritos's bondsmen were singing too, but whether it was the same song was totally beyond Dio's ability to discriminate. He was tired; his head ached; his stomach felt decidedly queasy, and he was trying to breathe through his mouth to minimise the stench of sweat, rancid oil and human waste. The wooden hall was thick with smoke that made his eyes sting and water.

Hearing a thunk, Dio looked around him. Neritos was now slumped across the table, seemingly insensible. He was at the head of a long, rough-hewn trestle, strewn with the greasy detritus of a gargantuan feast, with Dio in the place of honour to his right. The rest of the benches were crowded with Neritos's kinsmen, sub-chiefs and personal bondsmen, all equally filthy and pungent and now in various states of inebriation, one or two already stretched out amongst the soiled rushes on the hard earth floor and snoring contentedly.

A huge fire in the hearth that occupied the centre of one of the side walls and a handful of tallow candles provided the flickering light. Slave girls brought round earthenware bowls of the sour fermented mare's milk that was the Agrianians' national drink, warily dodging the grasping hands that reached out lecherously for them. Sometimes they were not fast enough, and Dio fastidiously averted his eyes.

It had been a long day. Someone had sharp eyes, because he had been met at the Skamandrian Gates by Chileos, one of Neritos's many sons, with a guard of sullen javelin men. Chileos was mounted on a shaggy mountain pony. As he took after his father in the matter of hairiness, the line of demarcation between man and horse was somewhat vague. He was surprisingly amiable and chatty, but his men were silent and surly.

It was a long ride to Amyklai, but they trotted alongside tirelessly. Dio had always argued that, with the right officers and a modicum of discipline, Agrianians would make the finest light infantry in the world. They were savage, tough, tireless and trained to the javelin from the moment that they could walk, so that, by adolescence, they could throw it forty paces with unerring accuracy. Which thoughts did nothing to lighten Dio's mood. He had a bad feeling about this, and both Chileos's odd affability and his men's overtly hostile demeanour sounded a warning call.

He should be safe enough. Twenty years ago, he had stumbled across a young Agrianian fighting for his life against three clearly experienced foes. Impulsively, Dio had gone to his assistance, and they had killed all three. That man was Neritos, caught up in the fratricidal bloodbath that invariably erupted after the death of an Agrianian kinglet. And it was Neritos who had eventually emerged triumphant and had sworn blood brotherhood with Dio. Considering his baleful relationship with his uterine brothers, however, Dio wasn't at all sure how much this was really worth. Never trust a live wolf or a dead Agrianian.

The Agrianian king had seemed pleased to see him, giving him a long and smelly bear hug and declaring a feast in honour of his great friend. They had talked that afternoon. Neritos had been guarded with his responses. The gist was that the Agrianian confederacy was unlikely to interest itself in the doings of the Troian Empire. He told a rambling tale of a stoat who lived quietly and well beside a lion's den. When another lion turned up to challenge the incumbent, the stoat decided to lend tooth and claw, and together they defeated the intruder. The lion, now aware of the stoat's existence, promptly killed it. The point of the story was clear.

However, Neritos thought that there would be no problem with recruiting Agrianian mercenaries if that was required. It was just as Dio had predicted. What really worried him was Neritos's attitude. It was wrong. He was normally foulmouthed and insulting, albeit in a jovial way, but now he was being polite and complimentary. He was being 'nice'. Aggies didn't do nice. It was unnerving.

The noise in the hall was becoming deafening; men were singing, a couple were fighting, to the cheers and encouragement of those around them; and several were rutting openly and shamelessly with slave girls. Dogs snarled and snapped over discarded bones, and a drummer was beating happily on a huge drum which seemed to be made of human skin, if the remnants of a hand hanging down one side was any clue. It was still early, but Dio had had his fill of Agrianian hospitality. He turned to Neritos, who lay forward on the table in a pool of spilt milk wine, his head on his arms and his eyes closed. Dio shook him by the shoulder. The King opened a bleary eye and gazed rather uncomprehendingly at him. 'I am tired, Great King,' said Dio in his best Agrianian. 'I would like to sleep now.' Behind him, he could hear scornful laughter. No doubt a comment on his barbaric pronunciation. 'My thanks for such a magnificent feast.'

'Pleased you enjoyed it,' mumbled Neritos, and his eyes closed again. Dio slid off the end of the bench and headed for the exit, stepping over a comatose man en route. He glanced back when he reached the door. Neritos was sitting up, and half-turned round to speak to a hulking warrior who wore the boiled leather cuirass of his Household Guard. The King appeared very much awake. Dio instantly looked to his front and passed into the wonderful crisp air. The vague feeling of unease had suddenly crystallised into real and immediate threat.

Outside, fronting the Feast Hall, was a large open area where the great meets of the Agrianians were held. In the middle, a bonfire blazed, tended by an elderly slave, the sign that the king caroused within. Beyond, amongst the untidy huddles of thatched wooden huts, a place of shifting shadows and uncertain shapes, someone moved back from the light. Someone enclosed within a dark cloak wrapped tightly around him. Someone whose size, form and movement looked strangely familiar. He was wearing greaves, so he wasn't an Agrianian; and as he stepped out of sight behind a hut, a flare of the fire cast a sudden light on his left leg, throwing a dent in the greave into sharp relief. That lazy bastard Gelon should have hammered it out long ago. That explained the unusual briefing Milt had demanded. It had given Gelon time to get to Neritos first. Dio had suspected that he was in deep shit, but now knew it was over his head.

He was careful not to react, not even to look towards the shadowed place into which Gelon had disappeared, but walked across the meeting ground to the hut that had been allocated to him. He stumbled a couple of times. It would not hurt to let the watchers assume that he was the worse for alcoholic wear, though he had been cautiously abstemious throughout the long feast. He fumbled with the door, then flung it open in obvious exasperation, flooding the interior with the ruddy light from the blaze. There was no-one there. He leaned against the lintel for a moment as though steadying himself, but in fact carefully studying the interior, marking down obstacles and gauging the positioning of his belongings, before standing upright with exaggerated care and stepping inside to close the door behind him.

He threw himself forward through the darkness, grabbed his sword belt and cloak and flung himself through the open window opposite. Sprawled in the muddy space between the surrounding huts, he rolled and scrambled quickly into the black shadow of one. He quietened his heavy breathing and lay still. He had only been there for a few heartbeats when two Household Guards, one the man who had been speaking to Neritos as Dio had left, slid silently into the space he had just vacated. They moved like ghosts to the side of one of the huts and squatted down on their haunches, javelins to hand and obviously intent on his window. As they were three-quarters turned away from him, Dio took the opportunity to creep away.

He trod a deadly balance. If he moved hastily, he could make a fatal noise. If not quickly enough, he could easily be run down when the hut was found empty. The hekates passed with the agonising slowness of shackled prisoners. Finally, he was sure that he was out of sight and far enough away to risk rising to his feet. He fastened his sword belt and wrapped himself in his black cloak before stepping out with a seemingly confident air. He made his way towards the central thoroughfare that ran to the main gate. It was now late, and the place was deserted. Nothing moved but a thin cat slinking across the muddy way. The sound of stentorian snores, a distant murmured conversation, a dog barking, suddenly ending with a yelp.

Ahead he saw the gate with torches on either side and the dark figures of guards. He immediately slipped to his left into the jumble of huts. He found his way through until he arrived at the perimeter wall. It was a palisade of sharpened stakes only ten hands high or so, but embedded atop a high and steep bank. He identified a section where the stakes had slumped forward a little. He waited as long as he dared, listening for any movement, but all was quiet.

He quickly scrambled up the bank to the rampart and hauled himself up the stakes. He swung up first one leg, then the other, to jam his feet between the crude points, then pushed himself up to teeter perilously atop the palisade. He jumped awkwardly down the other side, feeling a sudden jerk as his cloak, billowing behind him, caught on one of the stakes, and then a sharp, ripping sound as it gave, scarcely impeding his fall. He landed awkwardly on the scarp slope, which was even steeper than within, and slid helplessly down. He ended, with a loud splash, in the evil-smelling moat, the shock of the bitterly cold water making him gasp. He lay half-in and half-out of the scummy water, ignoring the pain as the chill struck at his skin, and listened intently. Not a sound.

He took off his torn cloak, which had trailed behind him and thankfully remained relatively dry, and rolled it round his sword and belt pouch. Then, holding it above his head, he slipped into the moat and struck out on his back across the dark waters. It only took a few kicks to gain the farther bank, and he hastily hauled himself out, numb with cold and shaking violently in the freezing air. Stripping off his sopping tunic and leggings, he weighted them with a convenient stone and drowned them in the stygian depths. Then, wrapping the cloak tightly round his wet and shivering body, he struck out to the northwest.

He had a long way to go. He assumed that the assassins would wait until the feast was over and everything was quiet before they struck. They would then waste time searching the town and sending men along the road to the Skam. They would never consider, or he desperately hoped they would not, the secret pass situated in the hills above Amyklai. The layer of cloud was shredding quickly and a three-quarters moon sailed serenely through the last fragments. By its welcome light, he was able to jog to make as much progress as he could, warming up nicely. He aimed for the sharp peak that cut a dark wedge from the star spattered sky and the tiny notch to its right that marked his goal. If he got out of this, there would be reckonings to be made.

THIRTY-ONE

THE EASTERN SKY was just beginning to lighten as he approached the summit of the pass. It had been a stiff climb, and he felt it. The years were finally catching up with him. All the way, he had been in an agony of indecision. To get across tonight, with the breaking dawn allowing for an easy pursuit if spotted, or to lie up throughout the day and attempt the crossing in the hours of darkness. Agrianians were the best trackers in Gea. His crossing of the moat had left clear traces. The spoor of his unintended slide would be a signpost as to his direction, and, if spotted, by tomorrow night the pass would be swarming with warriors, alert for any attempt. He would have to risk it now, but it was dangerously late, and he could waste no time.

The guard hut was silent, and he slipped past it in the waning darkness to follow the twisting path up to the stony col. Ahead, the unmistakable pillar of granite that marked the pass, and off to one side a flat slab of rock with a roughly built windbreak built upon it. Behind it, his back to Dio, stood a sentinel, wrapped in a warm cloak and gazing out across the valley beyond. Dio made no attempt to sneak up on the man but walked steadily towards him, the hood of his cloak obscuring his face, the knife in his hand hidden by the folds of cloth.

The man glanced behind him. 'That you, Arp?'

Dio grunted. He had learned the guttural language, but his accent was scarcely perfect.

The Aggie turned back to overlook the valley, yawned and stretched. 'You're early, but I'm not grumbling.'

A hand clamped across the man's mouth, and a heavy knife penetrated the side of his throat. He thrashed and juddered as blood erupted in a dark fountain, then slumped heavily. Dio heaved the body to the side of the rock and pushed it over. Anything that might delay pursuit for a few moments was worth the attempt. But the corpse fell onto some rocky crags below where it was still visible, even in the weak light of a burgeoning dawn. He swore under his breath, wiped his hand, sticky with blood, on his cloak, and set off immediately down the hillside, moving as fast as he dared. He followed a line just above the scree slope, where, even in the semi-darkness, he could see the evidence of a trail.

He was not far down when he heard a shout from above. With the light increasing inexorably, he began to run, jumping and stumbling down the grassy slope and praying that he did not turn an ankle. If the bastards saw him, they would be after him. Young and fresh, born and bred in the mountains, they would come bounding down like ibexes, needle-sharp javelins in their eager hands. He would have no chance.

He risked a desperate glance back, realising that he was already round the curve of the hill and out of line of sight. He dared not slow down but continued his rapid descent, repeatedly checking behind him. If he had not been seen, as seemed to be the case, the natural assumption would be that an intruder had penetrated the Agrianian heartland, rather than that someone had got out. Their attention would be in the wrong direction.

At the end of the scree, the trail turned sharply right and angled down towards the main track, once more in view of the guard post and fully visible in the spreading daylight, so he continued straight down the steep, grassy slope where he was out of direct sight. He had to measure speed against caution, zig-zagging endlessly, but nonetheless slipping and sliding most of the way. The track grew ever nearer as the hillside bottomed out. He ran the last few hundred paces down the now-shallow gradient and threw himself behind a boulder. He tried to catch his breath. His legs were cramped and trembling, and his lungs burned. He finally peered round cautiously. The slope behind was clear. Nothing. No pursuit. The wonderful slump of relief sank through his aching body.

Behind him was the coppice of trees where he had left his horse only the day before yesterday. It seemed much longer ago. He quickly made his way there, running between what cover there was, though his breathing was still coming hard, and his legs felt heavy with fatigue. Then he was in the gloom of the trees and pushing through to the clearing. Thanks be to Dyaus; his horse was still there, grazing placidly.

He retrieved his weapons, washed off the worst of the mud, blood and slime in the cold stream, and vigorously rubbed himself dry with his old cloak. He thankfully drew on fresh clothes, returning frequently to the edge of the trees to confirm that the pass remained clear. One last check. The slopes were devoid of movement, except for an undisturbed eagle wheeling slowly on broad, long-fingered wings.

He mounted his horse and returned to the track. Instead of turning for Gla, he swung his mount around and set off back towards the Skamandrian Gates, riding easily, but with his hood up, and making a point not to look at the col. Just one more traveller on the road. Once beyond their field of vision, he dismounted and led the horse across the bracken-cloaked lower slopes of the foothills, well above the distant fortress, until he cut the main track from the Gates. The garrison would assume that he was simply returning, with nothing untoward to report. He cantered back down to the fort; the gates swung open, and he was safe. For the moment, at least.

THIRTY-TWO

'You're back earlier than expected,' observed Theophanes as Dio dismounted. He wrinkled his nose. 'What a fucking stench! Is that you?'

'I'm afraid so,' said Dio. He looked around him to ensure there was no-one in earshot. 'Things got a little cranky.'

'You're not trailing a shitstorm in your wake, are you?'

'You have a wonderfully elegant turn of phrase, Theo.'

'Just naturally gifted. I repeat. Are the Aggies sufficiently pissed off with you to come calling?'

'I don't think so. But it wouldn't hurt to put the place on high alert for a few days.'

'Thanks a lot. Just what I fucking needed. A horde of irate Aggies descending upon me from a great height.'

'Is there any other kind?' asked Dio.

'There are worse things, though.' Theophanes sniffed ostentatiously. 'You could definitely do with a bath.'

'I could do with a bath,' agreed Dio. He drew Theophanes to one side. 'Between you, me and the horse piss, has anyone else passed through here to the Skam?'

There was no answer. Theophanes looked away, clearly discomfited.

'An overly large, red-haired officer from Gla as an example, taken totally at random, of course,' added Dio.

Theophanes looked unhappy. He said nothing.

Dio waited, then said quietly, 'Of course, if you had been ordered not to mention such things, you would be obliged to lie to me. I would understand completely.' He strongly emphasised the last sentence.

Theophanes looked at him sharply, then his face cleared, and he smiled slyly. 'No. No-one has passed through. Especially not that arrogant bastard Gelon. And that's the truth, because no-one would send me sealed orders instructing me not to mention it to anyone.'

'When did this non-existent person not pass through?'

Theophanes was beginning to quite enjoy this. 'He didn't pass through the day before you arrived.'

'Of course, Miltiades in particular would never send such orders.'

'He certainly wouldn't.' To ensure there was no misunderstanding, he gave Dio an outrageous wink. Subtlety was not his forte.

'Now, if the aforesaid non-existent person were not to pass through here in the next few days, you would have no reason to tell him that I have been through, with him being non-existent and not passing through himself and all.'

Theophanes screwed up his face as he disentangled the syntax, then said, 'Bugger it. I'm not to tell that bastard I've seen you coming out.' He frowned. 'But I can tell him I saw you going in?'

'That's the stuff. Thanks, Theo. I owe you. I asked you directly, and you denied it. All right and proper. But just keep your head down, old friend. I'm afraid I must deny myself the delights of your savoury mutton stew and be on my way, but point me to the nearest bath first.'

Theophanes wafted air from his offended nostrils. 'Thought you'd never ask.'

THIRTY-THREE

Dio chewed meditatively on a strip of boustria as he sat in the cover of a hawthorn thicket and surveyed the track to the Skam. This was his second day of patient waiting. His horse grazed quietly in the open woodland behind him.

He glanced at the sky. The sun was just dropping behind the broken skyline of the Panormus range, painting the sky a vivid red and silhouetting a passing flock of large gulls. Some cloud was building up over the Rhodopians to the north, but the wind was gusting from the west, so he would have no difficulties with the weather. Aphroditea shone out from the darkening blue and he could just make out the faint red-tinged scintillation of Aresia. Some might regard that the God of War looking down on them as an omen. The moon would not rise until later.

He turned his attention back to the track. It remained obstinately empty. He had seen no-one all day, except for a trio of Aggies on their shaggy ponies, no doubt going to lift a cow or two. Not his problem. Darkness enveloped the land, and he saw it.

Twenty stadia or so back, a small copse stood beside the track, and from its dark recesses flickered the dull red of a campfire.

Dio smiled grimly to himself and rose quietly.

THIRTY-FOUR

GELON AWOKE SUDDENLY and to terror, bathed in a cold sweat, his breathing short and ragged, and his heart pounding painfully. His campfire was guttering low, and against its ruddy light a figure was silhouetted. He could not see the face, but he knew instantly who it was. The point of a sword pressing against his taut throat was sufficient. He attempted to calm himself, forcing his breathing into a more regular rhythm and trying to get his rigid limbs to relax. Dio squatted down alongside Gelon, the sword keeping up an unremitting pressure on his larynx.

'I presume that it is unnecessary for me to tell you not to move. I will kill you if you do.' There was a slight emphasis on the *will*. His tone was chillingly conversational.

Gelon was beginning to gather his wits. Hidden beneath his blankets, his hand began to slide down towards his knife.

The sword cut into his flesh, and he felt a trickle of blood run down.

Dio shook his head. 'Don't be silly.' Gelon ostentatiously relaxed, and Dio nodded approvingly. 'Time that we had a little talk, I think. So, what was the deal with Neritos?'

The big man said nothing, but his eyes spoke for him. Dio simply increased the pressure on the sword a little.

It was enough. 'Two talents of silver, and a promise of support against Zarzed,' he said in strangled tones.

Dio was impressed. He hadn't realised that he was worth so much. Zarzed was the adjoining kinglet who was beginning to threaten Neritos's smaller territory. It wasn't a bad price for the murder of a man who had saved your life. For an Agrianian, that is.

'And the position of swordmaster for you?' There was no reply. 'I shall take that as a yes,' said Dio. 'And exactly who is in on the Laomedon plot?' He noted the flicker of surprise in Gelon's eyes.

'I don't know what you're talking—' he blustered, but stopped suddenly as Dio pushed forward again and more blood ran down. 'You can't kill me. It would be murder.' Gelon wasn't even convincing himself.

'So it would. Who's in on the plot?'

Gelon's head was thrust tautly back, the point of the sword now under his jaw. He found it difficult to speak, his voice strained and high pitched. 'Miltiades, of course, and Adrastus. And a man who carries messages between the holder and Raxamenes in Kadmeia.'

'Burly chap? Balding? Big wart on his chin?'

Gelon started to nod and instantly stopped as he felt the point of the sword bite. 'Yes.'

'Who else?'

'No-one else. Not as far as I know.' His tone was desperate. Sweat was running down his face.

'What about Patroclus?'

'I can't say. I'd guess he is. He's with the others a lot.'

'Why has that whoreson Laomedon not moved yet?'

'I don't know. I've only just been asked in. By Adrastus. I've been told nothing. Except it's for the good of the Empire. They're careful. Laomedon hasn't been mentioned, but I guessed it must be him.' For a moment, there was almost a look of pride in his eyes. It wasn't often Gelon worked anything out for himself. 'But I know it's worrying Miltiades and Adrastus. They're waiting for some sort of code word, though what it will mean I've no idea. Something's gone wrong.'

'So, you were invited into this select company because they wanted some evil bastard to rid them of my good self?' Dio said.

Gelon flinched.

'Why did Miltiades want me out of the way?'

'He wasn't sure his declaration of support would go down too well. They have some sort of cover story. But Miltiades said you can see trout in a muddy stream, and that you'd be the natural leader of any opposition.'

'He got that right.'

'He wasn't going to do anything, but Adrastus insisted.'

'So Adrastus sounds the salpinx?'

'Yes.' His voice sounded more strangled than ever. 'Miltiades just goes along with whatever he says. Adrastus sounds all humble, but you can tell he's commanding the army.'

'And Sofia?'

This time Gelon simply looked confused. 'Who?'

Dio gave him a grim smile, then tried a chance arrow. He had been thinking about the poisoning of the dog and the one scenario that seemed to fit.

'And they wanted the Lady Kalliste out of the way.'

He could see the terror twist the man's face. 'I have no part in that, I swear. It's Adrastus's doing. I told him that I wouldn't get involved.'

'In what, exactly?' A dark and terrifying suspicion was all but overwhelming him.

'In making sure that she had an accident.'

Dio had been schooled well. He did not visibly react in any way. But he stopped breathing. He had assumed that they had just wanted to drive Kal away from Gla. That her life was in danger came as a total shock. Radamanthus had even suggested it, and he had arrogantly pushed it aside as unworthy of consideration. Yet he managed to merely nod thoughtfully, as though he had known it all along. His face inscrutable.

Inside, across a sea of gut-wrenching panic, waves of anger surged and broke against the rocks of his fear, rebounding and roiling, like wild, gale-fed turmoil in a harbour, crashing from every direction against Gelon and Miltiades, Adrastus and Laomedon. But above all others, against himself. How could he have so blindly missed the threat, so misread the situation, so glibly drawn his facile conclusions?

The image of Pandarus seemed to rise before him, searching him out with cold eyes. 'When someone only has two options, they will take the third, boy. You examine every apple you buy, boy, and yet you leave possibilities unconsidered. You jump at conclusions like a witless grasshopper. Boy. Boy. Boy.' His words hammered into Dio's brains with the lash and sting of storm-driven hail. The old man stood on the farther bank of the Styx and shook his head in disgust.

Above all, his stupidity had put Kal in real danger. He fought the panic down. Pandarus nodded gravely. 'Not with your heart, boy, with your head.' Dio calmed himself.

Gelon was staring at him, his eyes big with fear.

'Tell me everything about it. You might know something I don't. In which case I will be duly grateful.' Lying bastard, he thought.

Gelon's face was ashen, evident even in the feeble firelight. 'I don't know any details. I'm telling you the truth. They weren't going to tell me anything. But Adrastus asked if I would ensure that the Lady Kalliste met with an accident when the time was right. I said no. I swear it.'

'What exactly did he mean by "when the time is right"? When is this planned to happen?'

'I've no idea. I swear by the Furies. I don't know. When I said no, he said nothing more about it. You have to believe me.' Dio did. Sham displays of such obvious desperation and fear could not be forged from Gelon's iron.

He pursed his lips and considered for a few heartbeats. 'Now I've got to decide about you.'

Gelon was terrified. 'I'll run. I'll run. I promise. I have to. They'll kill me. My only chance is to get to Leuctra, and get a boat to Dyaus knows where.' He made an involuntary little moan of distress. His eyes were pleading. The horror within was so manifest that Dio could not help but be moved by it.

He leaned back, slightly easing the pressure on Gelon's tight throat. 'I suppose you're right.'

Relief flooded into Gelon's face. He closed his eyes and exhaled with a long, shaky breath.

Dio thrust forward with all his strength. 'But I can't risk it.'

THIRTY-FIVE

He rode into Gla mid-morning as if nothing had happened, though he had pushed himself and his horse as hard as he possibly could through the terror-filled night. He dared not rush straight off to Kal, but a seemingly idle chat with the groom, as he stabled his horse, reassured him that she was well. For the moment, at least. He took his gear up to his rooms, then descended to the kitchens to scrounge a hunk of bread and wedge of cheese. He must appear his customary self. The iron self-control beaten into him by Pandarus asserted itself.

It was there that Patroclus found him. Dio had been sure that he would come: Miltiades would most definitely want to see him. This time he noted that Patroclus's tone was obsequious.

'My Lord Swordmaster, you are returned sooner than we anticipated.'

Dio noted the *we*. He looked up to stare, stone faced, directly into Patroclus's shifting eyes. 'There was good reason to leave,' he said, slowly and with emphasis, 'once Neritos told me everything.'

He saw the sudden tension in the man's shoulders and the widening of his eyes. The implications of Dio's words were obviously not lost on him. So, he was indeed involved. Dio popped the last piece of cheese into his mouth and took a drink of some watered wine. 'I told Miltiades they wouldn't play. Recruitment only. Besides which, they stink, their manners are atrocious, their food is putrid and their drink worse.'

Patroclus's relief was blatant. 'Miltiades would like to see you,' he said, hastily adding, 'At your convenience, of course.'

Dio sighed. 'So, no chance of some much-needed sleep, then. I'm on my way.'

He directed his steps up to Miltiades' office, Patroclus trailing along in his wake. Dio checked the two guards as he approached. Both simple, solid soldiers he knew well. It wasn't a trap. He returned their salute and passed through the open door. Patroclus entered too and closed it behind him. Miltiades was working at his table, and Adrastus was perched in the corner, quietly transcribing a letter from a wax tablet, looking as vulturine as ever.

Miltiades looked up. 'Dio,' he said warmly, 'you're back sooner than we thought.'

'It was hard to leave such lavish hospitality, but I made the sacrifice.'

Miltiades donned a mask of worry. 'There was no trouble, I hope?' He gestured to Dio to take a seat. This put

Patroclus immediately behind Dio, but the aide wouldn't have the guts to try anything. Nevertheless, Dio moved the chair slightly as he sat, so that he could see the reflection of the room to his rear within the polished surface of a hanging shield.

'None, unless you can describe an Agrianian feast as trouble, and I wouldn't quarrel with that. But there were only three fist fights and just the one man got knifed, so, as Agrianian feasts go, it was a model of civilised rectitude.'

'Neritos?' said Miltiades, somewhat impatiently.

'I talked to him the first day, and it was as I supposed. There's no way the Confederacy would, or even could, get involved. But if we want to recruit, he has no objections. There didn't seem a lot of point in staying. And, if you've ever drunk their fermented milk, every reason to go.'

'You've seen Gelon?' The javelin question was suddenly hurled at him by Adrastus, obviously hoping for a reaction, but Dio had been ready for it and did not betray himself by the slightest flicker.

'Gelon? Why in Hades' name should I have seen Gelon? I've only just got back. What's the idiot gone and done now?'

Miltiades exchanged glances with Adrastus, then spoke. 'It's just that he went out on a private hunting trip and has failed to return. As he was planning to hunt near Fort Skamander, we wondered if you had stumbled across him.' He rubbed the bridge of his nose.

'Not a sign. Knowing his sense of direction, he's probably got himself lost. I passed through the fort on my return. Theophanes never mentioned anything about him. I'm sure he would have, if he'd seen him.'

'Never mind. He'll undoubtedly turn up.'

Not from the depth I buried him, thought Dio.

'He's big enough to look after himself,' added Miltiades. Patroclus laughed ingratiatingly. Miltiades glared at him, and the laugh stopped abruptly.

'What news on the political situation?' asked Dio.

'No sign of any insurrection. The Grand Council has decided to formally name Troilus as successor. Looks like your theory about Laomedon was a trireme built without a keel.'

'Possibly,' conceded Dio amiably. But almost certainly not, he thought, though he did not understand the delay in acting. Something was badly out of line.

'Well,' said Miltiades jovially, 'go and get some rest. You've earned it.'

And he was dismissed.

But not forgotten. Of that, he could not be surer.

THIRTY-SIX

An armed hoplite barred his way to Kal's. Rather uncertainly. 'I'm sorry, sir,' he said, his voice shaking, 'but I've direct orders from Hyperetes Icarius that no-one is to enter without his express authority.'

Dio stopped. The orders of a watch officer could only be countermanded by the officer of the day or the holder himself. The man was staring at him, the unease transparent in his eyes. Just as Dio was considering simply disarming him, he heard rapid steps ascending the staircase behind. He swung round to see Icarius, puffing and red in the face, hurrying towards him.

'Swordmaster,' he gasped, 'a brief word, if you would,' and gestured Dio down the steps until they were out of earshot of a much-relieved guard.

'What in Dyaus's name is going on?' demanded Dio.

Icarius caught his breath. 'Thank the Gods that you're back. The Lady Kalliste's slave girl, the little one–'

'Dianthe.'

He nodded. 'She's been found raped and beaten to death in one of the back alleys of the town.'

Dio stared. At first simple shock, followed by wrenching sorrow. Only then did the implications all but overwhelm him, his mind racing to outpace the burgeoning fear. 'The Lady Kalliste?'

'She's safe. Very upset, of course.' He paused, then spoke urgently. 'There's more. I sneaked a look at the tag rolls for the period the girl was missing. There's no record of her leaving the fortress.'

The inference was clear. She had been killed inside Gla itself, and then her body smuggled out to make it look as though it was a random crime. Dio stood there for a few heartbeats, endeavouring to think it through while desperately trying to avoid the vortices of terror that coiled like poisonous vapours from fumaroles. He turned to the waiting Icarius. 'Have you been given any orders regarding the Lady Kalliste?'

'No, sir. Put the guard there on my own initiative.'

'Good man.' His iron self-control was winning the mental battle and his acuity of thought returning. 'I need you to do two things. Who's officer of the day?'

'Aeropus.'

'Dyaus's balls. He's one of Gelon's cronies.' He rethought quickly. 'Look, have you anything that can keep him involved for a time? At least ten, twenty hekates. But it's got to genuine.'

'The Gods must be with you. That fool Menester got fighting drunk in Fat Delia's last night. I was going to deal with it quietly.' Which meant beating him up behind the stables, thought Dio, well versed in the ways of hyperetes. 'But he's done it before, so perhaps it's time I made it official.'

'Can you try and get Aeropus to your office in a hemidekate? I can see your office window from the stable block. When he is arriving, just hang a cloak out of the window.'

'I can do that. No problem.' Icarius sounded confident.

'Then can you talk to Radamanthus? Make sure that he knows where you buried the dog. Ask him to be there in the afternoon of five days' time. That'll be Selenes. He's to wait as long as he can, and I'll contact him.'

Icarius shot him a look. He had obviously grasped the implications of what he was saying.

'If I don't, he's to return and then, when he's able, contact a man called Naukles in Leuctra. He has a small trading post down by the harbour. Use my name and mention the Battle of Naupraxis.'

Icarius carefully repeated the message, committing it to memory. 'Never heard of that battle,' he said, intrigued.

Dio clapped him on the shoulder. 'Nor has anyone else, except for Naukles and myself. You have my thanks. If you ever have need, you know I'll be there.'

'Be careful, sir. It's getting very nasty. And the Gods give you fortune.'

They walked back up the steps, and Icarius nodded to the guard, who smartly stepped to one side. Dio rapped on the door. There was no answer, so he opened it and went inside.

She was standing by the hearth, very upright, her eyes bright and one hand behind her back. He heard the clatter as the dagger fell to the floor, and she flew across the floor to cling to him with almost feral desperation. Her breathless words, buried as they were in his shoulder, were muffled and incomprehensible, but the relief in them was unmistakable.

He held her just as tightly, well-nigh overwhelmed by the way his self-control was all but swept away by the touch of her body and the anguish of her voice. He had felt fear before, in the press of battle, genuine stomach-voiding, skin-crawling, mind-freezing fear, but never like this. His iron refusal to face his emotions, the shield of analytical rationality he hid behind, his controlled persona, all crumbled like a dam before a torrential flood.

As always, he fought. Clawing his way back. Refusing to accept this surrender to the forces of unreason, he slowly and doggedly reasserted the needed mental discipline. Emotion would not save her. Judicious thought might. He made out what she was saying with difficulty.

'I thought you were dead.' She was sobbing now.

'Damn nearly was.' He realised the implications. 'What made you think so?'

She managed to gain some control over her voice. 'Patroclus. Antenor overheard him saying that, as soon as Gelon was swordmaster, there would be changes.'

She was calming down a little, but still hung on to him ferociously. She swallowed nervously. 'Was it Milt?'

'It was by his order,' he replied grimly.

Her voice was still thick with emotion and hesitant. 'You know about Dianthe?'

'Just been told. I'm sorry.'

She burst into tears again. 'It was my fault. I should have done what they asked. Herakla, the poor girl. What she must have suffered.'

'It wasn't your fault. Put the blame where it should lie.'

'I can't.' The tears died away. 'It weighs too heavily on me. It wasn't the work of some mindless thug. She'd no reason to be out in the town. I'm sure it was deliberate murder.'

'It was. But we've no time. We must get out now.'

She pulled back and stared at him, wide-eyed. ''How? Where?' He wasn't sure whether she was asking about Dianthe or their escape, but it didn't matter.

'Look, Kal, you're going to have to trust me. There's no time for explanations. Do exactly what I say and don't ask any questions. Save them for later. Now, dress for riding, grab a few travel clothes rolled in a good cloak and whatever jewellery and money you can easily carry. I'll be back for you in a few hekates.'

'What about Melissa? She's terrified.'

'She'll have to stay. She'll be of no interest to them, I promise you. Trust me, please, Kal.'

Kal nodded after a moment. 'I will.'

'Good. But now you must be quick.'

She pulled away from him and wiped her eyes, but, before she could say anything else, he was gone.

THIRTY-SEVEN

Dio acknowledged the salute of the guard and walked coolly down to his own rooms, where, true to his own dictum, he kept a scuttle bag packed and waiting.

He quickly crossed to the shelved alcove and teased out part of a supporting wooden batten to reveal a small cavity. He hooked out several leather bags heavy with coin and stuffed them in the bag. He snatched his thickest cloak and was back at Kal's before she had finished.

He simply gestured with his head towards the door, and she nodded, grabbed a last handful of expensive-looking jewellery, squirreled it away in a blanket bag and followed him out.

The hoplite looked up hopefully. 'Stay on guard until we get back,' said Dio easily. 'My Lady's slave is understandably frightened.' The man looked crestfallen, the prospect of an immediate release from boredom foundering on the rocks, but he nodded dutifully.

'If anyone wants the Lady Kalliste, she will be with the Lady Thais.' It never hurt to throw in some misdirection. He could hear the growl of Pandarus. 'Never approach anything directly. If you want a parsnip, look at the turnips.' They left by the main stairwell, but on the next landing he turned for the back stairs, normally used only by slaves and servants, and they hurried on down.

The stairs led to the bustling kitchens, but, before they were reached, a side door opened into the courtyard adjacent to the stable block. They slipped through it, Dio deliberately restraining Kal's urge to hurry, and into the stables themselves. It was gloomy and dust hung in the air, which was heavy with the sweet smell of hay and the less welcome acridity of horse stale. He asked a couple of grooms to tack up their horses and wandered, in an absent-minded manner, across to a window, from where he could see the inner guard room. He started to tell her about the Agrianian feast in great detail, though well aware that she was not really listening. Her agitation was all too evident.

'Their idea of a gastronomic delight is the stomach of a goat stuffed with minced lights, onion and barley,' he said, 'though, actually, it's surprisingly tasty...'

'Done, sir,' said the elder groom, slinging their blanket bags over the horses.

'Thanks, Peri,' he said. 'Would you get a step for the Lady Kalliste?' He heard Kal mount up behind him as he gazed across the yard, where Icarius's window remained obstinately cloak free. He swore to himself. Time was dribbling through his fingers.

Then he saw Icarius, hurrying out through the door and across the courtyard straight towards them. The bloody handle had come off the shield. He felt a nauseating emptiness. He turned to the grooms. Peri was standing holding Blackwing, who was tossing her head with eagerness.

'She seems to be favouring her front right. Could you just walk her, Peri, and give me your expert opinion?' He caught the look of horror on Kal's tight face but could not reassure her. Icarius appeared at the window. He could read the concern in his eyes.

'Swordmaster,' he said, with apparent surprise, 'I wasn't expecting you back yet.'

'Managed to drag myself away.'

The hyperetes spoke quickly and quietly. 'Aeropus is getting a squad together. I think they're coming for you.' Dio gave him a barely perceptible nod. He had been afraid of that. He could imagine the animated argument that must have taken fire the instant he had left Miltiades' office.

'Could you ask Antenor to report to me on my return?' said Dio more loudly.

'Of course, sir,' and Icarius hurried away on his imaginary mission.

Dio glanced behind him. Peri and the other groom were inspecting Blackwing's hoof. Kal sat on her horse looking as though she could shatter with the tension at any moment. Dyaus, but it was getting tight. His throat was dry, and he could feel the blood pounding in his temples. Then, across the courtyard, the door to the guard room opened, and Aeropus emerged, looking both self-important and inordinately pleased. Behind him, a file of sixteen fully-armed hoplites. Dio stepped back away from the window as they doubled away.

'How's it look, Peri?'

The groom sounded puzzled. 'Can't see a thing, sir.'

'She must have just stumbled. Thanks.' The hoplites disappeared around the corner, heading for the main entrance to the citadel. He caught the reins of Blackwing and led her out, with Kal just behind. The sweat was cold on his back, and the hekates seemed to stretch into dekates. Something inside was screaming at him to run. Pandarus was there again. 'Tell your body what to do; don't let it tell you.' He nodded within and forced himself to amble along. Kal, who must have been as taut as a kithara string, somehow managed to stay pace with him. It seemed as though he lived several lifetimes before the main gate loomed before him. He kept his eyes straight ahead, still smoothly describing to Kal what passed for culinary delicacies in darkest Agriania. The town was close now. So close. And a tetrarches stepped in front of him.

THIRTY-EIGHT

'SWORDMASTER,' THE TETRARCHES growled as Dio stopped in seeming surprise. He felt calmer, as though this had handed the initiative back to him. He could do something. He could act. He had some control once more.

'Tiro,' he said easily. 'Some problem?'

'I'm sorry, sir,' said the chubby man, pushing a stray hank of hair out of his eyes. He was going bald and was trying desperately to disguise the fact. 'I'm afraid the Lady Kalliste may not leave the post without express authority.'

Dio stared at him in perplexity, then smiled. 'Is this some kind of joke, Tiro? Not like you, that.'

'I'm serious, I'm afraid, sir,' said Tiro stolidly.

Dio was suddenly aware of Kal pushing her horse forward. He glanced across. Her mouth was set in a tight, straight line and her eyes flashed.

'Am I to understand that I am under arrest?' she demanded icily.

Tiro paled. 'No, my Lady, of course not—'

'Then on whose direct authority do you dare to stop me? I'll have you broken to the ranks for this.'

Tiro took a step backwards and looked wildly about him. 'I was informed by the hyperetes of the guard—'

'A hyperetes? Am I to be confined on the authority of a hyperetes? You are walking a dangerous line, young man.'

Sensing his moment, Dio stepped closer and took Tiro's arm in a friendly grip. 'Look, I'm authorising it, tetrarches,' he said. 'That'll get you off the hook. And it's a sharp one, believe me. I've been on it myself.' He winked at the flustered officer and unobtrusively ushered him further away from the idling men. Kal moved her horse forward, following them and continuing to transfix the discomfited officer with a basilisk stare. They were now actually through the gate.

Tiro gulped and looked totally lost. 'I'm not sure that you have the authority, sir.' He sounded unsure, but Dio could not afford the time to convince him.

'As swordmaster, of course I do,' Dio replied loudly and confidently. 'I exercise the personal authority of the holder.' He leaned closer and hissed, 'As well as this knife, and I'll gut you like a sea bream if there is the slightest move from you. Do you understand?' His smile never left his face.

Tiro swallowed hard and nodded. His face was white and sheening with sweat.

'No, that's all right, Tiro, you just didn't realise.' Dio spoke loudly for the benefit of the guards.

Their bored body language proclaimed that they were totally without suspicion of the quiet drama being enacted a few steps away from them. Kal had cleverly moved her horse to shield the two men from view.

'Hey, that reminds me,' Dio went on. 'I've a favour to ask of you. Just walk with us a few heartbeats, will you?' He manoeuvred the frightened officer down the track that led into the town. He called back over his shoulder, 'You have the guard, Xeno. Not to worry, I'm not kidnapping him at knife point.'

'Please do,' Tiro's dilochagos called back cheerfully, and the guards laughed dutifully.

They walked down the main street, Dio's knife pressed into Tiro's side. Behind them Kal followed, leading Blackwing. Dio looked back. She was as pale as snowfall but gave him a weak smile.

'Now, Tiro, listen carefully. I've got three choices. I can kill you now. Probably safest.' He still held the man's arm and distinctly felt his knees give. 'Or I can release you, and you can run back and sound the alarm as soon as you dare, but, by the time the duty plag is tacked up, we'll be long gone. Then you will not only have Aeropus's ire to cope with, but…' he paused significantly, then said, 'Look at me.'

Tiro instantly did so, fearfully. Dio caught his eye and spoke with quiet but convincing emphasis. 'I swear by the Furies that I will come back and gut you in the aforesaid manner. You know that I can, and that I will.' Tiro had no doubts. He was shaking. 'Or finally, you can pretend nothing happened, and that you simply accepted my authority, which you had no reason not to. You will probably catch a bollocking, but the alternative is so messy.' Tiro nodded with such enthusiasm that it was almost comical.

They were passing Fat Delia's. 'Now, if I were you, I'd go and have a krater of unwatered wine. You look as though you need it, and it won't be the first time you've availed yourself of a kylix on guard duty. I wouldn't come out for, oh, at least ten hekates. And, by the way, the favour was to tell Antenor that I would be unable to see him tonight as I had arranged.'

Tiro stared at him uncomprehendingly. 'Favour? What favour?'

'I told Xeno I wanted to ask you a favour,' said Dio patiently. 'That was it.'

Tiro continued to stare blankly at him.

'To cover your own arse, you bloody idiot. For Dyaus's sake, go and down some wine.'

The bemused man blinked, turned and stumbled into Fat Delia's, his long strand of hair floating behind him in the strong wind.

Dio swung himself up onto his horse, and they cantered down the main road leading from the fortress. He checked behind, seeing no sign of the terrified officer re-emerging, then glanced at Kal.

'You did well,' he said. 'I was impressed.'

'You'll never know how frightened I was.' She sounded a little more confident than before. She had reached for the iron within and found it.

There were few people around, some slaves returning from the agora laden with produce, the odd civilian and a small group of Monces, red blankets over their shoulders, chanting the Hymn to the One.

'Kal,' he said, as they rode past. 'Just in case we get separated, or something happens…' He deliberately did not look at her. He could not bear to see fear in her eyes.

'...find the stables of Misenus. Halfway down the Street of the Sirenoi. Keep your hood up. Make sure you speak to him alone. Tell him everything, and ask him to contact Radamanthus. Rad knows what to do. Trust him.'

He finally glanced at her for confirmation. She looked pale and tense but nodded quickly.

They arrived at the Southway, the main thoroughfare that led to the Great East Road, and thence to Leuctra. It was much busier, bustling with people moving amongst the brightly coloured stalls, the road clogged with the ox-drawn wagons of a trading caravan. To Kal's astonishment, he rode towards the nearest stall, the last in the line and facing the road to the fortress. He tossed the young woman an obol.

'A couple of your finest apples, my darling, as sweet and luscious as your pretty self.' She simpered at him, and he was uncomfortably aware of Kal's amazed stare. The woman threw him two sadly wrinkled specimens, which he caught deftly.

'Best I got,' she said. 'In apples, that is.'

He lowered his eyes to her well-endowed bosom. 'I might be back for a pear later,' he said, and winked, before turning away from the busy Southway and heading north. Kal, obviously taken by surprise, had to urge her horse forward to catch up with him.

'What was all that about?' she muttered, sounding rather cross.

'I want her to remember us.'

'I would think she'll have trouble forgetting,' she remarked acidly, and sniffed loudly.

They trotted along a little-used track that wound listlessly through a squalid collection of huts and poorly built houses, where the sour, pervasive smell of pigshit filled the air. The increasing wind was raising clouds of swirling dust that pricked their eyes. If they following this track out of town, it would simply wander off into the Vale for the benefit of a few isolated steadings.

'Where are we going?' she whispered urgently.

'A safe house, where we can go to earth for a while.'

'But there are few steadings out there. They will search them all.'

'I know, which is why we are not going there.' With that, he turned off down an evil-smelling alley, scarcely wide enough to allow them passage and hemming them in with the teetering walls of ill-built tenements. They emerged onto a wider street, whereupon he turned left again, heading back south.

She looked at him questioningly.

'Milt will expect me to throw a false trail, so I've done exactly that. But we're going to double back yet again. This time when no-one will see us.' It would also misdirect the immediate pursuit, but he wasn't going to tell her that. She did not know that the hunt was almost certainly already up, or, if not, it would not be long before it was.

'But won't he expect you to do that too?' she asked shrewdly.

'No. He will be so delighted at outsmarting me that he will never think through to the next step.'

She looked across at him. 'You play Milt like a trout on a line. You don't play me the same way, do you?'

He gave her a reassuring smile. 'Not a chance. I know who would end up being gaffed.' They followed the gradually climbing track through a thinning tumble of dwellings; chickens ran squawking from under their hooves, and urchins with bright, predatory eyes watched them go by.

Kal pointed out that their passing had been noticed.

'All the better,' he said simply.

THIRTY-NINE

THE UNTIDY SPRAWL of Glapolis was beginning to melt away into the surrounding Sea of Grass as their rutted track rose slightly to converge with the Southway again. Dio was increasingly tense, and Kal could see it.

'You've gambled on Tiro not giving the alarm, haven't you? They could be waiting for us.' Her face was strained and pale once more.

There was a moment's pause. 'Yes. I had to. If he did sound the salpinx, they would be breathing down our necks and too close for us to sidestep. But don't worry. He's not got the iron. And even if they have pursued, they'll be long gone, heading for the East Road at the ram, and we shall just quietly turn around and slip away elsewhere. It will be longer and harder, but we'll be fine.'

He was lying to her. There was no question but that there was already a pursuit, now that Aeropus was looking for him with an arrest warrant. He could only pray to Athen that they were sufficiently ahead of it to have a chance.

She smiled and nodded, but her frightened eyes belied her seeming reassurance. Without warning, the burden of her safety pressed down on him, thickening his thoughts and searing his brain with images that flung aside all other considerations and rampaged through his mind. He fought for calm and clarity. He could not afford these lapses. He needed to be focussed.

He stopped her short of the junction, where a last, solitary dwelling provided some concealment. 'Wait here.' He was conscious of some sharpness to his tone and made an effort to relax. 'If anything happens, get out of here and find Misenus.'

She nodded, and he rode on, his hood pulled well forward. He could but hope that Aeropus had taken the bait and was heading north, and that he had not had the nous to send men both ways. It had rained that morning, and Dio covertly studied the churned-up ground before quietly signalling her to follow. There was no sign of the passage of any substantial cavalry unit, the ruts of the ox-wagons unmarred. She joined him, and they finally cantered away from the town.

It was just before noon, and the day was dull and gloomy, with leaden grey cloud stretching from horizon to horizon. An unpleasantly cold and rising wind bit into them strongly from the northeast. Kal shivered and pulled her cloak more snugly around her. The road was devoid of travellers as they rode away, but he kept a careful eye behind him. As the track swung round a low ridge, they dropped into a shallow gully, down which ran a small, rock-strewn stream. He led her into its swirling waters, the banks barren of anything beyond an occasional small rowan tree, and they picked their cautious way along as it angled down and away from the road.

It was not long before they were out of view of anyone on the Southway, and Dio could breathe a heartfelt sigh of relief. But he kept them in the stream for some distance, before climbing out across a flat shelf of bare rock and taking to the barren heartlands of the Vale of Grass beyond. Some of the tension finally drained from his body. They were heading west, directly away from Leuctra, where the chase would surely assume they were making for. He glanced at Kal, and she smiled back. Her face had regained a little of its colour. She was beginning to feel safe. He hoped that she was right. It was one of those rare moments when he wished that he believed in the Gods.

It began to rain, though light and patchy. There was a touch of sleet to it, but the weather was behind them, driving in from the northeast. With their hoods up, they did not feel its worst. They said little. He concentrated on finding his way through the all-but-indistinguishable dips and hollows of the endless grassland, smeared into anonymity by the occasional drifts of fine rain. They kept going west, repeatedly deviating to avoid the odd isolated steading, making progress slow. At least the weather cloaked their passing, though the cold wind rose steadily until it was snatching fiercely at their cloaks and almost howling, and for any conversation they had to pull close together and shout to one another. It was gathering dusk when they came to a rise.

'The Great East Road,' he shouted. 'We need to cross quickly.' They urged their horses across the rough and rutted track, dropped into a hollow on the other side and drew to a halt again. He pointed to a low hillock beside the road with a surmounting cairn. 'The memorial to Aristamos; I was worried I might not find it in this clag, but now I know exactly where we are. We can't make the safe house today, but there's an abandoned steading ten stadia to the southwest. We can stay there overnight.'

She nodded. The strain was all too obvious in her face, and she looked cold and weary.

'Come on,' he said encouragingly, 'not far now.'

FORTY

They clattered into the steading yard as the rain finally began to drive down with real force. The sheds were sadly dilapidated, with doors slumping from their hangings or banging wildly in the gusting wind. But the central stone-built hearth home looked sturdy and undamaged, with solid shutters and a firmly closed door. Dio quickly bundled her inside with her blanket bags and went to find shelter for the horses.

When he returned, sheltering beneath his cloak the dry wood he had found in the old woodshed, he could scarcely see her in the gloom. He found his way across to the hearth and took out a small wad of kindling with flint and ironstone from his belt pouch. He soon had a modest fire burning, carefully feeding it pieces of wood of increasing size until there was a real blaze. The encroaching darkness in the room retreated in the face of a ruddy glow, and a wonderful surge of radiant warmth soon made itself felt. He glanced round to see her standing in the middle of the bare and dusty main room with her open bag in her hands, shivering with cold and almost in tears. She looked across at him miserably.

'Everything's wet through,' she said accusingly. The fire threw long, distorted shadows across the wall behind her.

'Not to worry, I've got dry clothes.' From a double-skinned leather bag, he drew a well-greased package of sheepskin, which had completely protected the contents.

'I should have known you'd be prepared. You could have told me.'

'Sorry. There wasn't time. Now I'll go and see to the horses properly. You get out of those wet things. Rub yourself dry with something, and put on whatever will fit you.'

'Bang on the door when you come back,' she said severely.

'I will put a blanket bag over my head if you would like.'

'What a good idea,' she said. 'Shame that you didn't think of it years ago.'

'I shall not stoop to bandying words with you,' he proclaimed grandly and turned to go.

'Which means you can't think of anything clever to say,' she called after him. 'Scarcely news from the agora then.'

'You said something funny?' he shouted back from outside, though the words were probably snatched away by the banshee wind.

Whether she heard or not, he felt better as he huddled deep within his cloak against the scything bursts of rain, feeling his way back through the congealing darkness to the horses. Weak and paltry fare the raillery may have been, but her old spirit was returning. That was good. He had never felt this frightening degree of responsibility for anyone before, and it dominated and warped his mind to such an extent that he was afraid that his usual clarity of analytical thought was suffering. Perhaps if she were her old, easy-going, assured self instead of the vulnerable, frightened and dependent woman he had seen today, he might find some ease.

FORTY-ONE

HE DUTIFULLY KNOCKED upon his return. Or, more correctly, hammered, as the demonic howling of the wind and the incessant banging of a loose door threatened to overwhelm any sound short of the stentorian. He faintly heard her call and gratefully tumbled inside, dripping water.

She was dressed in a tunic and some leggings of his, both rather too large but adequate, and was kneeling in front of the fire, spreading her hair out in an attempt to dry it. He had a strange and disturbing feeling seeing her in his clothes, one that he could not analyse. He busied himself by taking off his cloak and shaking it, then sorting out some dry clothing for himself. He went into the room at the end to dry off and change before he got too chilled.

He emerged to find Kal sitting cross-legged on the floor as close to the fire as she could stand to be.

'Now for a surprise,' he said. She looked at him questioningly. He went to one corner of the room, knelt down, and felt carefully along the bottom of the wall until, with a grunt of satisfaction, he found what he was looking for. He took out his knife, inserted it into a tiny crack and pushed. There was a faint metallic sound. He backed up a little, pushed his knife blade into a gap between two floorboards, and levered one up until he could get his fingers beneath it and throw back a cunningly concealed trapdoor. Kal came across to look. Underneath was an earthen floor. She looked puzzled.

Dio dug into it with his hands to reveal two buried handles, then, with a heave, lifted out what was effectively a six-fingerbreadth-deep tray of earth. 'Doesn't sound hollow if anyone starts tapping,' he explained. Beneath was a shaft with a wooden ladder attached to one side.

'It's a bolt hole,' she exclaimed delightedly. 'I've heard of them, but I've never seen one before.'

Most steadings had bolt holes. Cunningly hidden and well stocked hiding places for the isolated holdings at times of threat, usually made with impressive ingenuity and craftsmanship. There were several local men who made a good living fashioning them.

'How in Hades did you find it?'

'I probably would have never found this one. It's as good as they come. But I knew the steaders that lived here. Decent folk. They gave up and left. Lost their cattle too often to the Aggies. It's a perfect place for one of my caches.'

She raised her eyebrows.

'I have little bundles of clothes, money, weapons and food. Scattered all over. Some in Gla, some in the town, some hidden round the Vale in steadings or beneath boulders or even inside hollow trees. Bit like a jay burying nuts for the winter, I suppose. For exactly such an occasion as this. Always expect the unexpected, learn everything you can about every situation, and plan ahead. Those three rules were beaten into me. Sometimes literally.'

'How can you expect the unexpected?' Kal said. 'Even you must admit that that is a nonsensical thing to say. It's like knowing the unknowable or imagining the unimaginable. Or,' she added severely, 'saying the unsayable!'

He groaned dramatically. 'Sometimes I regret introducing you to elementary logic.'

'Elementary logic?' She snorted. 'I'm not talking such weak and paltry stuff. I'm talking of common sense. And that's something that I've been trying to introduce you to for many years. It's been a project of mine. Sadly unsuccessful.'

'Look, do you want me to go and produce some goodies, or are you going to stay here arguing logic all night?'

'Common sense,' she corrected him. 'Oh, the latter. You still have so much to learn.' She smiled happily at him.

'You're feeling better.'

She became serious. 'I'm away from Gla. I know we're not safe, but I feel safe.' She looked away. 'I always thought that I was a reasonably brave person. That I didn't frighten easily. But I was terrified. I couldn't sleep. I couldn't eat. I couldn't think, for Herakla's sake. I just stood there and waited for the scratch on the door. I didn't know such fear could exist.' There was a tremble in her voice. 'And I thought you were dead. That was…' She stopped and shook her head. 'I didn't know what to do.' She visibly took control of herself, drew a deep breath, then said, 'I should have gone to Leuctra some time ago. Poor Dianthe would still be alive.'

As always, he was unable to respond; the moment was too fraught with emotion, with possibilities. 'I'm not at all sure that that's true,' was the best that he could manage as he began to descend the ladder, 'but we'll talk later. There's much to do first.'

FORTY-TWO

THE WIND HAD dropped significantly, and there was no sound of rain on the roof. They sat facing the cheerful blaze, he cross-legged and she hugging her knees. The room was warm but humid; he had stretched rope across the rafters, and wet clothes hung from it, steaming gently. They had just finished a makeshift meal of ham, hard cheese and somewhat stale bread, as he had not had the time to replenish his scuttle bag. The room was well lit with a couple of oil lamps, and they were drinking a reasonable Apollonian red. This was one of his nearby 'earths', so he kept it well provisioned.

'Too close to Gla, though, for anything other than a temporary lying-up place. We move on in the morning.'

'Where are we going?'

'To a steading beyond Choraea. There's a couple there, Dymas and Phyllida. They'll shelter us. No questions asked.'

'Why?' Kal asked with interest.

'I once helped save them from an Aggie raid.'

'And?' she prompted.

He looked at her. 'What makes you think there's an *and*?'

'Because with you there always is,' Kal declared simply.

Dio looked heavenwards in a gesture of exasperation. 'They lost most of their cattle, so I helped them restock.'

'Meaning that you paid for them.'

'Not entirely. I told Milt that the steaders near Choraea were starving after Aggie depredations, and he authorised some military meat on the hoof. Eurybiades and myself made sure that it was decent stock.'

'But you paid for some.'

He made a dismissive gesture. There was silence between them for a while.

'What happened in Agriania?' she suddenly asked.

He told her. She shuddered slightly when he told her he had killed Gelon. 'Couldn't you have risked letting him run?'

'I could have risked it. If it had been just me, I probably would have. But...' Dio stopped.

Kal intuitively knew why he had ground to a halt and smiled. 'It's all right, Dio. I know that you're not putting the responsibility onto me, and I'm grateful for your protection.'

He smiled back, relieved. 'What about you? What happened in Gla while I was away?'

'Everything was fine until Adrastus came to call.' She pulled a face. 'He's a slimy little rat and no mistake. He was all very obsequious and solicitous. Wondered if I might not be happier in Leuctra. He more or less offered me a bribe, saying that Milt would transfer two talents to my name. I said that I'd think about it. I wasn't going to go until you came back and I could talk it over with you. But they told me yesterday about poor Dianthe.' Her eyes glinted with reflected firelight as they filled with tears. 'Then Thais told me what Patroclus had said.' She looked desolate. 'I wish I'd gone now.'

'You might not have made it there. I suspect that you would have mysteriously disappeared en route.'

She looked at him sharply, her face suddenly pale.

'The killing of Dianthe doesn't make sense as pressure. If Milt really wanted you gone that badly, he could have just put you out. Told you to go to Leuctra or to Hades. What did *he* care. I think Adrastus was behind the killing of both Kerberos and Dianthe and—' He stopped and considered how to say it. There was only one way. 'I don't know how you'll take this.' He was uncomfortably aware that she was staring at him intently. 'But I've good reason to think that Milt has been promised Laomedon's niece, Sofia, in marriage.'

She started, and her mouth fell open. 'You're joking.'

He shook his head resignedly. 'I wish I were.'

'So that's why he wanted rid of me. The bastard.' She sat in thought for a few moments. 'But why should he want to kill me?'

'I've been thinking about that. My best guess is that this Sofia is blowing up a storm. She doesn't want you around. Maybe she sees you as a possible rival, perhaps as a figure of sympathy to others that will detract from her standing, or she just feels it an affront to her dignity to marry a divorced man.' He paused. 'Rather than a widower.' Then he tried to lighten the atmosphere. 'Who can understand the mind of a woman?'

'Certainly not a man,' she snapped, then furrowed her brow. 'But I still don't understand. Why Kerberos? And why Dianthe?'

'The dog was an early piece of crude pressure. To get you out of Milt's hair. After all, if you were still around when Sofia showed up, there would be a lot of support for you. Particularly when people finally recognised that the divorce was no fault of yours. But I suspect that she, or her uncle, has become much more demanding, and Adrastus realised that he could put two shots in his sling.'

She looked puzzled.

'Think about it. Milt and Adrastus want to be rid of me because they see me as a focus for dissent in the garrison when they declare for Laomedon. Sofia wants to be rid of you. Let's say I'm dead at the hands of the treacherous Aggies and you're dead as the result of an unfortunate accident; Milt would come under the hard stare of suspicion. But if the rumours about us were to be,' he paused, searching for the right word, 'authenticated, shall we say, then the betrayed husband would, at the worst, be seen to have been dealing in justifiable revenge. I think Dianthe was supposed to provide that evidence, but she wouldn't do it. And she died for it. She must have been a very brave and loyal girl.'

Kal looked horrified; the blood drained from her face. 'Poor Dianthe,' she whispered. Then she gasped. 'We left Melissa at Gla.'

'I know. We couldn't have got out with her along. But she's no Dianthe. She would give them what they wanted.'

'But they might torture her.'

'I doubt they'd need to. And if she were not there, they would look to others to provide the evidence. Thais or Philomena. Anyone. They'll find somebody. If they bother. We've made it easier for them by fleeing together, but there was no choice. Once they had some so-called proof, it would just be a matter of time.'

She gazed at him, searching his face. 'Are they going to hunt us down, Dio?'

'I don't know. How demanding is Sofia? Or Laomedon? To what extent is Milt involved? My guess is this is down to Adrastus, but Milt must be agreeing to it. Can they afford for it to be so public?'

She still looked frightened.

'Look, Kal. The only way they could possibly track us is to get an Aggie tracker. That will take a few days at least. Even for an Aggie it would be slow and difficult along well-used highways like the Southway, and certainly not through water, so picking up our spoor where we left the creek will be all but impossible. Then, to be able to follow us after that torrential rain last night?' He shook his head. 'Not a chance. We could be anywhere in the Vale and, in a day or so, anywhere at all. So long as we were not spotted by anyone—and, in that weather, we can be pretty certain we weren't—they haven't a hope.' He stopped, then quietly added, 'And, whatever they do, we'll be safe with Phyll and Dymas.'

She gazed into the fire and said nothing. They sat for a while in silence. She looked weary, her face drawn, her eyes drooping. She had not slept the previous night, and it had been a hard ride that afternoon.

'Time for you to get your head down, I think.'

She nodded. He stood up and gathered five blankets that he had brought up from the bolt hole. He folded three and laid them atop each other before the fire to provide a modicum of protection from the hard, wooden floor. She watched, her face inscrutable. He laid a fourth blanket on top, and some dry clothes stuffed inside a tunic for a pillow.

'There's plenty of wood to feed the fire if you wake cold,' he said. He found that he could not meet her eyes.

'Where are you sleeping?' she asked. Her tone was carefully neutral, but he was aware that she was watching him closely.

'In what is laughingly called the bedroom,' he said lightly. 'Which is strange, considering that there is no bed. Is there anything that you need?' She shook her head. He picked up the last blanket, and finally looked at her. For a moment, there was something in her eyes. He assured himself that it was only his overactive imagination. He turned to the door.

'No,' she said sharply. He stopped. 'No,' she repeated, her voice now quiet and tremulous. 'Please.'

He turned back.

Her eyes were upon him. Large, pleading, the sleepiness departed. 'Please, Dio. Sleep in here. I don't want to be on my own. I'm still… frightened. Please.'

He was taken by surprise and nonplussed at the sudden inchoate clash of emotions. 'It wouldn't be proper,' he said, and winced at his own pomposity. Why, by all the Gods, had he said something so inane?

She laughed, but there was no joy in it. 'Herakla, Dio, we are on our own in an isolated steading for the night, and you worry about my reputation? It's shredded beyond repair. You can't patch it now.' Her voice softened. 'But you can give me sleep tonight. Feeling safe and secure. Knowing that my protector is there.' She paused. 'Please.'

'If that is what you want,' he said. Dyaus, why must he speak like a character in a third-rate tragedy at the Kalydonian Dionysia?

'It's what I want,' she said, smiling with relief. 'Thank you.'

He walked back and laid his blanket down on the other side of the fireplace, as Kal arranged herself as comfortably as she could on her meagre bed and covered herself with the blanket.

She giggled. 'Don't worry. I promise I won't molest you in the middle of the night. You're quite safe.'

He was bereft of words, completely unable to frame an answer, and she knew it. She chuckled again. 'Good night, Dio.'

He lay down and half-pulled the blanket over himself, feeling absurdly self-conscious. 'Good night, Kal. Sleep well.'

FORTY-THREE

H E GOT LITTLE rest that night. It was not the unyielding floorboards. He was used to sleeping on hard ground, and it was but small hardship to him. But the day had brought him to a sword clash between his greatest hopes and worst fears. He saw, only too clearly, that he was approaching an irrevocable decision, one that would set the course for the rest of his life, yet still did not know what he wanted. He knew now that Kal was much more important to him than he had ever realised. But in what way?

The shameful speculation that she might come to him in the night both enticed and frightened him. He tried to stop his ears to it, but it continued to reverberate through the long dekates. Every creak or sound had him instantly awake, lying rigidly in the darkness, fear and hope contending like two spear lines. But each time, there was just the gentle rhythm of sleep to her breathing. His seemingly innocent dreams of listening to the quiet susurrations of her sleep were mercilessly exposed as a self-deception that had cloaked his unfathomed and dark designs even from himself.

He rose a couple of times to feed the fire, and risked a brief look at her as she lay there, washed by the warm glow, her face gentled by repose and the soft light. One arm lay out on top of the blanket, her slim wrist and elegant fingers cupped within the shadowed valley of her breasts. He looked away. It felt as though he were violating her privacy, that he was looking upon her as an object of desire. It wasn't right. She was Kal, not a thing to be used and cast aside.

What more could she be? She lay there, sound asleep; secure in the knowledge that her friend, nothing more, was nearby. She had made herself more than clear. She wanted no relationships. He was creating gossamer castles from silken webs of surmise and wisps of insubstantial misinterpretation. And even these fragile constructs carried threat. Once before, long ago, he had laid himself open to scorn and had been lacerated. It would not happen again.

And yet, the image of her in his arms was one that he could not dislodge from his thoughts. No matter how he tried.

FORTY-FOUR

Dio rose before dawn, lighting an oil lamp. Kal slept on. He began to quietly sort things out and ready a modest breakfast of bread and cheese. The grey dawn had begun to infiltrate the gaps in the shutters when she stirred. He turned to find her eyes on him and a magical smile.

'Good morning, Lord Proper and Prim,' she said.

He had to smile ruefully. 'I do have a tendency towards the pontifical.'

'You keep it reasonably well hidden. When you're asleep, at least.'

'But you don't know what I'm dreaming about.' Nor did she. Thank the Gods. 'I dream in the pontifical.'

'I bet you do.' She sat up and groaned theatrically, stretching her back and grimacing. 'I'm amazed that herd of aurochs that ran over me in the night didn't wake me.'

'You slept right through it.' He took the pail of water he had drawn from the well the previous evening and carefully doused the fire.

She pulled a face. 'Dio killed nice fire,' she said in a childish voice. 'Bad Dio.'

'Bad Dio thinks it's time we were on our way.' He felt the clothes. They were still damp. 'I'm afraid that you'll have to wear what you've got on now.'

'Just my luck to be killed wearing a man's clothes. I'll feel bloody stupid at the funeral.'

'Don't joke about it,' he snapped, the tension within finally bursting the iron bar on his tongue.

Kal looked hurt.

'I'm sorry,' he said clumsily. 'Didn't get much sleep.'

'I slept like a child,' she said, then suddenly looked up at him, crestfallen. 'You were awake worrying and scheming and planning, while I was snoring happily by the fire. Then I make it worse by bragging about it.' She hung her head.

So much for his fervid imagination. 'Don't be silly; I'm just pleased that you got some decent rest. But we need to press on. The sooner we get to the steading, the better.'

She reached up, and he took her hand to help her to her feet, though he was still ridiculously aware of her touch.

FORTY-FIVE

They threaded their way along the shallow valleys; huddled deep within their cloaks. Dio was ever watchful, carefully avoiding the lonely steadings, sometimes making long detours to do so. He only allowed them to break the skyline when it was unavoidable, and then as quickly as possible, but he could do nothing about the imprint of hooves in the soft ground.

The downpour had long since ceased, though they could see the cloud shredding into rain to the west. The sky was a gloomy stretch of thick, roiling cloud, while the frigid wind still fetched from the north, if neither as strong nor as noisy as the previous day. There was thin ice on the sheets of standing water left by the torrential rain. Their breath clouded the pure air, and the ice cracked and splintered under their horses' hooves. He reckoned they would be at their destination by early afternoon. At least they could talk as they rode. Kal was worried about her children and how all this might affect them.

The elder, Aglaia, was twenty, had been married for three years, and was the proud mother of a fine toddler. She had wed into the ancient and wealthy Basilides clan, which was a coup for Miltiades—himself, like Dio, from but humble origins—and she seemed happy enough. She had been a lovely child, a mass of black waves of hair, huge intelligent eyes with a decidedly mischievous glint, and boundless energy that exhausted everyone around her. Antinous, Kal's son, was much more serious, lacking Aglaia's imagination and vivacity, but with a quiet determination that would see him do well in life. His father had recently managed to get him a prestigious position as a plagiophylakes in the Imperial Guard.

Dio had found, to his own astonishment, that he was gifted with a natural affinity with young children. The trick, he had discovered, was to be even sillier and more immature than they were, so there was no smack of adult authority about him. He cherished the memory of walking through the agora in Leuctra with Kal and a very young Aglaia. The little girl had firmly placed him between the two of them 'so that we can look after him'. They had spent most of the subsequent time creeping round the stalls behind an increasingly exasperated Kal who, unawares, was searching for them. When eventually cornered, they had accused each other with such enthusiasm that Kal had laughed until the tears came.

His relationship with Antinous, equally good, had been founded on the lad's interest in all things military. He had trained him to the sword, the spear and the bow, spent dekates poring over old histories together in the library, and knelt on all fours in Antinous's room pushing wooden blocks around to recreate the great battles. Kal always said that he had been the father they had never really had. Miltiades had loved them in his fashion, was undoubtedly proud of them, and did his best to advance them in life, but essentially children were an unwelcome distraction, and he was grateful that Dio could keep them amused and away from under his feet.

Dio was almost as concerned as Kal. Aglaia worshipped her father and Antinous his mother. Both were fond of Dio. What they would make of this chariot crash, he had no idea. It hurt him to imagine how they might judge him or their mother. But Kal was distraught, working herself up into a state of febrile distress, and it took him some time to calm her down. Eventually she relaxed a little, and he diverted her mind from the worry by telling her of their hosts.

'Dymas and Phyllida,' he said as they splashed through the shallow ford across the river Peiros. 'Phyll is pure steading; her family goes back generations; but Dymas is a city lad from Megara. He was with an archer auxiliary unit stationed at Gla during the First Thracian War. When he was discharged after an accident, he married Phyll, and they took over her grandfather's place. It's still called Glaukon's Steading after him. Dymas took to the life like a fish to water. Phyll's the one with the brains. She's very shrewd and acute; nothing much gets by her, and she's as strong as the sinews of the earth. Part of the land itself. Dymas is content to let her run things, but he's as dependable as they come.

'They have two kids. The elder, Gorgias, is like his father: stolid, unimaginative, but loyal and a hard worker. He's a good lad. Xanthos is a different bird altogether. He's quiet and unassuming, but he's never going to make a steader. He can't bear drudge, and he's happiest in his own company. He loves to be outdoors. He's a daemon of a hunter, and so they let him go his own way. Phyll worries about him, naturally, but he keeps them well supplied with meat and makes more than an obol or two with furs.'

Dio paused, then added, 'Xan is talking of leaving. He wants to see more of the world. Phyll won't stand in his way, but it'll hit her hard when he goes.'

'A quiet loner who goes his own way,' remarked Kal. 'I'd lay a drachma to an obol that he's your favourite.'

Dio made a noncommittal gesture. 'Perhaps.' He looked up at a high-flying skein of pink-footed geese, calling urgently to one another as their lines shifted and reformed incessantly. 'He'll travel with the wild geese, and he may achieve great things. He has the makings. If the Goddess of Fortune grants him reasonable luck, he may well be a name.'

'Is that what it's all about? Being a name?' There was a touch of asperity to Kal's tone.

'Not at all. I merely note it as a possibility.'

There was silence between them for a while.

FORTY-SIX

'But I still find the argument from first cause convincing,' Kal was saying. 'Everything must have a cause, so there must have been some special, primary cause, and that we call the First Cause, or just God if you prefer.'

She was doing what she was happiest at – arguing. He was happy too. It stopped her fretting. Though he wasn't at all sure how it had started. As far as he could recall, he had commented on the warmth of the sun.

'Why? Surely if you are referring to a cause, then we are justified in asking what caused that cause, and so on in an infinite regress. Why not leave it with the world as it is? Much simpler and more satisfying.'

'Not to me. It is surely reasonable to suppose the world needs a cause, just like everything in it. It is more reasonable to suppose that everything is of a universal nature, rather than the whole should be totally different from its parts.'

'But doesn't that dispose of this 'God' yet again?'

'Not at all. The concept of the First Cause is completely separate from the world. Read Bousaeus. And, according to Paleius, the intricate design of the world must require a designer.'

He pointed down at an isolated outcrop of rock that they were passing. 'Look at that puddle in the middle. It fits the hollow of the rock absolutely perfectly. It appears to be designed for the role.'

'Now, that's silly. Water flows to fill spaces. That's why.'

'So how do we know that the world doesn't somehow flow to fill spaces? That rabbits fill rabbit spaces and oak trees fill oak tree spaces?'

She furrowed her brow. 'That's hard to understand. It sounds profound, but I'm not at all sure what it means.'

'Because our tiny minds, and I am carefully not including yours in that general description—'

'Very wise.'

He continued, unperturbed, '—can't grasp ideas that are beyond them, does not mean that such ideas cannot be correct.'

'If you can't grasp them, then how can you even enunciate them? And it's difficult not to see a person, of sorts, behind the world, rather than some mindless principle.'

'But which person? Dyaus Pitar? Taranis of the Keltoi? The Thracian Zagreus? The God of the Monotheites?'

'Did you know that Theagenes is a Monotheite?' Kal changed the subject with one of her disconcerting jumps. Dio often told her that she had a grasshopper mind. She would simply point out that his tortoise brain was too pedestrian to follow the intervening links.

'I did, as a matter of fact. Talked to him about it a couple of times. Even read the Book of Truth. Well, a bit of it, anyway.'

'Believe it or not, Milt has a full set of scrolls. That funny little man in the black robes, the High Panjandrum or something, presented them to him when he came through Gla a couple of years ago. I caught him reading them one evening.'

'Milt? Reading?' Dio was incredulous.

'He said that he didn't think a lot of it.'

'I should think not. A total farrago of nonsense. Inordinately dull stuff. Packed full of ridiculous and arbitrary rules. They can't eat the white of an egg or touch wine or fornicate under a full moon. They always have to wear something red. And they must be clean shaven.'

'That would be just the women, I presume,' giggled Kal.

'You wouldn't like them. They're not at all keen on women. They can't worship with the men, and they must be totally obedient to their husbands.'

Kal tutted.

'They can't even speak to a man until spoken to.'

Her mouth dropped open.

'I'm thinking of joining,' he added blandly.

'You might, but I'm not,' she said darkly, 'so if you think that will shut me up, you have another and wiser thought to come.'

Dio pulled a wry face. 'Another wonderful idea founders on the rock of female intransigence.'

'I'll give you intransigence,' muttered Kal.

'You don't know the half of it. Have you heard of the Great Wakening?'

'No. But I have an uneasy suspicion that I soon will.'

'It is when the whole world will recognise the truth and acknowledge the greatness of Monos, the One. The world will thrive under the benign governance of his House. There'll be no more war, no famines, no sickness, no crime.'

'No bloody chance. And people are convinced by this?'

'More than you would think. And some of them names. Theagenes claimed that Charmides, the satrap of Lesser Troia, is a convert, and he reckons that one or two of the other satraps are attracted.' Dio shrugged. 'No-one ever said that an analytical mind was a necessary qualification for governance.' He pulled his horse to a stop and pointed to a distant cluster of buildings atop a small rise. 'We're there.'

'Thank Herakla. I'm hungry and tired. And I get cranky when I'm hungry and tired.'

'Really? I'd never noticed.'

Kal thumped his arm. 'That's for being sarcastic.'

He rubbed his arm with unnecessary vigour. 'Dyaus knows what I would have got if I'd agreed with you,' he grumbled.

'I could demonstrate,' she suggested helpfully.

'I wouldn't dream of putting you to the trouble.'

'No trouble.' She awarded him her most beatific smile.

Dio decided that a wise strategos knows when to leave the watch fires burning and slip away into the night. He pointed at the steading. 'Come on then, but carefully. I don't want anyone seeing us arrive.' As he urged his horse forward, something hovered on the edge of his mind, then flitted away like a dunnock into dense undergrowth and was lost.

FORTY-SEVEN

A DUMPY, MIDDLE-AGED WOMAN with lank brown hair, dimpled cheeks and a twinkle in her eye came rushing out of the house to meet them. 'Dio!' she shouted delightedly.

Dio swung down, and she grabbed him and gave him a bear hug. He felt uncomfortable as always, but Phyllida was either oblivious to it, or was simply not going to take heed of such a silly phobia. A couple of big, grey, rough-coated hounds charged up and leapt upon him with tail-wagging enthusiasm. He tousled their ears vigorously. Then a balding man with apple cheeks emerged from one of the outbuildings and limped up to grasp forearms. 'Dio,' he said. 'It's good to see you.'

A muscular young man came running round the corner of the large barn, a pitchfork in hand. He had the same rosy cheeks as his father but a shock of tawny hair. He grinned as he joined the throng and took Dio's wrist as a man should. 'Welcome, Uncle Dio,' he said, rather self-consciously.

Phyllida was looking up at Kal. 'This would be the Lady Kalliste, I presume?' she said, without any preamble.

'It would,' replied Dio, feeling a strange surge of proprietorial pride. 'Kal, this is Phyllida, the most formidable woman east of the Pot; Dymas, the luckiest chap; and this strapping young fellow is Gorgias, who has turned into a man since I last saw him, and a brawny one at that.' Gorgias looked bashful.

Kal swung herself down from her horse and was immediately engulfed by Phyllida. 'Any friend of Dio's is more than welcome here, my Lady.'

'Just Kal, please,' she said as she hugged Phyllida back. It was obvious that the two were going to get along famously.

'Come inside,' said Phyllida, her eyes searching the horizon. 'Gogo, see to the horses.'

FORTY-EIGHT

THEY SAT ROUND the large, roughly hewn wooden table, the axis about which their home life gently revolved. The steaders eschewed couches as effete and used three legged stools, though padded for comfort. Kal was working her way enthusiastically through a large platter of freshly baked bread and goat's cheese, watched by a benignly smiling Phyllida.

'Xanthos?' asked Dio, eating a little more genteelly.

'Guess.' Phyllida's response was unusually terse.

'Hunting.'

'How did you know?' said Dymas, a look of mock-surprise on his face.

'Just a lucky cast into the wind.'

Kal glanced up and said, through a mouth full of bread and cheese and in a most unladylike manner, 'He's a good hunter, I hear.'

'The best,' said Gorgias proudly. 'Last time, he brought back three bearskins. Three!'

'He could do with helping round the steading a bit more,' grumbled Phyllida.

'Let the lad be,' said Dio. 'He is what he is, and you won't change him.'

Phyllida sighed. 'You're right, of course. But it doesn't make it easy.'

Kal laid a sympathetic hand on her arm.

Dio caught Phyllida's eye. 'You knew who Kal was instantly. How?'

'Herodian. You know him, Dio. Three steadings over towards Choraea. He called in but five dekates ago, coming back from Glapolis. He told us the place was awash with rumour. I've been halfway expecting you ever since.'

'So, what's being said?'

Phyllida glanced at Kal, then drew a long breath. 'I'm sorry, my La... Kal, but the tale is that you and Dio have been deceiving the Lord Miltiades for many years and have finally run off together. Now, I know it's not true, because I know Dio, but that's what they're saying. I'm told they're searching for you. There's even talk of a reward.'

Kal put down the large lump of cheese she had been savaging. 'It's not true. Not at all. Milt decided to divorce me without giving a reason. Indeed, he has none. And Dio has been my friend and protector since.' She laid her hand on his.

He sat suddenly rigid.

'That's all. And that's the truth, I swear,' said Kal.

'I know,' said Phyllida quietly, taking Kal's white, long-fingered hand in her stubby, chapped ones.

Dio relaxed. He wondered if Phyllida had done it deliberately and knowingly. It would be like her if so.

She looked across at Dio. 'So, you want to go into hiding here for a time.' It was a statement rather than a question.

'I know it is a great deal to ask—'

'Diomedes of Gla!' thundered Phyllida with a voice that could stop a phalanx. 'If you say anything like that again, I shall fetch you such a clout round the ear, you won't know whether you're in this world or the next!'

'And she will too,' chimed in Dymas, rubbing his own ear to make the point.

Dio made an open-handed gesture of submission. 'Point taken, Phyllida of Glaukon's Steading; but, seriously, you do know there will be danger.'

'Of course I know,' she snapped. She turned to Kal, who had returned to the bread and cheese with renewed purpose. 'Men!' she declared, with a resounding sniff. 'And they consider that women are stupid.'

Kal nodded vigorously.

'I know enough to know when I'm outnumbered,' observed Dio.

'There are three of you, and only two of us,' Phyllida pointed out.

'As I said.'

'I presume no-one saw you arrive?' asked Dymas.

'They didn't.'

'Then I can see no problem.'

'The horses will have to disappear,' said Phyllida.

'I can put them in the west pasturage,' suggested Gorgias, looking to his mother for confirmation. She nodded.

Phyllida looked out of the window to the small wooden

building across the yard. 'We have the guest house, which has its own bolt hole. So long as you keep your head below the parapet, you should be safe.'

'Nevertheless,' insisted Dio, 'it remains dangerous. It can be mentioned to no-one.'

Phyllida regarded Gorgias sternly. 'No-one,' she repeated meaningfully. She glanced across at Dio. 'Got himself a lady friend, would you believe? Young Hebe from a couple of steadings away. Nice girl.'

Gorgias flamed red. 'We're just friends,' he muttered.

Dymas laughed. 'So, what were you doing in the hay barn that left bits of straw sticking in your hair?'

'Only checking the apple store.'

'That's what they call it these days, is it?' said Dymas, enjoying himself hugely.

'I'm pleased for you,' said Dio, 'but you mustn't mention us, even to Hebe.'

'But Hebe said we couldn't have secrets between us,' Gorgias said without thinking. He glanced quickly at his father. The blush that had been fading returned with renewed vigour. 'She wouldn't say anything.'

'She can't tell what she isn't told. I'm sorry, Gogo.' Dio drew his sword and placed it carefully on the table. 'On the blade,' he said.

Gorgias stared at the sword with horror. The Great Oath was not to be sworn lightly. One did not mock the Furies. He looked desperately at his mother, then his father, for support, but their faces were implacable. He reluctantly placed his right hand flat on the sword.

'Swear by the Furies that you will speak to no-one of our being here.'

His face seemed to sag, and his voice shook, but he did so.

Dio returned the sword to its scabbard. 'There you are, Gogo; now, if it ever comes out that you have kept a secret from Hebe, you can blame me and the terrible oath you had to swear.'

Gorgias gave him a weak smile.

'He probably just saved your life,' said Kal and tore off another hunk of bread.

FORTY-NINE

THE GUEST HOUSE was a steading hearth home in miniature. The central living area was dominated by a large fireplace, with kindling and logs in the box to one side. Gorgias had already lit the fire for them. A small bedroom with just room for a double bed was at one end and an even smaller bedroom for children at the other. Noting Phyllida's speculative look, Dio quickly commandeered the latter. Dymas showed them the bolt hole. The entire hearth could be unlocked and slid to one side, allowing access. Like all steading bolt holes, it was cramped but well stuffed with essentials. Phyllida brought across bread, cheese, wine and milk.

She pointed to a small bell above the door. 'Gogo is rigging up the rope. If it rings, douse the fire; get down in the bolt hole, and wait. Don't come out until we come and get you. Try not to leave any clues that the place is occupied. But you know how to throw the javelin, Dio.'

Dio nodded. 'Thank you, Phyll.'

'Not necessary, and you know it.' She hugged Kal. 'We're going to be great friends, I'm sure.'

'I do hope so. But was I awfully greedy? I feel ashamed of myself now.'

'Nonsense,' laughed Phyllida, 'I like someone with a good appetite. I won't hug Dio. I only did that when he arrived to keep him in practice. He needs a good hugging from time to time.' She looked slyly at Dio, who felt his face warm.

Dymas came in with the bedding.

'We'll say goodnight, then. Sleep well and soundly, both of you.'

'Thank you,' said Kal. 'And the same to you.'

The door closed behind them. Dio placed the tray of food beside the hearth so they could take it with them in an emergency.

Kal flopped down on a cushioned chair beside the fire and looked around her. The place was warm and cosy in the glow of the fire and of a couple of oil lamps. 'Do you know,' she said, almost dreamily, 'I feel warm and snug and sleepy. Perhaps I might have eaten a mite too much, though,' she added after a moment's reflection.

'I should think so,' said Dio as he went into Kal's bedroom to make up her bed. 'I've never seen such a rapid demolition job of a platter of food. It reminded me of the old Norther tale of the God losing an eating competition with a young boy.'

'What was that?'

'A God visited the Land of the Giants and was challenged to various tasks. He had the eating competition, a race against a toddler, a wrestling match with an old man, and a piece of rope to lift. He failed them all.'

'Not much of a God,' she exclaimed derisively.

'They had tricked him. It was all illusion. The race was against rumour, the old man was death itself, and the rope was the World Serpent that encircles the earth. He terrified the Giants when he managed to lift it a finger's breadth. The whole world moved.'

'What about the eating?'

'His opponent was famine.' He came back into the room.

She pulled a face. 'Anyway, when you've stopped being rude about a girl's slight peckishness, I was trying to say that this feels like home. It feels homelier than my rooms in Gla. Isn't that strange?'

'You're safe here.'

'Yes, that must be it. Along with other things.'

He chose not to pursue that enigmatic comment.

She curled her legs under her in her characteristic pose and looked at him as he sat down in the chair opposite. She yawned mightily. 'So, what's going to happen?'

'We stay here for at least a few days, probably longer. We're as safe here as anywhere.'

'I feel safe,' said Kal. 'Perhaps I shouldn't, but I do. I feel warm, and nicely full, and—there will be no impertinent comments—and…' A smile spread over her face. 'Happy. Yes, I feel happy. Isn't that strange?'

Dio sat down on the other side of the fireplace. 'Perhaps it is more relief.'

'No,' she insisted. 'Happy.'

'Then hold onto it. There isn't a lot of it about.'

'I will. That's sound advice. There are times when a flicker of common sense gleams momentarily in a man, but then is gone. Such times are rare but give one hope.'

They sat there before the cheerful flames that painted their faces in rubicund tones, listening to the fire crackle and chitter to itself, saying nothing. Dio glanced up and realised that she was sleeping. He gazed at her face for a while, though it felt almost like a violation; then, with a great deal of trepidation, he got up, went over and slid one arm beneath her knees and the other round her back. She murmured something but did not wake. He lifted her, and she reflexively put her arms round his neck, saying something else in her sleep that he could not catch. She felt warm and solid in his arms, and he could smell her musky odour with overtones of her favourite cedar perfume. Her breath was gentle on his cheek, and her hair caressed his neck.

He carried her through to the bedroom and laid her down on the bed. He didn't know whether he wanted her to wake up or not. But she was sound asleep. He pulled the covers over her and reluctantly walked away. Behind him, she snuggled more comfortably. This time, he caught what she murmured.

'Goodnight, Milt.'

FIFTY

'Mmm,' mumbled Kal, 'this is delicious porridge.'
Phyllida beamed.

'Do you know I had to wake him up this morning? Hammer on his door. Dead to the world and snoring.'

'I wasn't snoring,' Dio muttered. Neither of them had mentioned anything about how she had got to bed the night before. Perhaps she thought she had got there by herself, but had fallen asleep immediately and forgotten the going.

'How, by Dyaus, would you know?' demanded Kal reasonably.

Phyllida shook her head sadly. 'He's getting old, poor thing,' She reached for the pot of honey. 'He'll soon be having a regular afternoon nap.'

'Snoozing peacefully in the sun,' added Dymas.

'I'll make him a thick woollen shawl,' said Phyllida.

Gorgias was laughing. 'I'll make him some bearskin slippers.'

'You too, Gogo,' said Dio acidly. 'Why does the image of a bison set about by a pack of wolves come to mind?'

'Would that be that old, grizzled bison with the rheumatics?' said Phyllida, and hooted with mirth.

'Wearing a shawl, bearskin slippers and a grumpy scowl,' cried Kal, and they both collapsed in helpless laughter.

'If I can be the cause of a little merriment in life, then my living will not have been in vain,' declared Dio sententiously.

'Well, you've certainly lived a worthwhile life, then,' said Kal, winking at Phyllida and scarcely able to get her words out for bouts of giggling.

'I was going to give you a hand round the steading, but I suppose I'd better go and have a lie-down instead.'

Phyllida looked serious. 'It's too dangerous for you to be out. What if someone comes?'

'There's five of us, so there's plenty of eyes, and as long as we stay close to the steading itself, there should be no danger. And you're one worker up.'

'We could do with some help with the stable roof,' said Dymas quickly. 'I can't get up there easily with my leg.'

Phyllida considered. 'All right,' she said somewhat grudgingly, 'I know you'll only fret else. But Kal is a proper guest, so no work for her.'

'Nonsense,' insisted Kal. 'I'll die of boredom. What are you planning for today?'

'Making bread.'

'Fine, I can help with that. Is there any more porridge?'

FIFTY-ONE

THEY SAT ROUND the remnants of a fine meal. Phyllida had always been an excellent cook. It had been a good day. Cold but sunny. Dio had enjoyed the simple, hard physical graft of repairing the roof with young Gorgias. Enough to keep his mind occupied. There had been a regular accompaniment of merriment from the house: the rumble of laughter from Phyllida overlain by Kal's musical giggle. But the laughter and joking had died away, and the evening had taken on a serious cast. Dio briefed them, calmly and efficiently, as to the present situation. Phyllida, Dymas and Gorgias listened intently, but exchanged worried looks when he spoke of Laomedon.

'There have been rumours,' said Phyllida, 'but I thought it was just silly gossip. Though I did wonder when we heard of the assassination.'

'Why didn't Laomedon strike immediately?' asked Dymas shrewdly.

'I don't know,' admitted Dio. 'I can only suppose that the handle came off somewhere. But he must move sooner or later.'

'So, what are you going to do?' demanded Phyllida, direct as ever.

'I don't know that either,' said Dio. 'It depends on how actively are they searching for us and where they are looking.'

Kal immediately argued that they should head for Leuctra and take the first ship out of there. Phyllida hotly supported her. Dio disagreed, and Dymas doggedly backed him.

'I would lay a silver talent to an obol that it is closely watched, but covertly,' said Dio. 'It's the obvious place, and there'll be more spies than fleas on a hedgehog. It's too dangerous. I'm sorry.'

Phyllida patted Kal's hand, and Kal smiled wanly at her. 'We could head north for Antenopolis,' she persisted.

Dio demurred. 'It's a long way, and we'll have to pass through the Thebeaid. Raxamenes will be on the lookout. With us taking it on the scuttle, along with Gelon's disappearance, they have to assume we know something. They won't know what, but that'll make them even more desperate to stop us. At the moment, it's too dangerous.'

Dymas pushed his empty wooden bowl away from him and sat back. 'So, sit tight, and when things have quietened down, make for the coast.'

Dio reached for the iron within and cleared his throat. 'I must return to Gla. I've arranged to meet Rad outside the town. I need to know the situation.'

Kal's eyes were suddenly wide open. 'You're going back? You can't.'

'I have to.'

'You can't. I won't let you.'

'I've no choice, Kal. I have to know how things stand. We can't just sit around waiting for them to scoop us up. Besides which, while we stay here, we are putting Phyllida and her family into the arena.'

'Diomedes,' said Phyllida in her warning voice.

'It's a fact, Phyll. You can't deny it. And you tell me that you wouldn't be saying exactly the same thing if the situation was reversed.'

Phyllida looked down and sighed. Kal's eyes were fixed on his, but he dared not meet them.

'Look, I'll be seeing Rad well outside of the fortress. There's no danger.'

'Of course there'll be danger. How could there not be?' said Kal. He could hear the strain in her voice.

He said nothing. He still would not meet her stare.

She opened her mouth, then closed it again and sighed. 'There's no point in arguing, is there? You've made up your mind. I've seen that look before.' She spread her hands in a gesture of hopeless resignation.

'I'm sorry, Kal. But I have to go. How else can I keep you safe?'

He could feel the strength of her stare, and he realised how perilously close to the rocks of self-exposure he was sailing. Then her shoulders slumped, and her head dropped.

'You will be careful. You won't go and do anything stupid?' Her voice trembled slightly.

'When have you known me do anything stupid? Don't answer that.'

She smiled, but it was an unconvincing attempt.

There was a hard and painful silence for a while, then Dymas challenged Kal to a game of tilia and Gorgias went out to coop up the hens. Dio took the opportunity to suggest to Phyllida that they go and light the fire in the guest house. They walked across through a crisp, moonlit night.

'The answer's yes,' said Phyllida as she laid the fire.

'I haven't even asked the question,' said Dio wryly.

'I'll see that your Kal is kept safe if anything happens to you.' The phrase 'your Kal' burst like kindling in his heart. 'I know you, Dio. You're gambling on somehow sorting all this out, at a much greater risk to yourself than you've led her to believe, because, if you try and run for it together, she'll be at risk.' She stopped and turned towards him, looking him straight in the eye. 'Whatever happens, she'll have refuge here, but you go and get yourself killed, and I'll never forgive you.'

'Is this where the bit about clouts and ears comes in?' he asked, using the oil lamp to ignite the fire.

She harrumphed. 'It ought to be. She's a good woman. I like her. She told me about that feeble bastard of a husband. She's had a bad time. She also told me how good you've been to her. What I don't understand is why I'm making up two separate beds.'

'Phyll!' He should have expected such outspokenness; he had known her long enough, and she had an earthy common sense that had no truck with anything as wishy-washy as tact. But it took him by surprise, and he was embarrassed.

Phyllida shrugged. 'Well, you're both adults and should know your own minds.' Then added, 'I suppose.'

Dio went to his blanket bag. 'There's money in there, if anything happens to me.' He drew out a small scroll and gave it to her. 'Those are the details of a man in Leuctra and how to contact him. If the worst comes to the worst, he'll get her out of the country. He can be trusted.'

She took the scroll, and her face softened. 'I'll look after her. Have no fear.'

She turned to head back to the hearth home. 'But for an intelligent man, Dio…' She sighed and left the unfinished observation hanging in the air as she walked out.

FIFTY-TWO

RADAMANTHUS STRODE UP and down, beating his arms against his chest and swearing horribly. Despite his thick hooded cloak and woollen mittens, he felt that he was freezing to death out here in the chill wind. It was a desolate, open spot. The little-used track wound its perfunctory way past a small outcrop of limestone pavement, in the midst of which a scrawny hawthorn tree, embedded in one of the deep grykes that cleaved the uneven surface, struggled for existence.

On one of the flatter clints, a neat cairn of stones marked Kerberos's nearby resting place. A few hundred paces to the north stood a small clump of fir trees, but otherwise nothing except the featureless roll and swell of the endless grasslands. He had searched the outcrop and the copse assiduously, but there was no sign of Dio. Radamanthus swore again and swung round to continue his relentless march for warmth.

His heart lurched. Dio was sitting on a clint and grinning at him.

'Dyaus's balls,' exclaimed Radamanthus. 'I was bloody nearly in the grip of Herakla then. How did you do that?'

By way of answer, Dio kicked at the small rise of vegetation before him, and it unrolled to reveal a loosely woven cloak in which were embedded twigs and tufts of grass. Radamanthus examined it with interest. 'Where did you get that from?'

'Made it myself. Even the Aggies have a thing or two they can teach you.' He stood up, and they grasped wrists.

'You look a bloody sight warmer than I feel,' observed Radamanthus. Apart from a woollen cloak, Dio was wearing a thickly-padded tunic and trousers, fur-lined boots, huge oiled woollen mitts and a sheepskin hat with long, snug ear lappets.

'Cold enough. Thanks for coming, but let's get into that copse just in case anyone happens by.'

'How's Kal?' asked Radamanthus as they walked across.

'She's fine. And safe. In a good place where she is being well looked after.'

They found what shelter they could against the wind and sat down on a tumbled trunk. 'So, what's the situation?' asked Dio.

'That idiot Aeropus followed your bloody great sign saying "we went this way" like the cretin he is. By the time he finally worked it out, you were long gone. They brought in an Aggie tracker on the sly, but even he can't pick you up.'

'What's the buzz in the agora?'

'Confused. The place is agog with it. The general opinion is as you would expect, but those that know you don't hold to it. Most officers in the garrison have heard about the poisoning of the dog and the death of the slave girl and know which end of the horse eats the hay.'

'What has Milt done about it?'

'On the face of it, nothing. Even that imbecile Tiro got away with a minor dressing down. Lucky bastard. But there's been a sudden outbreak of transfers between Gla and Kadmeia. Strangely enough, it's old, loyal units, especially those trained by you, that are being given their marching orders. Both Antenor's eile and Ilus's tag have been reassigned. They know what they're doing.'

'But that would require specific orders from the Imperial Army Staff.'

'Supposedly so. But Eury has a pet clerk on a leash, and he swears that no such orders have been received.'

'Unless they were classified – for the holder's attention only.'

'But there have been no Imperial messengers, and what would be the point? The transfers can't be kept hidden, can they?'

Dio nodded thoughtfully.

'There's more,' said Radamanthus. 'The new units are being sent on a lot of "familiarisation exercises". They're looking for you. Eastward towards Leuctra, it seems.' Radamanthus's homely face split into a lopsided grin. 'And Miltiades has thrown out patrols northwest, ostensibly to check on reports of Thrak depredations, but no doubt thinking you might have doubled back and are on the scuttle for Antenopolis. They won't find you in either place. I reckon you're tucked up safe and warm with a reliable friend way off in the southwest.'

Dio made a noncommittal grunt.

Radamanthus's smile grew even broader. Then it faded. 'There's something odd about this new lot. They keep themselves to themselves. They don't even go to Fat Delia's. I don't like it.'

'Well, it helps in one way. I need to get into Gla. And they won't know me.'

'Well, isn't it fortunate that I've just done the duty roster, and by sheer chance, it's all the new units on the rabbit watch.'

'You know, you could make a decent officer one day, if you work at it.'

'Thank you. Too kind. But just wait and see what else I've got for you.' He delved into his belt pouch and produced a small parchment roll, handing it to Dio with a flourish.

Dio unrolled it, glanced at it, raised his eyebrows and looked across at a beaming Radamanthus. 'By the teeth of the Furies, where did you get this?'

'To be honest, it was Eury's doing. Though I helped a bit. When all this began, Eury came up with the idea. As being of some possible use one day. How right he was. So, the next time that prick Pheidon came through, I lifted his messenger pass. I have some unusual accomplishments even you don't know about. Eury's tame clerk is a decent forger. By the time a groom found the original in the stables, we had this. More than passable. If you'll forgive the remarkably clever pun.'

'That's brilliant. Not the bloody pun. This.' He waved the pass. 'This makes it easy.'

'Not too easy,' warned Radamanthus.

'I need to think.'

Radamanthus got up and stamped about a bit.

'Does Pheidon come the same night every se'ennight?' Dio eventually asked.

Radamanthus stopped stamping and considered. 'Pretty much. It's almost always Heliou. He was here last night.'

'Does anybody else bring messages?'

'Occasionally.'

'At night, like Pheidon?'

'Usually, though I remember one arriving in the middle of the day.'

'And does Adrastus still make his se'ennightly trysts at Cybele's house of ill repute?'

Radamanthus stared at him for a moment, slightly bemused by the change in subject. 'He does. Never misses. He's there every Aphrodites, appropriately enough, a dekate after sunset. Doesn't return until next morning. Wearing a self-satisfied smirk.'

Dio smiled. 'Better and better. I am right in supposing that you know Cybele?'

'I most certainly do,' replied Radamanthus, a little belligerently, 'and I'm not ashamed of it.'

Dio held up a placatory hand. 'Have you any grip on her? An owed obligation? Unpleasant little secrets? The ability to squeeze her operation until it brings tears to her eyes? Simple friendship?'

'All of those, plus I'm a damn good customer.'

'Excellent. Finally, can you get a blank official arrest warrant?'

'Can a dog bark? Nothing easier. Miltiades signs them by the handful. He'd sign his own and never notice. Easy to slip in an extra one. And lots of them are blank, as Periphetes only knows some of the villains by their street names.'

Dio nodded with satisfaction, then looked down at the ground. 'Rad, I'm going to ask you to do some things. You will be wading into very deep water, and it may get risky. If it works, we could turn Laomedon's stampede. Or we might find ourselves right in its path. It's for you to decide, and no recriminations if you sensibly choose not to have anything to do with it. I would just ask, in that case, that you forget everything that's been said.'

'Don't be a daft bugger,' growled Rad. 'I'm with you. Every bloody step.'

Dio looked up at him and smiled. 'Thanks, my friend. Then here's what I want you to do.'

FIFTY-THREE

DIO FINISHED OUTLINING his plan. Phyllida was aghast, Kal almost in tears, Gorgias's eyes sparkled with excitement and Dymas looked thoughtful.

'It's far too dangerous,' blurted out Kal. 'And why? It's not our responsibility to save the Empire.' She remembered one of Dio's favourite arguments. 'How can we possibly know the consequences of whatever we do? They might well be for the worse as for the better.'

'The chances of Laomedon being a better proposition than Troilus seem somewhat minimal. What did Kymon say? "It cannot be good to ignore the bad."'

'It's not about bloody philosophical aphorisms,' she snapped and burst into tears. Phyllida leaned across and engulfed her in her brawny arms, glaring at Dio.

'I'm sorry. But it's as good a chance as we can hope for. The tide's running with us. I have no choice.'

'There are always choices,' retorted Phyllida acidly, still holding a sobbing Kal to her ample bosom.

Dio said nothing.

'When is this going to happen?' asked Dymas, ever practical.

Dio braced himself. 'I head back tomorrow.'

Kal stopped sobbing and regarded him with horror. 'Tomorrow?'

'Speed is essential.'

She bit her lip. 'But you can't. They'll recognise you. How can you expect to get back into Gla and not be recognised? It's just not possible.' There was desperation in her voice.

'The guard won't know me. They'll be these new replacements from Kadmeia. And it will be in the middle of the night. There's no-one around at that time.'

'What if there is?' demanded Kal.

'I'll deal with it according to the circumstances.' It sounded weak even to him. 'Rad will be on one of his legendary snap inspections, so he'll have my back covered.'

'I still don't like it.'

He was silent.

'It's no good, pet,' said Phyllida resignedly. 'He's going, and you won't stop him. But I can help a bit.' They all looked at her. 'My grandma worked with a travelling mummery troupe when she was young and wild. She could alter your appearance so your own mother wouldn't know you. She once worked on old man Aster, as a joke, and his wife chased him out of the house with a broom. She showed me some of the tricks when I was a kid. I've still got some of her stuff. I can make him unrecognisable, even to those who know him. I'm going to have to get busy, though, if he's going tomorrow.'

'Not a large wart on the end of my nose, if you don't mind.'

'You'll get what I shall be pleased to give you,' said Phyllida in a tone that brooked no argument.

For the first time, Kal smiled. 'Do you think you could make that two warts?'

FIFTY-FOUR

PHYLLIDA CAME ACROSS with him to the guest house again to light the fire, leaving Kal and Dymas engaged in their evening duel over the tilia board in the hearth home.

'He loves that game,' she said. 'I got tired of it years ago.'

She worked on the fire, building a little pyramid of thin sticks above the kindling, then using the lamp she carried to ignite it with a spill.

She looked up at Dio, determination in her face. 'It's a little late now, and perhaps I shouldn't say this, but that never stopped me. And I doubt it'll have any effect anyway. Those that won't look, don't see. Kal is a fine woman, and she thinks a lot of you. You should think on. Chances of happiness do not come often into this life. And, without being insulting, at your age they're not likely to come again.'

'She's made it clear that she doesn't want anything to do with men,' he said, secretly wanting her to gainsay him.

She duly obliged. 'What women say and what women do are two entirely different things. And no smart answers, if you please. When this is over, if you two are not in bed together before the se'ennight is out, I'm coming across and carrying you there regardless. One under each arm. And don't think I won't. And I've told her the same.'

Dio was shocked. 'Phyll! You haven't.'

'I bloody well have.'

He stared at her.

She looked at him incredulously and spread her stubby hands in a gesture of encouragement. 'Well? What did she say?' she prompted.

Dio swallowed. 'What did she say?' Hope and fear.

'She said that you had done so much for her, but you were a man happy with his own company, and she would not trespass on your privacy. Trespass on your privacy!' Contempt quivered in her voice. The fire was blazing nicely now. She turned to go. 'You're both purblind idiots. I've told you. You've a se'ennight to frame yourself. Then you'll have me to reckon with.' She marched off with a determined mien.

Dio watched her go, his mind racing as freely and uncontrollably as a runaway horse.

FIFTY-FIVE

K AL WAS COMING across as Phyllida left, a shawl wrapped round her shoulders. She was seemingly pleased with the fact that she had beaten Dymas two games to one, but the look in her eyes belied the buoyant gilding. There was a tension between them. He did not know how to deal with it. He fussed around with trivialities, collecting gear for the morrow. Kal sat by the fire; her false air of good cheer evaporating, and watched him miserably.

'When you get to Ilios,' she said tentatively, the slight emphasis on 'when' betraying that it had been 'if' that had formed in her mind, 'will you see Antinous?'

'I should think so.'

'Give him my love. Tell him I love him more than he knows. Men never seem to recognise love fully.'

He covered his confusion by delving within his blanket bag to search for he knew not what. 'I will.'

There was a long silence between them.

'You really think that this will work?'

'It has every chance,' he replied, choosing his words with care.

She tensed. He could see it in her sudden stillness. Her eyes were wide.

'Dio,' she said, then paused. 'Dio, that is the entire plan?' She paused again. The silence was painful. 'You are not planning to kill Milt?' she burst out.

He met her gaze for once. 'It's a possibility,' he said evenly. It was more than a possibility. Dio had been betrayed, and there is no acid more caustic to the soul than betrayal and no better balm for its burn than revenge. And the bastard had planned to murder Kal. Better yet, removing him would undoubtedly thrust a pole through Laomedon's chariot wheel. The chances were that Miltiades had been keeping the possibility that Dio was possessed of important information under a cloak. He would have no doubt as to Laomedon's likely reaction to such news. With Miltiades dead, Radamanthus would become temporary holder and undoubtedly deal appropriately with that rat Adrastus; the search would be stopped and Kal would be safe. Killing Miltiades was most definitely more than a possibility.

She sat forward, her eyes locked with his. 'You mustn't.'

Any measured thoughts about possible advantages were wiped instantly from his mind like a wax tablet swiped by a scribe. All he could think was that she still loved Miltiades. The feeling of shock and despair struck him with almost physical force. It left him without words, his mind reeling with the implications.

She took his silence for simple intransigence. 'He's the father of my children. I was married to him for over twenty years. I know that he has changed, but he was a decent man.' There was a long pause. Then she whispered, 'It will come between you and me.'

The implications of her final words hit him. He felt he was tossed in some savage maelstrom, first drowning in the white waters, then hurled into the life-giving air. His natural response to such uncertainty was to sit stone-faced, shutting out any clue to his emotions or thoughts. She must have interpreted it as obstinacy.

'Dio, please.' Her eyes were desperate, her voice beseeching. 'Please, Dio. Please.'

He finally realised what he was doing to her. 'I'm sorry,' he said gently. 'I won't kill Milt. I promise.'

She let out a juddering sigh of relief. 'Thank you,' she whispered and began to cry.

He awkwardly went across and offered her a cloth to dry her eyes. The thought occurred that she might embrace him, though whether he feared it or hoped for it was not at all clear. And she did, indeed, scramble to her feet and cling to him, sobbing. He patted her back ineffectually.

'I'm sorry,' he repeated over and again. 'I didn't mean to upset you.'

He was preternaturally conscious of the press of her body, the surge of animal warmth between them, the light touch of her hair against his face, the musky sweet smell, the tight and desperate grip in which she held him. He felt ashamed that these dominated his mind rather than her obvious distress, but he felt transfixed. The heaving sobs that racked her body slowly subsided, and she pulled away.

She sniffed loudly. 'I'm sorry. I know that you find it difficult, but there are times when I can't help myself.'

'I promised you a hug whenever you needed one.'

'I know, and it was very noble of you, but I could see it in your face. You just freeze. I won't do it again.'

He didn't know what to say. Or to think. Because the surge of disappointment was so intense that his last desperate defences wobbled. He suddenly knew, regardless of his neuroses and phobias, that he wanted to hold her again. That the thought of losing her was unbearable. And yet. And yet. Somehow the discipline that he had imposed upon his mind held. In the face of such a realisation, he knew that he should say something. The words formed but immediately seemed trite and false, and he could not bring them to utterance. Only spontaneity could burst the barriers that enclosed his words in a ring of iron, and he could not be spontaneous. He said nothing. And that nothing was as hard as granite and as heavy as lead. The moment faded, and he felt weak, pathetic and useless.

Kal sat down again, dabbing at her eyes. 'If your plan works, Milt will be implicated.'

Still concerned about Miltiades. The uneasiness remained. Why could there never be certainty? 'There's no way past that. But if we manage it, then Troilus will owe us. And I promise you that I will use whatever influence I have to save Milt.'

'Thank you.' She rose from her chair and moved towards her room. 'What time are you leaving tomorrow?' she asked. Now that Miltiades was safe, she seemed calmer.

'Early morning.'

'And just when I was looking forward to a pleasant time in our own little home. It's the birth of the sun tomorrow.

A new year. New beginnings.' Then she sighed. 'Same old endings.'

The world shifted again, the enigmatic phrasing making his heart race. And there was a note of wistfulness, even longing, in her voice. Or was it purely in his own mind? She stood by her bedroom door. The fire cast its magic and she looked beautiful. He looked away.

'You will be careful,' she whispered.

'Of course.'

'And come back to me. Please.'

He knew that he should have gone and held her, comforted her, but he couldn't. He had sworn to himself that he would say something, anything, but all he managed was an abject, 'I will. I promise.'

She nodded slightly, unconvinced. Her eyes still searched for his, but he kept them resolutely fixed on the fire. He was helpless. She turned to go. Her body spoke of misery.

'Are you all right, Kal?' he burst out. 'You seem upset.'

She did not turn. 'Of course I'm upset. What did you expect?'

There was no way he could answer. 'Do you need anything?' It was weak beyond belief, but it was the best he could do.

She finally turned and looked at him. He could not read her expression. 'Yes,' she said quietly, 'I do. But I'm afraid that it is not available.' She walked quickly into her room and closed the door behind her.

He stood by the fire for some time. Desolate. Self-recriminatory. He thought about going to her, but knew he wouldn't, and turned to walk dismally to his own room.

FIFTY-SIX

He could not sleep that night. The moon slid long fingers of cold light across his small room, and the wooden building murmured to itself in the light wind, creaking and grumbling. His mind was full of Kal. He had finally accepted that he wanted her. He had fought obstinately against the acceptance, but the time had come to yield. He found it hard to say, even to himself, that he was in love with her, but it was true.

He suspected that he had been in love with her for a long time, his feelings suppressed and enclosed within a bronze corselet. He had been lying to himself. Pandarus, as always, had known. 'You believe your own nonsense too easily, boy, and that makes you vulnerable. You stop asking just as soon as the hard questions arise. It will kill you one day.'

Nevertheless, he was still not sure of her feelings for him. She had said, so often and so definitively, that she would never get into a relationship with another man, and every word returned to haunt him. Every utterance of hers that had seemed to speak of feelings for him could so easily, in retrospect, be but innocent comments coloured and twisted by wishful misperception. Words that had broken upon him like a storm, undeniable and seemingly beyond misinterpretation, now twisted and mutated like passing clouds and drifted by, rendered bland and innocuous.

How would he ever find the courage to broach this to her? If he was wrong, how endure the humiliation? How survive the dreadful wake from such a dream? Dyaus Pitar, but he would rather face a massed Dryopian charge than this. The moonlight had begun to take on the leaden hue of dawn as he finally fell into an exhausted sleep.

FIFTY-SEVEN

Even Kal had to laugh. Phyllida had worked all night. She had stained his face with a solution of boiled bark, giving him a sallow complexion. She had dyed his hair black and combed it forward, plastering it down with goose fat, which not only altered his appearance remarkably, but had the advantage of hiding his forehead scar. She had disguised the scar on his cheek beneath a straggly, black false beard, sticking it to his face with an evil-smelling concoction.

'Pooh,' said Kal, wrinkling her nose, 'I suppose the idea is that no-one will dare get near enough to him to recognise him.'

'It won't come off easily, mind,' Phyllida warned. 'It'll sting a bit when it does.'

'Good,' pronounced Kal with some satisfaction.

Phyll had made him a couple of pads to slip into his cheeks, altering the shape of his face and making him mumble. The whole ensemble was completed by a padded tunic and leggings, covered by looser clothes purloined from Dymas.

Kal clapped her hands delightedly. 'Age and girth await all men,' she quoted.

'I'm not wearing these until I need to,' he grumbled. 'I'll melt.'

'Stop moaning,' demanded Kal severely. 'It was your idea.'

'Actually, it was Phyll's.' He went to remove the offending articles. They followed him to the door. Kal's smile died on her lips as she watched him go, her eyes anguished.

'He'll be fine, pet. He's overcome far worse odds in the past.'

'But sooner or later, the gambler always loses,' observed Kal moodily.

Dymas came up with the pack horse. 'I think we've got everything.'

Dio returned and stuffed the clothes in a blanket bag. There was an awkward silence. 'I should be back in about two se'ennights. Three at the most. If not...' His voice trailed away.

'You'll be back,' declared Phyllida confidently.

'Winter always returns,' added Dymas, grinning.

Kal's face was ashen, her smile a rictus. She reached out and took his hands, then suddenly pulled him forward and wrapped herself round him. Her face was buried in his shoulder, and her voice was muffled. 'You come back, you hear. I want you back safely.'

'I'll be back.'

She reluctantly released him, and for a moment they gazed into one another's eyes, before he turned abruptly to

Gorgias, who held Blackwing ready. He swung himself up onto the saddle cloth and took the lead rope of the pack horse.

He did not know what to say, so simply said, 'May the Gods protect you,' and urged Blackwing on. He looked back at the steading from the top of the rise. Kal and Phyllida were still watching. He rode on, descending the farther slope, his face set, Kal's last words ringing in his head.

FIFTY-EIGHT

It was late afternoon, and Misenus had just finished mucking out the last stall when a man entered. He was a rather chubby individual with sallow skin and an untidy black beard.

'What can I do for you, friend?' Misenus asked, laying aside his pitchfork.

'I'm looking to buy a horse,' said the man, his voice slightly slurred and unclear. Misenus wondered whether he had been drinking.

'Well, you've come to the right place,' declared the stable owner cheerfully. 'You won't find better horses and better prices anywhere in Glapolis.'

'A decent horse, mind,' said the man. 'Not those broken-winded jades that you keep for passing idiots.'

Misenus bristled. 'All my horses are decent. I've sold horses to senior officers of the garrison, many times, and never a word of complaint. Ask anyone.'

'Horses like Blackwing?'

Misenus stood as though turned to stone. 'What do you know about Blackwing?' He stared suspiciously at the strange visitor.

'Quite a lot, actually.' The man spat two pads from his mouth into his hand, pulling a face as he did so. 'As I do about you, you old swindler.'

Misenus gaped. The voice. Even then he could not believe his eyes. 'Dio?'

'The same,' said Dio, sounding tolerably pleased with himself. 'So, a decent horse, mind.'

'By all the Gods.' Misenus grasped forearms, shaking his head in wonder. 'What in the name of the Furies are you doing here? They'll kill you if they catch you.'

'Then I shall have to make sure I stay uncaught.'

The horsemaster dashed over to the stable door, closed it and dropped the locking bar into position before drawing Dio into his small workroom. He produced an amphora of wine.

'By Dyaus, but it's good to see you. How's the Lady Kalliste? I've told everyone that that story was the biggest pile of horse droppings I've ever shovelled up. And I've shovelled up a few in my time.'

'She's safe.'

'What are you doing here?'

'Unfinished business.'

'You're here to kill that bugger Miltiades, and bloody good riddance.'

'No, but I do need your help.'

'You've got it.'

Dio took out a bag heavy with gold pieces.

'I don't want your money,' said Misenus instantly, sounding offended.

'Yes, you do, because it was given to you, not by me, but by a long, thin streak of a man, with a nose like a vulture's beak and looking as though he had an egg stuck in his throat. He kept himself covered by a dark blue cloak. He had a slight accent. Do you know a Phthian accent?'

'Certainly do,' said Misenus, giving it the characteristic nasal cast and the upward stress at the end.

'Well he had one, but only slight, mind. He came to you last Aphrodites, about a dekate after nightfall, and gave you this gold to have a horse ready and tacked up tonight. Together with a travelling kit in blanket bags. And with clear instructions not to be around. You asked the obvious questions but got nothing.'

'I remember him well. I presume the horse is still required?'

'It is.'

'It won't be Blackwing, but she'll be a good one.'

'And I'll leave a pack horse with you for the moment, if it's calm water.'

'No problem.'

Dio clapped him on the shoulder. The first piece was in play. Now it began to get more difficult.

FIFTY-NINE

Adrastus hummed to himself as he approached Cybele's. He felt the familiar shiver of anticipation. The burly doorman nodded to him respectfully as he entered. Inside, the atmosphere was warm and bright, if slightly fuggy, lit by a myriad of oil lamps. The walls were painted with lurid, pornographic depictions of sex positions, each carefully numbered for the convenience of customers. The brothel heaved with customers and girls, was cluttered with couches and cushions, and overspilled with kraters of cheap wine. Everywhere the bounce of bare breasts and wriggle of fleshy buttocks, the flow of diaphanous chitons that left nothing to the imagination, and the musky smell of sex. Cybele came across, her red hair vivid in the lamplight, dripping with jewellery and heavy with make-up.

'Mopsus!' she cried, as though she didn't know his real name. 'Welcome.'

A slave offered him some wine, which he refused, as always.

'And which of our beautiful girls has caught your fancy tonight?'

'I thought, perhaps, Doris?' His voice was husky.

Cybele nodded briskly. It usually was. 'Leda fine for you?' she enquired, referring to the room.

Adrastus nodded.

'I'll send her in a few hekates.' She held out a peremptory hand.

Adrastus dropped five didrachmae into her palm, which disappeared with impressive speed, and turned swiftly for the door decorated with a gilt swan.

Across the room a well-made, dark-haired girl wearing a sullen expression and a wisp of a chiton watched him go, then looked reluctantly across at Cybele. The madam beckoned her across.

'That fucking pervert again,' she grumbled. 'I've still got the bruises from last time.'

'It's your lucky day, dearie. He's arranged to meet someone. You won't be needed. Thought that you'd like to know.'

Doris smiled with relief.

Leda was a small room, lit by a single oil lamp, with a large mattress on the floor. Behind it, on the wall, was a substantial wooden panel painted with the rape of Leda. Few of the customers who used the room suspected that the graphic portrayal concealed one of Cybele's bolt doors. Adrastus closed the door behind him and shrugged off his cloak, then suddenly swung round in panic as he sensed, rather than heard, a movement. A wicked-looking spatha was pointing directly at his throat. His knees buckled, and he pissed himself.

SIXTY

Priskos was lounging comfortably in prime position before the small fire. He was just quietly fading into sleep when the call jarred him back to full wakefulness. 'Officer of the Guard!'

It brought him to his feet. He swore, grabbed his cloak and went straight out of the guardhouse, leaving his dilochagos to roust the men.

It was the still of night and bloody freezing. He shivered and wrapped his cloak more tightly about him. Three dekates of the rabbit watch still to go, and, he noted with some alarm, that evil sod Radamanthus had appeared from nowhere. Priskos walked over to the two hoplites on guard. There was no need for anything to be said. He could hear the approaching hooves for himself.

He remained silent as the rider appeared, emerging from the black shadow of a building into the cold, bleached moonlight. As the rider crossed the open killing ground, Priskos glanced behind him to make sure the guard had turned out. Someone approaching at this time of night could always be trouble. And that bastard deuteros was standing off to one side, watching, just waiting for him to make a balls-up. The rider was engulfed in a dark hooded cloak, and all Priskos could make out in its shadow was a black beard. The man thrust a small scroll at him without a word. Priskos beckoned to a hoplite carrying a torch. As expected, it was a messenger pass. Why they had to appear at this godless time of night was beyond his understanding. He checked it carefully, then handed it back and waved him through. Neither said a word. He cast a furtive glance at the lurking deuteros. Radamanthus was simply watching, his face expressionless.

'Well, fill in the tag roll, lad,' Priskos murmured to one of the guards and went back to his fire.

SIXTY-ONE

DIO WALKED SILENTLY along the corridors, passing through the long stretches of dark shadow between the scattered flares of light thrown by the occasional splutter of moribund oil lamps. He had rope-soled his boots so there would be no noise, but, as expected, the place was deserted.

Nevertheless, he was apprehensive, his eyes probing for the slightest movement, his ears straining for any barely perceptible sound, his whole body as taut as the string of a kithara. To be discovered in the very heart of Gla would offer no chance of escape. He had no illusions as to how they would deal with him if he was captured, and so was determined not to be. Any man could be broken, and Kal had to be protected. He momentarily touched the hilt of his sheathed dagger. If he was discovered, he would kill. If he could not kill, he would die. He had walked with death all his life. It held no fears for him.

He paused for a few heartbeats as he passed the stairs leading to the holder's rooms. The temptation to revenge himself on Miltiades surfaced, rising like some fearsome monster from the abyss of the sea. It was so powerful and immediate that he found himself with his dagger in his hand and his foot on the first step before his thoughts finally caught up with the impulse.

There was no light from the landing above. It should have been torchlit. He slipped out of the line of sight from the stairs and listened. After a few moments there was the faintest murmur of a voice and a slight scrape. They had laid an ambush for him. That bastard must be shitting his loincloth. He knew, better than most, what Dio was capable of. Dio sincerely hoped that he lay awake this very moment, his heart lurching at every tiny creak and groan that an old wooden floor is heir to. The monster slid back quietly into the black depths. He had promised Kal, and the words of Pandarus echoed through his mind. 'Revenge should be all ice, boy, never fire.'

Arriving at the small room just beyond the holder's office that he had described to Radamanthus, Dio checked carefully behind himself and then slipped inside. It was small, dusty and neglected, with some surplus furniture stacked untidily in one corner and nothing more.

Dio felt above the lintel, and there was the key, together with a duly seal-stamped arrest warrant and a small, inscribed wax tablet. He cautiously emerged and walked quickly toward the door to his destination, where he inserted the key through the horizontal slit cut into the door beneath the bolt. When it would go no further, he twisted it through a quarter-turn and pushed upwards, the now vertical pegs lifting the locking pins until the bolt could be withdrawn. He stepped inside, then quietly pushed the door to.

It was pitch black within, but he knew Miltiades' office and felt his way across the room to unfasten one of the window covers. It let in some diffuse moonlight, and he waited for his eyes to adjust before going over to the writing table. He put his hand underneath and felt around until he detected the tiny catch. There was a click, and he was able to jiggle out the drawer hidden within the ornate carvings on the side. He pulled it wide open, gathered up all the scrolls that were within, and pushed them into his belt pouch, sliding the drawer shut. He went over to the window and, by the moonlight, examined the keys he had appropriated from Adrastus until he found the one that was for the man's personal chambers. He rehooked the leather window cover in place and stopped. The distant sound of footsteps.

He acted instantly, moving cautiously but swiftly across the darkened room, familiar enough with the place to know that there were no obstacles in his way, and silently pressed himself against the wall beside the door. A very narrow strip of light screamed that the door was slightly ajar. Stupid. Stupid. He could feel the sweat prickle on his back and the blood pound in his temples. He forced himself to breathe slowly and deeply. The footsteps were near now, two people and the murmur of conversation. He grasped his knife in a reverse downward grip. If it was needed, it would be at close quarters and would have to be swift and brutal. One of the voices was female. Dyaus have pity. Would he have to kill a woman?

'Not that you care,' said the woman, her tone sharp and embittered.

Dio closed his eyes in despair. A bloody lovers' tiff.

'Of course I care,' said the man. 'It's just impossible.' Dio stiffened. The light, emollient voice was unmistakable. Patroclus. As Miltiades' aide, his quarters would be further down the corridor.

'Why? Why can't you marry me? You were quick enough to leap into my bed.'

'It's complicated. I can't explain now, but I promise that I will in two se'ennights.'

They were directly outside. They stopped. A faint wash of light from one of the few lit oil lamps seeped under the door. Shadows broke across it, and the vertical shaft of light suddenly disappeared. Dio lifted his knife, brought up his other hand for balance, and waited.

'Some careless bugger has left the office unlocked.'

'Go on, change the subject, why don't you?'

Dio flattened himself against the wall. The door abruptly swung open, spilling in a flood of light and two warped and elongated shadows that wavered across the room and part way up the opposite wall. The door was now slowing to a halt at an angle that would expose him to view by the briefest of glances. He quickly caught the handle and smoothly eased it further back until it concealed him as much as it possibly could. He was now effectively blind, staring at a panel of wood, but not deaf. He listened intently to the quiet footfalls as Patroclus stepped inside.

'Doesn't look as though anyone's been in.'

'Hadn't you better search everywhere? Look under the tables? Behind the door? See if an assassin is hanging outside the window by his fingertips? Perhaps he's hiding under that cushion? Then you won't need to expend all that mental ingenuity on reasons why you can't marry me.'

Patroclus sighed loudly. Dio desperately controlled his breathing.

'Oh, that's right,' the woman continued. 'You didn't come up with any reasons, did you?'

From the sounds, Patroclus had turned. Dio anticipated his response to detection, rehearsing the probable scenarios in his mind. He would have to down Patroclus instantly and then grab the woman before she could start screaming. Despite the tension, he felt a calm settle over him at the prospect of doing something, rather than waiting helplessly for discovery like a snared animal.

'I said I would tell you the reasons in two se'ennights, all right? You'll understand then.' Anger was creeping into his voice. There was movement as Patroclus left the room.

'Wait,' cried the woman shrilly. 'You haven't checked everywhere.'

Dio stopped breathing.

'He might be inside that papyrus roll.'

The door swung closed, and darkness shrouded the room once more.

'Hilarious,' said Patroclus, his voice now muffled.

There a scrape and a click as the bolt was pushed back and the locking pins fell into place.

'And why can't you tell me now?'

Dio's heart started beating again. He leaned back against the wall and let his pent-up breath escape in a long, noiseless exhalation.

'I can't. I've told you. There are reasons. You just won't listen.'

'Crap,' she declared.

'Dyaus, I've had just about enough of this.'

'That's not what you said when you were on me like a bloody priapic rabbit.'

'Oh, fuck off, for Dyaus's sake.' There was the sound of steps continuing down the corridor.

A pause. A muttered 'Bastard.' Then other steps returning to whence they had come, but more quickly. Somewhere a door banged shut with an air of pointed finality. The other steps faded, and all was silent again.

Two se'ennights. That must have meant that something was going to happen within that time, almost certainly something to do with the plot. Something significant. This puzzled Dio. It was nowhere near the campaigning season, and for Laomedon to march at such a time of year was incredibly risky. Feed and forage for a large army would be all but impossible. And why it should have anything to do with marriage was totally beyond him. He dismissed it. He would soon enough know the answers. He finally moved.

His legs still felt decidedly shaky as he lifted the restraining pins on the bolt and slid it to one side. He listened, alert for the slightest sound. The faint scuttle of a rat. A monotonous drip of water somewhere. Nothing. He opened the door and came out quickly, his knife now forward. The corridor was empty. He slid the bolt across until he heard the restraining pins drop, and was gone.

SIXTY-TWO

Patroclus stood uneasily before Miltiades' desk. Miltiades stood staring out of the open window, his hands clasped behind his back. Patroclus shivered at the cold air spilling in.

'You have spoken to the madam of this establishment?'

'Yes, sir. Apparently Adrastus—he called himself Mopsus, by the way, said—'

Miltiades made a small disapproving shake of his hand at such unnecessary trivia.

Patroclus swallowed and continued. 'He said that he just wanted the room in order to meet someone, and paid handsomely for it. He never emerged. When she finally scratched, it was empty. There was a concealed door in the room. He must have known about it and had a key. Cybele suspects a doorman who walked out about ten days ago and took some keys with him. The doorman has since disappeared.'

'Was anyone other than Adrastus seen entering the room?'

'I don't know. Certainly, Cybele didn't see anyone. But she did say they were very busy. I didn't want to ask too widely. You said to keep it under a cloak.'

'And this stableman?'

'Cybele said that Adrastus had asked her about a reliable man, and she had recommended Misenus. You've bought horses from him yourself, sir.'

Miltiades nodded in a slightly irritated way.

'So, I went to question him. Adrastus threw money at it like water. A horse and travelling bag waiting and no questions.'

Miltiades, his face set in stone, turned and looked directly at the anxious aide. 'What about this mysterious messenger?'

'He had a genuine-looking pass. No-one had reason to question it. He was in the fortress for less than a dekate. When he left, he asked the way to Cybele's. When I searched Adrastus's rooms, I found this on a table.' He stepped forward to hand a small wax tablet to Miltiades.

Miltiades took it and scanned it. It was unmistakably Adrastus's writing, instructing someone to meet him at 'the suggested place'. It was all too obvious where that was. He walked across to his desk and sat down heavily.

'There was no sign of his door being forced, so the messenger must have been provided with a key.' Patroclus was certainly not going to mention the unbolted door to Miltiades' office last night.

Miltiades said nothing, but rubbed the bridge of his nose.

Patroclus waited. Uncertain. 'Should I organise a search?'

There was something like despair on Miltiades' face. 'No point. He's long gone.'

'But what's he doing?'

'He's going to the emperor with evidence of the plot. Why, I've no idea. Unless he was a traitor from the start. Or,' he paused in consideration, 'he's got the scent of failure, he sees the whole thing unravelling and is on the scuttle. But then why take the scrolls? And who is this contact?' He rubbed his nose again. 'No. He must be going to the emperor. Buying his pathetic life with ours.'

Patroclus blanched. 'Are you going to inform Lord Raxamenes?'

'That would be the sensible thing to do.' Miltiades' tone was sarcastic. 'At best, I would be regarded as an incompetent liability, and one surplus to requirements at that. At worst, they would assume that I'm involved and have betrayed them. No. I think I might visit Leuctra and make some arrangements instead. A touch of sea air might do me good.'

He rose and walked towards the door. 'You are sure no-one else knows anything of this?'

'Absolutely,' said Patroclus confidently. 'I did all the investigation on my own.'

'Good.' Miltiades opened the door. 'Come in, Leodes.'

A large form shambled in. A vacuous, lumpen face and a grubby hoplite tunic strained tightly across the massive frame beneath. Immensely strong, but with seriously limited intelligence, he was totally loyal to the holder. Miltiades had taken him on as his personal bodyguard since Dio's flight. At least he could be sure of instant obedience and no questions asked. He nodded at Patroclus.

'Kill him.'

SIXTY-THREE

THE COLD WAS so intense that Dio had risked making a fire in the abandoned steading that he was using as his base. Adrastus lay on the hard, wooden floor some distance from the flames, gagged and trussed, shivering in the glacial air. His panic-stricken eyes never left his captor's face. Dio was quite happy to keep him cold and hungry, cramped and pained, and all but frightened to death. When it came time to question him, he would be like wet clay in his hands.

For the moment, however, Dio was going through the scrolls yet again. When he came to question Adrastus, he wanted to know some of the answers already so he had some way of authenticating the slimy little worm's story; but the scrolls still weren't making sense.

The code seemed straightforward enough; there was just nothing to get a grip on. The letters were riddled with references to wolves and warthogs, snakes and skylarks, lions and lampreys. It was a bloody zoo. But who was who? They could be satraps, or at least holders like Miltiades, functionaries at court, or even field commanders. Some were clearly places. But the number of possibilities was limited. Dio estimated sixty or seventy individuals who could be involved at this level. He had thirty-three code names, of which only eighteen were apparently active participants in the plot; but, however he tried to make them fit, they came out wrong.

And what was really puzzling him were a couple of references that were transparent. He could interpret L at K as nothing other than Laomedon at Kerakos. Which seemed indefensibly sloppy.

He rubbed his eyes savagely and started going through them once more.

The Lamprey reports that all is ready, and the Warthog has contacted the Wolf. Three thousand has been transferred to the Pig. The Manticore will not disturb the Dolphin again and can be discounted for the time being. The Snake to report on preparations.

He stopped and went back.

The Manticore will not disturb the Dolphin again and can be discounted for the time being.

It was glaringly obvious. Like lightning searing an entire scene onto his retina, he suddenly knew what it was. He hastily searched for the date. The eleventh day of Metageitrion in the year 499. Last summer. The clash between Laomedon and Lycidas, when Laomedon had taken a real beating. He would certainly not be disturbing Lycidas again after that. Not for a long time. So, Laomedon must be the Manticore. Which meant—

By the Gods, but the traitor wasn't that bastard Laomedon at all. The seemingly overt references to him had been deliberate disinformation, designed to divert attention from the plotters. He began to reread feverishly. If Lycidas were the Dolphin, then the Cockerel, who would not move without the Dolphin's approval, must be Mikkos of Phthia. Which meant that the Wolf, apparently so concerned about the Cockerel at his back, could only be Isodemos of Thalassa. If the Manticore was Laomedon, then the Lion, carefully watching a mutual border with the Manticore, was Charmides of Lesser Troia.

Excitement mounting, he grabbed a piece of charcoal from the hearth and scrawled a rough map of the Troian Empire on the old wooden table, putting in the satraps' names and their code names as he deduced them. They slotted into place perfectly. There it was. At least a partial picture. Another group of coded names, probably high-ranking officials at Ilios or possibly even army commanders, remained beyond his reach. For the moment. But he was confident that the terrified Adrastus would provide. And the outline was there.

He laid down the charcoal and straightened to look at the map he'd drawn. The man who would be emperor was the Lion, Charmides of Lesser Troia, nephew to Aristogeiton and Troilus. With him stood only four satraps. Antikles of Mykerenos; the new satrap, Inachos of Lakadaemon; Raxamenes of the Thebeaid; and, somewhat cautiously, Isodemos of Thalassa. Lethos of Korinthia was characteristically waiting to see what would happen before charging in on the winning side. And with them his old friend Miltiades, of course. He smiled mirthlessly at

Miltiades' code name. They could not have come up with anything better than the Snake if they had tried.

The puzzle was why they had done nothing after the assassination. They effectively had Ilios at the vulnerable centre of a semicircle of inner provinces. A converging thrust from Lesser Troia, Lakadaemon and the Thebeaid should have toppled the capital in days. And bloody Laomedon had nothing to do with it!

A memory suddenly took him, jogged by the name of Charmides. Talking to Kal just before they got to Phyllida's, discussing this new sect of Monotheites. 'Theagenes claimed that Charmides is a convert.' He could hear himself saying it. Then Radamanthus's comment about Monce units in Mykerenos muscled its way into the torch glare of his consciousness. Pandarus's cube suddenly shifted into a new perspective. A mass of trivial anomalies crystallised into a shape. And a fearsome one. There was no doubt. It was a moment of pure revelation.

He got up and strode over to Adrastus, whose eyes bulged with terror. Dio reached down and tore open Adrastus's tunic to reveal a small amulet. To his astonishment it was a skull, the symbol of Hades. He was thrown off balance for a heartbeat, his newfound certainty faltering. He violently yanked the god guard off, snapping the fine silver chain, and inspected it closely. On the back of the pendant, carefully inscribed, was a tiny letter mu within a circle. Mu for Monos, the God of the Monotheites.

What had Radamanthus said? The new replacements kept themselves to themselves and didn't even frequent Fat Delia's? Because they were forbidden wine. It was a bloody religious plot. The Great Wakening, no less. How could he have been so wrong? So convinced of his reading of the situation that he never even considered other possibilities? He'd forgotten Pandarus. Pandarus hadn't forgotten him. The old man glared at him with pure disgust.

'By the testicles of Toros, boy, you've the mental acuity of a brick. No matter how strong or beguiling the evidence, always allow for other possibilities. Never blind yourself. Use your god-given eyes.' Dio closed his useless eyes and swore fiercely. He had them, and he hadn't used them.

So many seemingly meaningless, but now significant, things fell into rank. Miltiades' sudden aversion to wine. The curious disappearance of Patroclus's beard. Adrastus's red band round his ponytail and Patroclus's boots. An image of Miltiades reading the Book of Truth, clad in his red sash of office, sipping water and rubbing his beardless chin, loomed before him. How could he have missed it?

His stupidity could have got Kal killed. He knelt and savagely ripped the gag from Adrastus's mouth, giving vent to the anger before it consumed him in its incandescence.

'First question,' he snarled. 'How come you don't carry the poles and blanket?'

Adrastus was almost incomprehensible as he fell over his tongue in trying to answer as fast as he could. 'We have a special dispensation from the high priest.'

Dio held up the god guard, showing him the reverse. 'But you are required to wear this symbol of your faith nevertheless?'

Adrastus nodded frantically.

'So, who is Sofia?'

Adrastus looked even more terrified, which Dio would have sworn was impossible. 'The stepdaughter of our leader.'

'Who is?'

The man's eyes flicked desperately around the room as though looking for some miraculous salvation. Which he probably was, thought Dio. And wasn't he going to be disappointed?

'Who is?' barked Dio in his best exercise ground voice.

'Charmides.' It was an involuntary response, the tongue leading the brain. The secretary winced, then added, in a less-than-enthusiastic tone, 'The Chosen of the One.'

Dio nodded. He was not going to have any trouble with this one. 'And that's why you were planning to have the Lady Kalliste murdered. Sofia can't marry a divorced man while his ex-wife still breathes.'

Adrastus said nothing. His face was absolutely bloodless.

'Planning to murder Kal makes me angry. Very angry. I would bear that in mind.' He sat back. 'Now it's time for more questions. A lot more.' He took out a wicked-looking knife and idly cleaned his nails. 'There's not going to be any difficulty, is there?'

Adrastus shook his head furiously.

Dio's smile was not a pleasant one. 'Good. I have a bit of a headache, and I really could do without the screaming.'

SIXTY-FOUR

THERE WAS NO screaming. Adrastus volunteered information with a pathetic eagerness. He gave up all the satraps immediately. But Dio was now hunting bigger game. Charmides, the Lion, was to be emperor, but the Lamprey seemed to be the puppet master, the man who had to be kept informed, from whom the decisions emanated, the real centre around whom the plot revolved.

'And who is the Lamprey?' He kept his questions even-toned, his face blank, never allowing Adrastus to see what he knew and what he didn't know.

'Apollos.'

Dio had begun to suspect as much. Apollos was a courtier who had climbed high. The leader of the Imperial Council, he was technically the man who would take over as interim ruler should the emperor be unable to perform that function for any reason. But even more significant was his relationship with the pliant Aristogeiton. He had been a major power behind the throne, and when Aristogeiton had spoken, more often than not it had been with Apollos's words.

Now Dio understood things that had puzzled him. The sheer inertia of the Imperial Court. Apollos had been deliberately allowing a drift towards chaos, a perception of ineptitude, a burgeoning unease in the country, to smooth the way towards the usurpation. And it explained the surprising elevation of a mediocre strategos to the position of polemarchos, the commander of all the armed forces, as well as the ease with which the assassins had got to Aristogeiton.

'So which animal is the polemarchos?'

'The Warthog.'

'And that transfer of the main field army to Phthia is nothing to do with countering Eretrian threats, but simply a move to get it as far from Ilios as possible.'

'Yes. Apollos generated false reports of Eretrian forces massing on the frontier.'

'Charopos?' That was the imperial spymaster.

Adrastus shook his head. 'Not one of us.'

'Just bloody incompetent, then.' Dio sat back in thought. 'So, Apollos was behind the sacking of Anastasios of Lakadaemon and his replacement by that nonentity Inachos. That gave you four provinces with direct invasion routes into Greater Troia and to Ilios. If Korinthia came in, then even better. But you can't have that many men.' He stood up and walked back to his crude map on the table and studied it for a few moments. He swung round. There was only one answer. He walked quickly back to the petrified secretary and crouched down.

'What have you got?'

'I don't…' and screamed. The knife blade quivered in the wooden floor, almost touching his ear.

Dio shook his head. 'Bugger. Missed.'

'The Household Guard!' Adrastus was shouting at the top of his voice in terror. 'The Imperial Guard commander. He's a Monist. We're packing the Household Guard. The emperor's personal guard. And the Imperial major-domo is ours too. We control the entire household.' There was almost a note of triumph beneath the screeching panic.

Dio sat back and swore. He was surprised by the ease with which Adrastus had spewed up everything. He had expected a little more divinely conferred backbone. But he believed him, and he did not like what he had heard. Not at all.

Apollos was bringing pieces into play, cleverly and stealthily, and surrounding the emperor with a ring of iron that would be hard to penetrate. He frowned as he tried to find a way through. Who could get him inside? Antinous would be there, but he was a junior officer with no real authority, and Dio could not put Kal's son in harm's way.

Then it struck him. Zeuxis. The Imperial swordmaster. A dour, humourless individual, a man who was not exactly on friendly terms with Dio, though they respected one another. He was not the type to get involved with anything so fatuous as new-fangled cults, and his pennant was firmly fixed to Troilus's banner. He had authority and access. Zeuxis it would have to be.

It would still be hard. Hard? Damn near impossible. But he had to try.

SIXTY-FIVE

Two days later, in the early morning, Dio rode up to the Great Gate of the Imperial Palace in Ilios. His beard had gone, as painfully as promised, and his hair was washed clean of the dye and goose fat, but his face remained a sallow colour. He had balanced speed against caution, paralleling, but avoiding, the Great East Road and bypassing all significant habitation.

He had left the broken, abject Adrastus with an old comrade, a retired hyperetes, who ran a wine shop on the Attic Way. Podargos was now in his sixties, but still as tough as a leather cuirass and totally trustworthy. He would have no trouble with the thoroughly cowed secretary, and Dio had left the duly completed arrest warrant with him as his safeguard.

The Imperial Guardsmen stood at the gates in their scarlet cloaks and nodding horsehair plumes, carrying silver shields with the black sigil of an eagle. As he approached, they formally crossed their spears before him to deny him entrance. A young red-haired officer strolled across, his gleaming helmet casually tucked under his arm, obviously none too impressed by this travel-stained and unshaven visitor. He was visibly taken by Blackwing, though, eying her enviously.

'Your business?' he demanded curtly. His accent was patrician, and he exuded an air of arrogant authority.

Dio wondered how to play it. He looked at the brand-new yellow shoulder sash with its polished command brooch in the form of crossed spears. The man was a lowly tetrarches, for all his superciliousness, and newly appointed too, by the look of it. His eyes kept nervously straying to his veteran hyperetes, who was standing to one side and watching closely. He sensed the underlying insecurity beneath the swagger and decided. He swung down from his horse.

'Put your helmet on, man,' he barked. 'Where do you think you are?' He thrust his mace of authority at him. 'Diomedes, swordmaster to Miltiades, holder of Gla. I need to see Zeuxis, your swordmaster, immediately. On important Imperial business.'

He had read the situation well. The officer hastily fumbled his helmet on, and the guards tried to conceal their delighted grins. Dio followed up his advantage, in accord with the best military precepts, by peremptorily handing Blackwing to the first of the guards and snarling at the second to go and get Zeuxis at the ram. The man doubled off without waiting for his officer's command. The tetrarches remained standing stiffly to attention.

'Name?' demanded Dio.

'Maro, sir.'

Dio beckoned him away from the watching soldiers. 'Speak softly. Do you wear a god guard?'

Maro looked puzzled. 'Yes, sir. Apollon, sir.'

'Let me see it, but do it unobtrusively.'

Maro hesitated for a heartbeat, then carefully drew an amulet from under his tunic. It was a golden sun. Dio took it from his unresisting hand and turned it over. The reverse was pristine. He handed it back and took a deep breath. He would have to trust this young boy with the fuzz still on his chin. It was like charging into battle with a willow switch.

'Now, Maro, let's forget your unfortunate beginning and start again. The way you act from now on will either result in you being a hero, basking in the Imperial sunbeam, or very dead. There's a plot to kill and usurp the emperor.'

Maro remained rigidly at attention, though the blood seemed to drain from his face.

'The traitors are all Monotheites.' The tetrarches opened his mouth to say something, then slowly closed it again. 'Have you any Monists in your section?'

'Only one, I think. Nisos. The men are always offering him wine.'

'Then I want him detained and kept out of communication with everyone. The story is that there has been a murder, and the murderer is known to be an Imperial Guardsman with a particular god guard.' Dio produced a scroll from his pouch, unrolled it and waved it under the young officer's nose as though it meant something. "This is my authorisation as a special investigator appointed by the emperor. You are hereby ordered to inspect every god guard and detain all who have pendants that fit the description.'

Maro was sweating, and his eyes had a hunted look. Dio knew he was terrified, caught in a situation where he had no grasp on what to believe or what to do. Like a frightened rabbit, he could leap in either direction at any moment, or just stand there wavering. Dio softened his voice.

'Look, lad, I know you're in a hard place. Will you accept the orders of Zeuxis?'

'He isn't really one of my superiors, sir.'

'But he carries the emperor's personal authority in matters of discipline and training.'

Maro nodded reluctantly.

'I'm sorry, lad, but you must choose. All you have to do is detain those with suspect god guards. On orders. Then stay quiet.' He looked the young man straight in his eyes. 'Can you do it, Maro?'

There was a moment of hesitation that stretched Dio out on the rack of time.

Maro suddenly nodded. 'Yes, sir. I can do that.'

Dio felt his legs wobble with relief. He was aware that the guard were all surreptitiously watching, but if Maro played it confidently, that would be all to the good.

'Who can you trust?'

'The hyper, sir. And there's a couple of lads who would follow you to Hades if it was needed.'

'Right. Get those three and check their god guards just to be certain. Look carefully on the back. Do you know the Monist symbol?'

'It's a mu, isn't it, sir?'

'A mu within a circle. Anyone wearing that is to be detained. Anyone with it inscribed on the back of another god guard is to be kept totally separate. That person will almost certainly be a conspirator. The others may be innocent, but we can't risk it. Once you've done that, then close the gates, and don't let anyone in or out.'

Maro hesitated. 'I don't think I can do that, sir, not without Imperial authorisation or direct orders from the polemarchos.'

'The polemarchos is one of the conspirators.'

Maro managed to look even more astonished, which was no mean achievement.

'Will you take Zeuxis's orders?'

The man's face glistened with sweat.

'You have to decide. The fate of the Empire rests on you.' Perhaps not the best thing to say, he belatedly reflected.

'I just don't know, sir,' the young officer burst out desperately.

'Thanks be to Athen,' muttered Dio as his attention was caught by the figure striding across the courtyard with a small soldier almost running in his wake. A large, muscular man with a reassuring black spade beard, cropped hair and fierce eyes.

Zeuxis arrived and grasped wrists. 'What's all this about?' he demanded without preamble. Zeuxis had never forgiven Dio for beating him in a bout two years before.

'We need to talk in private.'

Maro took them to the guardroom office. 'Well, get on with checking your guard, then,' said Dio, and the young officer scuttled off. Zeuxis closed the door behind him and turned to find a sword at his throat. He froze.

'I'm sorry, Zeuxis, but I have to check something.' Dio could see the leather thong round his neck. 'Could you, very slowly, produce your god guard?' The beard was not enough. He had to be certain.

Zeuxis glared at him, but did as bidden with exaggerated care.

'Now sit on your hands on that stool, and wrap your feet round the legs. You know the procedure.' Dio kept carefully to one side, the sword at the point of Zeuxis's jaw and, very cautiously, turned the pendant over. He sighed with relief, took the sword away and slid it into his scabbard. 'My apologies again. You can give me a good kicking later. But for now, listen.'

'Don't think I won't,' growled the big man, snatching back his amulet.

Dio launched into a concise explanation. Zeuxis listened, his eyes growing wider. 'Hades, man, you're fucking serious.'

'I couldn't be more so.'

'And you have this conspirator who is willing to talk, along with these scrolls?'

Dio nodded.

'I'd think it was donkey carrots if it was any other man, but, even so… It can't be true. It's just too… too…'

There was a rap on the door. Maro stood there with two hoplites holding a third in a very firm grasp. The young officer's face was a picture as elation and fear chased one another across his features. He held out a pendant, a trident of Poteidan. Dio took it and turned it over, then showed it to Zeuxis.

'I bought it off a man. I didn't even know there were anything on the back,' said the restrained man truculently.

'Who sold it to you?' snapped Maro.

'A man in a wine shop. Don't know his name.'

'So, you are not a Monotheite?' asked Dio quietly.

'I am not.' He was belligerently defiant.

'In which case, you would undoubtedly agree with me that the Book of Truth is a compendium of lies and this Monos just a piece of pigshit.'

The man's eyes took on a hunted look. He hesitated, then suddenly but ineffectually lunged against the hold they had on him. 'Bastard,' he spat. 'You can kill me, but when the Great Wakening comes, and come it will, I will appear again to live in the New World with joy and happiness—' his voice rose and rose to a hysterical shriek '—whereas your name will be obliterated from the scroll of life. As if you had never been.'

Maro was horrified. 'Dyaus's balls, he was to be transferred to the Household Guard on Selenes.'

Zeuxis looked at Dio. 'I'm convinced.'

SIXTY-SIX

Dio and Zeuxis hurried through the palace. 'We have to assume that all the white cloaks are Monces,' muttered Dio.

'There've been a lot of changes recently. Men transferred out and new ones drafted in. I thought it excessive, but assumed it was the new commander eager to make his mark.'

'New commander?'

'Anchises was forcibly retired by the polemarchos. Lot of bad feeling.'

'And the polemarchos is a conspirator.'

Zeuxis said nothing.

They were almost running in their haste. 'We might be lucky,' said Zeuxis. 'He'll still be breaking his fast. Once he gets the whole court round him, we won't have a chance.'

'But will he see us?'

'He'll see me. I have privileged access. And I'm pretty sure he'll see you too. He's a keen spectator of swordplay. He's mentioned your name several times.' There was an edge to Zeuxis's voice.

They arrived at a pair of carved and gilded doors. Two of the Imperial Household Guard, impeccable in their snowy white cloaks and triple ostrich-plumed helmets, stood outside with crossed spears.

'Swordmaster Zeuxis to have audience with His Imperial Majesty.'

There was no hesitation. They took his proffered sword, opened one of the doors to allow him entrance, and then closed it behind him before looking the somewhat bedraggled Dio up and down with open contempt. Dio waited, seemingly patiently, but in an inner state of almost unbearable tension and fear. This was the crucial moment, when the axle pin could fail on the chariot, and it would all have been for nothing. Worse, Kal would remain in danger. Somehow, he had to persuade Troilus not only to listen to him, not only to believe him, but, against his reputed nature, to act quickly and purposefully. He would have bare hekates in which to work. He could only hope that Zeuxis managed to get the message through that Troilus needed to listen to him.

The hekates passed so slowly it seemed that time slept. The guards continued their insolent scrutiny as he tried to look nonchalant, but his skin crawled, and his stomach was an empty void. He almost jumped when the door opened suddenly, and Zeuxis beckoned him within. One of the guards held out his hand for Dio's sword, and then Dio stepped inside.

The massive room glowed with wall paintings and rich hangings, one wall dominated by a huge window that overlooked the main gate. Its marble mullions were sculpted into a riot of luxurious vegetation and the spaces between filled with thin, translucent horn. Some panels were covered with carved oak boards instead of horn, and two had been opened and supported on thin struts to allow fresh air into the room. Another large wooden door stood opposite the window, decorated with gilded eagle motifs, next to which two white-liveried servants stood to rigid attention, their hands behind their backs, their eyes unwaveringly to the front. The back wall was hung with vibrantly coloured and thickly-woven tapestries.

A small, middle-aged man with mousy brown hair and a fringe of a beard sat in an elaborately carved oaken chair that towered over and dwarfed him, at a massive table that was so polished Dio could see the man's reflection. He was eating a boiled egg. He wore a simple white gown and was possessed of a nondescript face, though with kindly eyes. Round his neck hung the huge golden Imperial Seal, the only sign that he was anything other than a small, middle-aged man eating a boiled egg. He looked worryingly relaxed.

Zeuxis was standing at the window, seeming to be idly looking out through one of the opened panels, but keeping an eye on the gate. Behind the emperor, and far too close, were two of his Household Guards, and a tall officer stood to one side. Dio swore inwardly. He was desperate to keep the conspirators from realising that they had been sprung from cover. It would almost certainly force them to act precipitately. This could get very chancy.

He bowed. 'Your Imperial Majesty,' he intoned. Troilus waved away the ceremony.

'"Sire" will do perfectly well,' he said, 'I would be perfectly happy with "Troilus", but the court would have a collective fit. Come over here, Diomedes of Gla. I have heard much about you. Anyone who could beat Zeuxis must be a great swordmaster indeed.'

From the corner of his eye, Dio caught the wince. Zeuxis drifted across the room to the two servants and had a quiet word. They quickly disappeared. The officer, whose attention was directed at Troilus, did not notice, nor did the emperor.

'Sit down,' Troilus said expansively, waving at a cushioned stool alongside him. 'Some wine?'

'I thank you, Sire, but no.'

'We must organise a bout. I would love that.' He carefully spooned out the last bit of egg.

Dio pulled a piece of parchment from his pouch. 'Perhaps your Majesty would like to see the plan for a tournament that I have sketched out.' The narrowed eyes of the tall officer were fixed on Dio now, and his body was tense. He clearly knew something was amiss. He moved forward.

Troilus glanced up from the screed. 'Yes, tetrarches?'

The man stopped. 'Nothing, your Majesty.'

'Then move away. You make me feel nervous, looming over me like a watch tower.'

The emperor flapped his hand at the officer, who, visibly reluctant, withdrew. His face was tight, and his eyes darted suspiciously from Troilus to Dio and back again.

Troilus glanced at Zeuxis now standing alone near the door and froze momentarily. Then he went on as if he had noticed nothing. 'Zeuxis, come you here,' he said easily. 'We must discuss this.'

Zeuxis wandered over. Troilus went back to his reading. After a few moments, he shook his head and looked up. 'And what do you think to all this?' he demanded of Zeuxis, tapping the scroll with the back of his hand. 'To be able to involve so many in such a tournament seems somewhat unlikely, does it not?'

'By no means, Sire. Diomedes is certain that all those who have said that they are willing to participate will do so. I have spoken to one myself, and one of the chief organisers will be happy to confirm the arrangements. I have no doubt that all is as Diomedes has described.'

Troilus nodded and reached for the wine. 'Perhaps we can arrange it then. It would be wonderful to see such masters so matched.' He pushed the golden egg cup away and turned to the guards. 'No bloody serving men! Go and see if the kitchen can manage another egg. A little less runny this time. And fetch a small kylix of fresh milk, if you would be so kind.'

'Your Majesty,' said the officer, aghast. 'They cannot leave you.'

'Pooh,' said Troilus scornfully, 'with the two greatest swordsmen alive as protection? Don't be imbecilic.' He looked back at the pair of guardsmen. 'Now run along, or I might get tetchy.' They glanced at one another, then left, closing the doors behind them. Zeuxis inconspicuously moved round behind the indignant officer.

'Now, if your Majesty would be so good as to order this officer to show us his god guard,' said Dio clearly, watching the man's face. The shock and sudden fear were all that was needed. The tetrarches immediately went for his sword, but, before it was half-way out of the scabbard, Zeuxis had him in an arm lock with a great hand over his mouth, stifling any cries. Dio strode over to the struggling man and yanked off his amulet. He stepped back to the emperor, turning it over for him to see. 'There, Sire, you see…'

And stopped. The reverse was totally unmarked. His mind reeled. Emptiness yawned in the depths of his stomach and sweat sprang from his brow. He swung round to stare at the officer, still tightly in Zeuxis's clutches, but whose eyes held the unmistakable gleam of triumph, his hand making a white-knuckled fist.

Behind him, the emperor's voice. 'What's going on? There's nothing there. Zeuxis, release that man.'

'Wait!' shouted Dio, jumping forward and grabbing the officer's clenched hand. He forced it open, the man grunting with pain as Dio bent his fingers back and twisted off the wide gold ring he had been endeavouring to conceal.

'There, Sire.' And there it was, neatly inscribed on the inside: a mu in a circle.

'On second thoughts,' said the emperor, 'best hang on to him, Zeuxis. There's a good fellow.'

Zeuxis suddenly took away his hand and hit the man hard on the side of the head. The officer's knees buckled, and he shook his head groggily. Zeuxis looked disgusted and hit him again. This time, he slumped to the floor. The Troian swordmaster quickly gathered some of the restraining cords from the hangings and roughly bound and gagged the officer before dragging him out of sight behind a curtain. He came back and threw the man's sword to Dio, who caught it deftly. Troilus swung round to face Dio; his face had hardened, and his eyes were quick and intelligent. 'I think you had better explain all this more fully.'

Dio did so, as rapidly, clearly and succinctly as he could. Zeuxis backed him up. The emperor listened, then looked pensive, rubbing the back of his neck.

'The Imperial major-domo, the polemarchos and the leader of the Grand Council? All in a conspiracy. It beggars belief.' He looked straight at Diomedes, who had broken out into a sweat, convinced that it was all going to crashing down around him. 'But I believe you. It's too bizarre not to be true, and I never trusted any of them. What do you suggest I do?'

Feeling weak with relief, Dio walked across to the window. He had to take a deep breath before he could trust himself to speak. 'Give Zeuxis the Imperial Seal and written authorisation. In your name, he'll close off the palace, ensure that we have trustworthy units to hand, and arrest all known conspirators. I believe it is just the Household Guards who are involved. The rest of the Imperial Guard knows nothing of it. If Zeuxis can get to the barracks, we can get a ring of loyal troops round you.'

Dio glanced through an open panel and froze.

'Shit.' He spun round. 'Some Household plumehead has just arrested that young officer.'

'Give me authorisation, and I'll try and get out via the kitchens,' said Zeuxis.

'Until then, we need a defensible room,' said Dio.

'My bedchamber,' said the emperor decisively. He had had already taken off the Great Seal from round his neck and went to a graphotrapeza on the window wall. He hastily found a scrap of parchment on the writing table and scribbled on it, 'By my personal order. Troilus.' Zeuxis took the seal and parchment, then slipped out of the room via the side door.

Troilus went to a large drape on the back wall and pulled it to one side, revealing a door that was a riot of fantastic carvings. Outside of the main door, there was a sudden commotion.

'Quickly,' said Dio. 'I think the handle's going to come off.'

SIXTY-SEVEN

They dashed down the long corridor beyond, past doors off to left and right, and through the one at the end. The emperor's bedroom was another oversized room but with just a single entrance and no windows for security. The unadorned bed was large and heavy, but still looked out of proportion with the overweening dimensions of the place. Beyond that, there were but a couple of delicately carved tables and a gilded, well-upholstered klismos. Four lit golden lamps were suspended on chains that hung beneath small smoke holes. The room lacked any other decoration and was surprisingly spartan.

Dio slammed the door and dropped a solid locking bar in place. It looked as though the place had been designed as a last refuge. The door was thick oak, and the floor and walls marble. The two tugged and pushed the heavy bed until it jammed the door. Breathing heavily, they stood back.

Dio began to stretch and work his muscles. 'That should slow them down.'

Troilus felt under the pillow and drew out a heavy kopis sword in a tooled leather scabbard. 'I don't intend to die like a sacrificial ox.'

Dio pulled a sheet from the bed and wound it round and round his left arm, tying it off to make a makeshift shield, for whatever good it might be. The emperor watched him, then followed suit. Dio drew his knife with his left hand and stood waiting. They could hear nothing. Perhaps they had misinterpreted the noise.

'Interesting morning,' observed Troilus. 'Not at all my usual regime.'

Dio grinned at him. 'It could get even more interesting.'

'I was afraid of that.'

'If I may speak freely, Your Majesty?'

'Just Sire,' insisted Troilus again. 'Under the circumstances, I think candid speech is permissible. Not too candid though, I hope.'

'It's just that I thought I would have great difficulty persuading you to act. But you were impressive – decisive, quick thinking and no mean actor.'

Troilus chuckled. 'Thank you, but say what you mean. You thought that I would be weak. That's what everybody thinks. Indolent, I'll grant you, but I was always the stronger of the two. Ari never gave me a chance. He knew, only too well, how weak he was. I suppose he didn't want any comparisons.' There was a thread of sorrow in his voice. 'So, never seeing me do anything, people jumped to the obvious conclusion.'

They waited. There was still no sound. Every hekate was pure gold.

'Now, *I* have a question,' said Troilus. 'From what you have said, these...' He looked questioningly at Dio. 'Monces?' Dio nodded. 'These Monces seem to capitulate very easily. Not what one would expect from your standard religious fanatic.'

Dio grinned. 'Bad psychology. Adrastus said their priests had told them the Monos had them under his personal protection and nothing, but nothing, could harm them. Any threat would be instantly eradicated. Gave them tremendous confidence, I've no doubt, but the moment there was a knife at their throat and a distinct absence of divine thunderbolts, it rather sank their boat. Almost instant deconversion.' He considered. 'Well, for some. Others seem to be able to happily make anything fit into their belief system. They're your unalloyed religious fanatic.' He continued to loosen up with some practice swings, familiarising himself with the weight and balance of his sword. 'Besides which, I've a suspicion that not a few are aboard just for the ride. Using this cult as a bridge to power.' He still couldn't believe in a Miltiades in the grip of genuine religious fervour.

Troilus nodded. He sat down on the bed. 'If they don't come soon, I could miss my lunch. And I never got my second egg this morning.'

Dio held up a warning hand. There were finally sounds outside. Men were searching, and it was not long before someone tried the door. Troilus stood up, sword in hand. They could hear voices and movement, then a man calling through the wooden door.

'Your Majesty, open the door. There's a dangerous assassin in the palace. We must protect you.'

'I'm having an imperial nap,' shouted back Troilus. 'Go away and leave me in peace.' His eyes gleamed. Dio got the sense that he was almost enjoying himself.

'We can't do that, Your Majesty. We are sworn to protect you.'

'So, stay outside and protect me.'

'We've reason to believe that you are under threat by a traitor.'

'Rubbish,' snorted the emperor. 'Just bugger off and let me sleep.'

'Your Majesty, we cannot,' the voice insisted.

'Cannot? *Cannot*? Which particular moron is that?'

There was a pause. 'The polemarchos, Your Majesty. Anaxis of Attica.' Diomedes could hear indignation in the voice.

'Snivelling little rat,' muttered the emperor. 'You are no longer the polemarchos,' he shouted back grandly. 'I dismiss you. You are now Lord Usher of the Imperial Pisspot.' Dio laughed out loud.

There were the sounds of excited voices outside. They had obviously decided that they were just wasting time. It went quiet for a while, then there was a scuffling. Troilus and Dio glanced at each other, stood back and readied their weapons.

There was a tremendous blow, and the door shook on its hinges. A pause and another huge crash. Dust drifted down from the ceiling. A third. The door held. And again. And again.

But on the seventh blow one of the bronze metal hooks, into which the locking bar dropped, began to show signs of strain, small cracks radiating through the wall around it.

Again and again the ram battered the door, which was now slightly proud of its frame, the metal hook partly out of its seating.

A strange but familiar calm came over Dio. He was aware of fear and pain, but somehow they were divorced from him, separate shadowy entities that were with him, but not of him. Feelings that could be disregarded for all their clamour. The world became slower and sharper, his mind focussed with a single purpose and driven by cold calculation. The very antithesis of his usual self-questioning and insecurity. He was born for this.

The bar seating suddenly gave completely, and the door opened a crack. Dio leapt forwards and stabbed through the gap. There was a scream of agony. He jumped back as a couple of sword blades thrust through in retaliation.

Dio flung himself at the bed and heaved. It shifted back, trapping the swords, but then Dio was knocked back bodily with the next blow of the ram. The bed had been thrust backward into the room, leaving a gap of a few fingers. There was no way they could stop them. Several more violent impacts and the gap was wide enough to squeeze through.

Some idiot tried it, and Dio simply slit his unprotected throat. Blood fountained across the marble floor. The methodical ram started again, each time shifting the bed and door further into the room. Dio prayed that they had not thought to bring archers.

A man with shield and sword suddenly leapt through, jumping over the corpse of his predecessor and swinging his sword wildly. Dio smoothly parried and gutted him. He fell screaming to the floor, clutching his entrails, as another was already clambering over his writhing body. They lacked armour, thank Dyaus. Dio immediately lunged and took him in the thigh. The man cried out and stumbled forward, and Dio savagely slashed at the back of his neck.

He bent swiftly to scoop up the shield of the first man and fling it back to the emperor, before using his own makeshift shield to fend away the downward cut of another assailant. Two quick parries, a feint, and the man staggered back with a killing thrust to his chest, knocking the man climbing in behind him off balance. Dio smoothly dispatched this one with a clinical lunge to the heart. But two more were now inside and a third was forcing his way through the door.

One tripped over a body, and Dio opened him up from the belly to the sternum with a vicious rip of his knife while blocking the blow from the other with his sword. He caught the sword of his second opponent on his hilt, then his feet hit the awful mess of slippery intestines and shot out from under him.

He landed heavily on his back, knocking the wind from his body, and his death loomed over him, a heavy kopis lifted for the killing blow. Reactions honed over years took over, and he somehow got his sword up and across his body to stop the descending edge with jarring force. The man lifted his sword again, and then suddenly stiffened and collapsed. Behind him stood the emperor with a bloody sword and a rather pleased expression.

Still they came. Dio managing to scramble to his feet as he warded off a late cut with his knife, spun away from a clumsy thrust, then kicked out at the back of the unbalanced man's knee and stabbed him in the kidneys as he went down. Instantly, he dropped down on one knee to avoid a savage swing that hissed over his head, and thrust up into the man's unprotected belly. His assailant staggered back and sagged against the wall.

There was only one guard left in the room that was now thick with bodies and slippery with blood, and he was pressing the desperate emperor hard. Dio leapt forward and buried his sword in the man's back, and it was all over.

The flood had stopped, and outside was the clash of steel and shout of men. Zeuxis had arrived. Dio and Troilus stood there, breathing heavily, unable to believe that they had survived. The emperor looked at Dio with real admiration. 'I've never seen anybody fight like that. You were so fast it was incredible. I thought I wasn't going to have a chance. To get involved, I mean.'

Dio shrugged. 'They were fighting at a disadvantage, Sire. Coming through that narrow gap. And they hadn't had time to get their armour on.' Outside the noise subsided, though someone was sobbing helplessly.

'But isn't stabbing someone in the back regarded as somewhat unsporting?' A smile hovered on Troilus's lips.

'A wise man once told me, take every advantage you can, fairly or not.'

'Wise indeed.' The emperor wiped the blood from his face with the sleeve of his gown.

'Your Majesty, are you safe?' The anxious voice of Zeuxis.

'I am indeed.'

'Thank the Gods.' There was a sharp cry and the sobbing ceased.

'Thank you and Diomedes.'

They unceremoniously pulled aside the corpses, and the two men who were still alive and groaning, and dragged back the bed. The door fell off its hinges with a crash.

The corridor was full of sprawled bodies, a heavy wooden bench lay tipped on its side, the walls ran with blood and the air was heavy with its metallic tang and the smell of urine and faeces. Two men were held firmly by tough-looking guards. One was a small man with a tousle of grey hair and watery blue eyes. The other a craggy-featured officer with a hate-filled expression, resplendent in a sculpted breast plate and the imposing uniform of the Imperial Guard. Zeuxis stood beside them, wiping his sword with a piece of cloth.

'As you thought, the entire Household Guard were Monces,' he said. 'There are still some holed up in their barracks, but most are dead. Sorry that we took so long.'

'Don't worry about it,' said Troilus airily. 'We weren't too bored.' He shook his head. 'Every one of my personal guards a traitor? Including the commander of the Imperial Guard himself, sworn to die in my defence?' He looked reproachfully at the defiant officer, who glared back. He shook his head again. 'I suppose with their commander a Monce, and backed up by the polemarchos, it would not have been too difficult. I recall complaints about replacements and forced retirements, but Ari did nothing about them. As usual.'

He turned to the smaller man, who cringed. 'Well, well, the Lord Usher of the Imperial Pisspot, is it not?' His voice was suddenly harsh. 'Take them away. I want answers. A full account of everyone involved. And I don't care how you get it.' The hoplites dragged the two away, none too gently.

Troilus looked around him at the scene of mayhem and death. 'Is it time for lunch?' he inquired hopefully.

SIXTY-EIGHT

VERY EARLY NEXT morning, with night still crouching over the land like a lion over its prey, they gathered in a briefing room in the strategion of the Imperial Guard. They stood around a large circular table upon which was painted a detailed map of the Troian Empire, with coloured blocks showing the position of forces. Troilus, Diomedes and Zeuxis were there, together with four others.

The first, Anchises, a tall, man of imposing build, with cropped hair and neat moustache, was studying the map with intense concentration. He was the previous commander of the Imperial Guard, hastily brought out of resentful retirement and reinstated. The second, Charopos, a short, round man, tufts of grey hair behind his ears marring the otherwise perfectly smooth sheen of his bald pate, was the Imperial Spymaster; his men were working on the unfortunate conspirators even as he spoke. He looked somewhat subdued—as he had cause to be, considering the scope of the revolt and the infiltration of the Guard that had happened on his watch.

Then there was the holder of Ilios, Dorian, a slight man with a surprisingly babyish face upon which a bushy beard looked ill at ease, but a man with a good martial reputation. Finally, Parmenio, a spare, rangy figure with the black hair and blue eyes of the true-born Troian, a young and upcoming strategos who commanded a small field army stationed just outside the capital—the only troops in their immediate vicinity.

At Dio's urging, they had already sent a force at ram speed to the Military Academy at Megara to secure the safety of Troilus's son, and now Charopos was briefing them. He and his men had not slept that night. Nor had his prisoners.

'It seems that the nucleus of the revolt is extremely limited. They have relied on converting satraps, putting secretaries and aides in place, and slowly and carefully creating special units of fanatics with the dispensation to hide their faith. It has been remarkably successful in terms of keeping the plot secret, but means that the real core of their support is numerically very weak. Their assumption is that the bulk of Troian forces will do as ordered. They are relying on a prepared cover story to convince the regular forces that they are fighting for the Empire. Once the emperor and his family had been assassinated, they would claim it was an internal coup, and Charmides, as the senior male representative of the house, would lead the charge to the rescue.'

'Cheeky buggers,' growled Anchises, 'using themselves as the excuse for their own actions.'

'But why haven't they acted before?' interrupted Parmenio, staring at the ring of angry red wooden blocks that encircled Ilios with its two solitary blue ones.

Dio took over. 'You will probably find this hard to believe. Their high priest had a revelation. Apparently one of the more obscure verses in this Book of Truth talks of the Great Wakening happening after seven times seventy years, and another says that it will be ten years in the waking.'

'Sounds like me in the morning,' muttered Anchises.

'So, he decided, in a pious exercise of arcane arithmetic, that it must come to fruition in the year equal to seven times seventy, plus ten.'

Everybody's faces took on a look of concentration as they struggled with the maths. Dio put them out of their mental misery. 'Five hundred. This year. Clearly a significant year in any case, which must have bolstered confidence in the prophecy. They are ready to move in ten days. On the anniversary of the birth of Zeuxidamos, the founder of the cult.' He shrugged. 'They like that sort of thing.'

'Then why did they assassinate Aristogeiton last year?' persisted Parmenio.

'Simple cock-up. The charge had already been sounded when the high priest belatedly got around to his adding up. Usual divine bureaucratic muddle, by the sound of it. The fanatics tasked with the murder of Aristogeiton just didn't get the message that rescinded their orders. Those that were to kill you, Your Majesty, fortunately did.'

Troilus blanched. 'They were going to kill me too?' He thought for a moment. 'I suppose it makes sense.' They all looked back at the threatening map. 'So, "What do we do?" is the question.'

No-one spoke. As usual, Dio was unable to stop himself taking charge, despite his preference to remain quietly in the background. 'We cut off their heads.'

'We have to catch them first,' snapped Dorian.

'No,' explained Dio patiently, 'I mean that we need to move very fast and take out the main conspirators. Significant forces at ram speed to each of the provinces, bearing the Imperial Warrant, and simply arrest the leaders before they realise what is happening.'

Parmenio shook his head. 'They will have their fanatically loyal units with them. There will be resistance, and the forces we can muster could well be overwhelmed.'

'It's a gamble. What we can't afford to do is wait for them to get news of what has happened and come at us with everything they've got.' Dio nodded towards the ominous map. 'We haven't the forces to hold, and they could still persuade the rest of the army to follow them. But attacks *on them* by Imperial troops, with the emperor still alive, will break the spokes of their chariot wheels and no mistake. They'll be off balance and scrambling to come up with a viable explanation. There's a good chance that most commanders will sensibly stand aside until they know what's happening.'

He scrubbed his hand through his cropped hair. 'And I believe them weaker than you imagine. My guess is that Miltiades will have read the liver about Adrastus's disappearance and is probably boarding a ship at Leuctra as we speak. Raxamenes is a coward and, without Gla behind him, will probably also scuttle, or at least do nothing. Antikles is strategically isolated in Mykerenos and can safely be left to wither. Lethos, we know, won't move until he knows who's going to win. So that just leaves Isodemos in Thalassa, Inachos in Lakadaemon and, of course, Charmides as the heart of the revolt. He is at Caria, just over the border in Lesser Troia, at the moment, I believe.' He glanced at Charopos.

'He was, four days ago,' the spymaster confirmed.

'Close enough to Ilios to be able to act swiftly when the time comes. But that sword is double edged. We are equally close to him. If we can take him down quickly, it will all be over. Or, if we can remove the other two from the equation, the revolt is dead. Even if we only succeed in taking one out, that gives us more than a fighting chance. Especially if we send immediate requests for forces from Argos, Attica and Chalcidike, and orders to the reserve army at Delos to move here at best speed.'

Parmenio gave him an appraising look, then nodded approvingly.

The rest looked to Troilus. He stared at the map for a few hekates, then abruptly said, 'We'll do it. Dorian, I want all available forces here as soon as possible. No delays. Zeuxis, you take complete charge of my personal security and the remaining Imperial Guard. Charopos, you round up every suspected Monce. Parmenio, you take Inachos. Anchises, Isodemos is yours. Mounted forces only for speed, so you will have limited numbers. Sort out amongst yourselves the division of forces. But do it quickly.'

'Charmides, Sire?' said Dio.

'Well, it's only right and proper that the big one should be left for the polemarchos, is it not? So, bestir yourself.'

This made Dio the supreme commander of all Imperial forces. He looked round him in shock, then stared at Troilus, who was smiling benignly at him.

'Yes, Polemarchos? What is it?' he said with a twinkle in his eye.

'Might we discuss this, Your Majesty?'

'Not at the moment. You have a traitor to apprehend, and time is short.'

SIXTY-NINE

D<small>IO CANTERED THROUGH</small> the main gate of the fortress at Caria with an officer and eight troopers of the Imperial Guard behind him. The rest of his force, three eiles of cavalry and one of mounted archers, remained waiting quietly out of sight round the street corner. An officer and two hoplites strode up. There were no obvious signs of alarm, but the officer looked understandably concerned. Dio dismounted and presented a parchment bearing the Imperial Seal.

'Imperial inspection,' he snapped, 'and I'm not happy with what I've already seen!'

'Imperial inspection?' repeated the officer incredulously.

'I presume that you have ears, even if you lack brains. Why have you done nothing about the trouble in the agora?'

'What trouble?' The man was floundering.

'So, you don't even know when you've a riot on your hands.' He shook his head in exasperation. 'Call out the guard.'

The officer yelled an order to his signaller, the salpinx sounded, and thirty hoplites tumbled out of the guard house and into line, hastily fastening cloaks and jamming helmets on their heads. Dio strode down the line, looking suitably appalled at the state of their uniforms and dressing.

'By the Little Gods and the Great, I've never seen such a badly turned-out bunch.' He swung to face the flustered officer. 'They're a bloody disgrace. But I haven't time now. Get that crowd sorted out in the agora. But flats, not blades. Send your hyper with a file and a half.'

'But, sir—' the officer began to protest.

'Now, man! Now!' roared Dio.

The officer muttered to his hyperetes, who numbered off twenty-four men and set off at the run. Straight into the waiting arms of his cavalry, thought Dio with due satisfaction. He turned to the remaining half-file of eight hoplites, standing rigidly to attention.

'You four across to the main gate in case the trouble floods up here, you two remain here in case I need you, you two to the watch tower.' He glared at the officer. 'And you with me; I want to inspect the tag rolls. Come along, Agetos,' he added, and the young-looking taxiarches came trotting after them. They entered the guard office, and Dio slammed the door behind him as Agetos smoothly placed a very long knife across the officer's neck. Not surprisingly, the man turned to stone. Perspiration flooded his face. Dio pulled out his god guard, turned it over, nodded, then perched himself on the edge of the small table.

'I presume all the men in this detail are Monists?'

The man said nothing, but looked up as though expecting something to happen. Agetos casually nicked him with the knife, and blood flowed down his neck.

The officer winced but remained silent.

'Shouldn't I be dead?' enquired Dio. 'Struck down on the spot by an avenging god? Something seems to have gone wrong somewhere. Now, I'm going to ask you once more.' He drew his spatha and pointed it straight at the man's genitals. 'But this time, no answer and I'll cut off your balls. Are your men all Monists?'

'Yes,' the man croaked.

'How many units are Monist? One lie and I'll have you crucified, and your body cremated.'

Dio had discovered that the great fear of the Monces was cremation. Their body could not be regenerated at the Great Wakening if it had been reduced to ashes. Which seemed remarkably limited of such an omnipotent God, but he wasn't complaining. It proved an extremely effective way of persuading them to talk.

The man swallowed, then reluctantly spoke. 'Three.'

'Who and where are they?' prompted Dio.

The officer looked wildly around him, then sagged. 'First plag, out on patrol at the moment. Dmetor's taxis…' Dio raised an eyebrow. 'That's our unit; they're in the second barrack block. And the Black Guard, Charmides' bodyguards.'

'How many in the Black Guard?'

'An understrength taxis. Hundred and twenty men or so.'

Far less overall than he had feared. If the man was telling the truth, of course.

'Put him in the holding cell. We'll get more later.' As Agetos thrust him inside the barred cage, and none too gently at that, Dio wagged an admonitory finger at him. 'One sound, and it's a nice cosy funeral pyre for you. If you're lucky, we might kill you first.' He opened the door and yelled across the yard, 'Dilocho, here at the ram.' He turned to Agetos. 'Get ready with that pig sticker. Then we'll call for those two waiting.'

Within hekates, they had all the remaining hoplites jammed miserably and uncomfortably in a cell made for one. 'Couldn't squash another one in, even if we wanted,' said Agetos happily. 'Not even a little one.'

'Thinking about it, you could pull a couple out to act as guides.'

The cavalry filed through the gate and quickly dismounted, and the officers gathered for a hasty conference.

'We're in luck,' Dio told the first eilarches. 'Their cavalry plag is apparently taking the air. Take your eile and this miserable wretch—' he thrust a trembling hoplite forward '—to the second barrack block. He will show you where. They're all Monces. Go in hard and fast. Kill anyone who blinks. Don't hesitate. I want them taken out.

'Monomachus, you and the first plag of your eile will hold the gate. Close it. No-one enters or leaves. No exceptions. Second plag goes with Agetos. Third eile.'

'Sir,' responded a handsome young officer crisply. Every time Dio looked at him, he saw Kal's eyes. 'Antinous, you and the archers with me.'

Agetos held a small, squirming hoplite by the scruff of the neck. 'Lead on,' he said amiably. 'We'll follow.'

SEVENTY

Accoring to their informants, Charmides was in the Great Hall, apparently involved in a meeting with some senior officers and a trio of black-cloaked priests. Dio and his men moved quickly across the courtyard, at double pace and in open order. He dared not let them go faster or they would lose cohesion.

To their left was a series of square, functional barrack blocks, towards the second of which the first eile was already swiftly angling. To the right, by the large strategion and small villas for senior officers, groups of bemused soldiers and civilians gathered to watch and wonder. Ahead, Dio could see the Great Hall, a large double door set at the top of some steps and flanked by a portico of fluted columns, a triangular, carved architrave above. Standing by the doors were half a dozen hoplites carrying black shields with a golden lion sigil and wearing black leather cuirasses and

Korinthian helmets surmounted by three black feathers. Obviously Charmides' Black Guard.

A self-important chiliarches, ablaze in his red sash of office, came bustling up, all peppery indignation. 'Who, by the satyr's swinging dick, do you think—?' At a gesture from Dio, the two nearest hoplites delightedly grabbed the senior officer and hustled him onwards, cutting him off in mid-complaint.

'What do—'

'Shut up,' said Dio and shoved the scroll with the Imperial seal under the officer's nose. The man gaped, then yelped as Dio reached out and tore his god guard from his neck, glancing down at the man's hands to ensure he wore no rings.

He looked at the back. 'Not a Monotheite, then?'

'Certainly not,' spluttered the chiliarches.

All was confusion as they pressed farther on, roughly pushing tardy soldiers aside. Ahead, one of the Black Guards was gesturing urgently towards them, another racing off towards the nearest barrack block.

Dio pointed at the running man and swept his hand across his throat. Immediately, a flight of arrows sang across the yard. The hoplite spun and despairingly thrust his shield forward towards them, but there were too many, and he fell and lay still, several shafts protruding from his body.

Mayhem erupted from the second block as the first eile piled inside; shouts, screams and the ring of iron.

'Cover those blocks,' shouted Dio to the hekatonarches of the archers. 'Antinous, protection.'

'First plag, double shield line, close order,' the young man snapped, and, in the midst of the urgency, confusion and danger, Dio had time for a glow of pride.

The eight left-hand files split away and in heartbeats had reformed as a double line, shields interlocked, in front of the archers. Black Guards began to tumble out of the final block and into a hail of arrows.

Dio bawled for the troopers to halt. The doors of the Great Hall were closing. They were too late.

Dio spun round to the chiliarches, whose eyes were wide and face pale. 'Imperial edict. Charmides is a traitor. More Imperial Guards are on their way.' They weren't, but it wouldn't hurt to say so. 'Now get everybody back in their barracks, and they stay there until I say otherwise.' He could hear Antinous yelling for his third tet to extend the shield line right. 'Check their god guards. If there's a mu on the back, you arrest them.' He tossed the officer's god guard back to him, only for him to fumble and drop it.

He looked round at the sudden clash of arms. Charmides' Guard were big men, obviously skilled and imbued with a manic intensity. Many lay across the courtyard transfixed by arrows, but the bulk of them, forty to fifty, had smashed into Antinous's shield line and were hewing their way through it. He heard Antinous shouting for his men to hold.

'How many other exits to the Great Hall?' Dio had to yell above the dreadful din.

The idiot was scrabbling on the ground for his god guard. 'Just a side door. On the right.' He scrambled to his feet.

'Send me a good officer as soon as possible. Now go.' He shoved the chiliarches on his way, then swung round, drawing his sword. 'Agetos, take your men and cover that side door and any windows. No-one comes out.' He looked round to Antinous's last reserve tetrarchia. The Imperial line was buckling under the frenzied assault. 'Fourth tet. On me. Form wedge.' A couple of desperate heartbeats as they formed up behind him in triangular formation, and then he flung himself at the flank of the Black Guards – just as the Imperial line broke.

Dio's men smashed into the side of the rampaging hoplites and clove into them like a butcher's axe, stopping them exploiting the line break. Antinous was desperately trying to reform his men. Then the formation around Dio splintered like an eggshell as a group of Charmides' men appeared seemingly from nowhere and drove into their rear. Now it was just man to man, all formation lost. Just a massive brawl. The Imperial troops flung away their useless spears and drew their kopoi. Everywhere the clash of steel and the scream of men.

The battle calm enveloped him. Everything was clear, distinct, moving slowly as though through water. He easily blocked a sweeping cut aimed at his head and drove for his opponent's midriff. But the hoplite smartly jabbed his shield downwards, and Dio's spatha slid from its bronzed surface. He flung his own shield outwards to batter away another cut and leapt backwards as the man tried the old trick of hooking his shield behind Dio's. The Black Guard tried to follow up his seeming advantage, but Dio unexpectedly sprang forward again with full force and buffeted the shields together, the shock jarring his arm. Taken by surprise, the hoplite staggered back, and Dio instantly drove his sword across the top of his shield, through the helmet's narrow vision slit and into the man's eye. He fell away, screaming.

Dio took a moment to look around. Numbers were telling, and the Black Guard, now significantly fewer, were beginning to yield ground. But off to the right, in a clear space, Kal's son was battling a positive giant of a man and clearly losing, frantically staving off the rapid, savage and powerful blows that were driving him inexorably backwards. Dio saw the inevitable happen—the retreating Antinous tripped over a corpse, landing sprawled on his back, his kopis skittering from his hand. The giant loomed above him, reversing his sword for the killing thrust.

'No!' screamed Dio and hurled himself across the intervening gap, his spatha perilously over-extended. The giant must have heard the shout and hesitated for a heartbeat before stabbing his blade down. That heartbeat was the saving of Antinous. Dio's despairing lunge caught the hilt of the descending sword and pushed it away, just enough for it to plunge harmlessly into the beaten earth by the side of the helpless youth. Dio executed an instant reverse cut across the man's momentarily exposed throat, and the guard fell to his knees, clutching his neck, blood spurting through his fingers.

Dio quickly looked around again. It was almost over. The last few hoplites were being hunted down without mercy, the troopers swarming over them like deerhounds on their quarry. The second barracks was clearly under control and the Great Hall surrounded by an iron ring of Imperial Guardsmen. He reached down and hauled Antinous to his feet. As his combat calm faded, the realisation of how close Kal's son had been to death rose within him, and he could feel his legs tremble. He forced the emotion down.

'Thanks, Uncle Dio,' said the shaken young man. 'I owe you.'

'Self-preservation, lad,' said Dio. 'Your mother would have killed me.'

'Sir.' A fresh-faced tetrarches saluted. 'I was told by the chiliarches to report to you.'

'Excellent,' said Dio, and regarded the large double doors to the hall. 'Now, where might one obtain a really nice battering ram?' It would make a refreshing change to be on the other end of one, he thought.

SEVENTY-ONE

CHARMIDES STOOD, WITH the remnants of his bodyguard, at the far end of the Great Hall. The few survivors were crouched behind upturned tables, trying to find what shelter they could. But Charmides, a tall, handsome man with the characteristic black hair and blue eyes of the Troian aristocracy, scorned such cowardice. He could not have known that Dio had given strict orders to avoid him as a target. Around Charmides lay mounds of bodies, some still moving, but most in the sprawling slump of death, porcupined with arrows. He grimaced and yanked out a stray arrow that had just penetrated one of the shoulder straps of his thick linen cuirass.

At the other end of the hall stood a quadruple rank of Imperial troopers with a fearsome forest of spear points protruding from an impenetrable row of gilded shields. The spear heads were dark with blood after the last desperate attack by the trapped bodyguard. Behind the shield wall, archers were nonchalantly nocking arrows, choosing their victims and loosing.

'Enough,' said Charmides and dropped his sword.

Behind him, the clatter of falling steel. The rain of arrows petered out, and for a moment all was still and silent. Then the moans and groaning began. Someone was calling for his mother, another choking horribly on his lifeblood.

A man stepped forward through the parting ranks of the Imperial troops, a tall, middle-aged man with greying hair and a scarred, angular face, spattered with blood. There was a darkly stained sword in his hand, and he looked as though he knew how to use it.

'And who might you be?' said Charmides. He did not seem overly interested.

'Diomedes, swordmaster at Gla.'

'Never heard of you.'

'That makes no matter.'

'No,' said Charmides, his tone one of weary resignation. 'It doesn't. If you will forgive me, there is something I must do.'

He pulled a man forward, a stooped, frail, white-bearded man in a long black robe, calmly took him by the throat and lifted him off the floor. The old man scrabbled desperately, but vainly, at the strong arms, kicked and flailed and struggled, but to no avail. Charmides simply held him, his own features expressionless, until the agonised face darkened, the eyes bulged and the struggling stilled. Dio watched impassively. The would-be emperor finally let go, as though dumping some rubbish, and the lifeless body collapsed on the floor.

Dio leaned on his sword. 'That would have been the high priest, I presume?' he asked conversationally.

Charmides nodded slowly, then looked up from the shapeless heap at his feet. 'To Ilios, I suppose?'

'Indeed,' agreed Dio, 'To Ilios.'

SEVENTY-TWO

Blackwing was tired, and Dio dismounted and walked for a while. The weather was just as it had been when they had first arrived, bright but very cold. He was not far from the steading now, and he welcomed the time to sort out his thoughts. Though he had been doing nothing else since leaving Ilios, and they remained obstinately unsorted.

The collapse of the revolt had been spectacularly swift and complete. Apollos had committed suicide, and the major-domo was under arrest. Isodemos had got the scent of what was coming and had simply fled before Dorian's arrival. They were still searching for him. Parmenio had fought a savage and bloody battle to take the fort at Pylos, killing Inachos in the process, and Miltiades was long gone from Leuctra, as Dio had predicted.

But Raxamenes was a mystery. He had taken it on the scuttle from the Kadmeia, but had been arrested in Cyzicus, where he claimed that he had been heading for Keltia. Dio, recalling the surprising ease with which Adrastus had given up the details of the attempted coup, suspected both Raxamenes and Adrastus had been Laomedon's creatures all the time and that Raxamenes had actually been heading for his real master. A suspicion that had hardened when the satrap was found, the next day, poisoned in his cell. Dio wondered if Laomedon, or someone with brains acting for him, could have infiltrated the conspiracy and used it as a staked goat. Plots within plots. He was still convinced that the brutal Warden of the Debateable Lands was looking to revolt.

But for now, that left only Antikles in his mountainous province of Mykerenos to deal with. Most of the conspirators were in prison awaiting trial. Charmides and Adrastus had already suffered the dreadful fate of crucifixion along with three Monist priests. The Book of Truth had been banned, the Monotheite Church proscribed; it was haemorrhaging supporters faster than a severed carotid artery, as Troilus happily described it. The Great Wakening had already been derisively renamed the Great Yawn.

Dio had finally managed to persuade Troilus that he did not want the position of polemarchos. Nevertheless, he had only been allowed to leave Ilios on the understanding that he and the Lady Kalliste would return in due course. He thought that he had said nothing about Kal that might suggest a relationship, but the emperor was far too astute.

'The Lady Kalliste must be very special,' he had said with a characteristic twinkle in his eye, 'and I look forward to meeting her. I hope that you will do me the honour of accepting me as her wedding father.'

Dio had instinctively begun to deny it, but had thought better of it and thanked Troilus with a decidedly sickly smile. But whether it would even happen was now too close. Living with fear and uncertainty was bad, but confronting reality could be worse.

So, he had to prepare himself. Saving an emperor's life, foiling a countrywide plot, destroying the odd religion, just a day's work. Telling a woman that you loved her. That was hard.

He rehearsed phantasmal conversations in his thoughts, witty and urbane, caring and loving, measured and elliptical. His imagination conjured up the responses, delighted acceptance, shocked surprise, instant rejection. Laughter. It could be laughter. Dio closed his eyes, as if that could shut out the images that rampaged through his helpless mind. He tried to be analytical, manipulating possibilities and permutations until his head hurt, and swore to himself that he would speak, but knew that he would not. He cut and polished poetic phrases, constructed brilliant arguments and dreamed fabulous metaphors, knowing that they would languish and die and never live in the real world. He longed to see her with all his heart and dreaded it with all his mind. He wanted to run madly to be with her again, resenting every hekate away from her, desperate for her presence. But then he wanted to turn Blackwing round, just ride into the calm of renunciation and leave it all behind him as if it had never been. Dio had never felt so frightened in his life.

SEVENTY-THREE

Eventually, the familiar cluster of buildings grew above the skyline. There was no longer reason for caution, so he simply rode in.

He had scarcely set foot on the ground when Kal came flying out of the hearth home and flung herself upon him, nearly bowling him over. Phyllida followed a little more sedately but with a huge grin across her broad features. Kal clung tightly to him as he held her in his awkward way, uncomfortably aware of the press of her against his body, as well as of the knowing smile on Phyllida's face. He wasn't at all sure that he wasn't wearing an inane grin himself. Kal's face nuzzled into his shoulder, and he could feel a dampness on his neck. He did not know whether to be relieved or disappointed when she finally stepped back. She kept hold of his hands and shook her head helplessly, totally unable to speak.

Dymas had come up behind him. 'Well, you've been busy and no mistake. Uncovering the dastardly plot.'

'I stupidly got it completely wrong.'

'Defending the emperor single-handedly against hundreds of assassins.'

'Only a few before the whole of the Imperial Guard poured in.'

'Capturing the traitor in hand-to-hand combat.'

'I just shot arrows at him until he surrendered.'

'And now the polemarchos, no less.'

'A temporary position only.'

'Well, I prefer my version,' declared Dymas obstinately.

'As will most people,' said Phyllida, elbowing in to give Dio a huge hug.

Kal finally found her tongue. Her eyes searched his face. 'You're not hurt?' Her voice was scarcely more than a whisper.

'Not a scratch. At least, not until Phyll just crushed my ribs.'

'Did you see Antinous?'

'He was with me at Caria. He's fine. He did well.' Beneath the simple words, a muted pride. 'I spoke to Aglaia too. I told her that the emperor had promised to pardon her father, and that you were safe and well. She sends her love and says that she wants to see you as soon as she can.'

Kal smiled her thanks.

Gorgias had appeared, pleased and excited. 'Everyone's talking about you, Uncle Dio. Mum said I could tell Hebe. She was very impressed.'

'Well, I'm glad it was of some use to someone, then.' He was aware of Kal's eyes still searching his face. He forced himself to look back at her. 'Are you all right, Kal?' he asked softly.

She nodded happily. 'Never better.'

'Let's inside,' said Phyllida, 'and you can tell us all about it.'

Kal smiled at him as he stepped forward. It was almost a shy smile. Dio stepped up and into the hearth home and was suddenly grabbed from behind, his arms trapped in a bear hug.

'Got you,' said a familiar voice. Dio laughed and thrust up with his arms against the hold as he dropped down on bent knees. Twisting, he slid his left leg round behind his attacker, reached down and grabbed him at the back of his knees to lift him up and casually tip him over his back, continuing to turn to break his fall. The young man hit the floor with a whoosh of exhaled air. Still laughing, Dio put his arm down to pull him back to his feet.

'Will you two stop it?' said Phyllida wearily, coming in after them with Kal. 'You're just big kids.' She looked at Kal, and they both shook their heads in resignation.

Dio released his grip and grabbed the shoulders of the young man who had attacked him. He was a slight but wiry youth, with a rather long face and brown hair tied in a ponytail. 'Xan, it's good to see you.'

'You're still too good for me, Uncle Dio,' said Xanthos breathlessly, slightly winded. 'But you were supposed to throw yourself forward to lift me off my feet.'

'Rule seventy-three—we are up to rule seventy-three, are we not?'

'Seventy-four, I think,' chimed in Gorgias, pulling up a stool to the table.

'Rule seventy-four. Always do the unexpected. Then there's rule seventy-five, of course. When they expect you to do the unexpected, do the expected.'

'Well, then it would be unexpected, so that's still rule seventy-four,' said Kal primly.

'Oh, Dyaus,' groaned Dio. 'She's been at the elementary logic again.'

'Sound common sense,' she corrected him. 'I don't often admit defeat, but my project to teach it to a man was doomed to failure from the start.' Phyllida, working at the table behind her, nodded vigorously. 'I'll start Blackwing on basic geometry in the morning. At least I'll have some chance of success.'

'One to you, Auntie Kal,' laughed Xan.

Auntie Kal. Dio wisely chose to say nothing, though uncomfortably aware of Phyllida's shoulders heaving helplessly.

SEVENTY-FOUR

They had an early meal, and he told them what had happened, and they oohed and aahed and fired questions at him and told him what had really happened and laughed a lot. He was aware that Kal said very little and that her eyes rarely left his face. Whenever he looked at her, she smiled at him. He suddenly found himself surprisingly eager to retire to their 'home'.

'I have something for you all,' he announced and went across to search in his blanket bag until he found four linen bags, tied with silken ribbons and with attached tags bearing their names. He handed them out. They were heavy and clinked.

Phyllida immediately looked angry. 'Diomedes,' she began warningly.

He held up his hands in a placatory gesture. 'Nothing to do with me, Phyll. I promise. They're from the Emperor.'

She looked at him with horror, then untied and upended hers. A pile of large golden coins spilled out onto the table, together with a small leather case. Their eyes widened. She took the leather case and opened it with shaking hands. Inside was a golden medallion. They crowded round to look at it. It bore the embossed profile of the emperor and, inscribed round it, the words, 'For Phyllida, wife of Dymas. With eternal gratitude for her bravery and loyalty. Troilus III.'

For once in her life, Phyllida was struck dumb. Eventually, she managed to say, in a remarkably weak voice, 'The emperor had this made for me?'

Dio nodded, smiling.

Dymas and Gorgias had already dived into their bags and were gazing at their own medallions.

'Dyaus's balls,' breathed Gorgias.

Phyllida instantly boxed his ear. 'Language!'

'Sorry, Mum,' said Gorgias, rubbing his ear, 'but this is really going to impress Hebe.'

Dymas made no attempt to suppress his laughter. 'But a single arrow in his quiver.' Phyllida frowned at him, but Dymas just grinned back.

Xanthos looked concerned. He had not opened his bag. 'Why me?' he asked Dio. 'I did nothing.'

'You were here too, as we knew you would be. And if Kal had needed it, you would have been there for her. You shared the danger. How could we leave you out?'

Xanthos smiled. 'Thanks, Uncle Dio.'

Phyllida carefully replaced her medallion in its case. 'The emperor does know that it wasn't loyalty to him personally?'

'I should think so. He's certainly no fool. But he is grateful nevertheless. As am I, Phyll. For everything.'

He must have put more meaning into it than he intended, because she shot him a peculiar look and smiled knowingly.

'Well, I think that that's enough excitement for one day,' Phyllida said, 'if not for the night. I know it's early, but I'm sure Dio and Kal would like to go to bed.' She didn't actually wink, but she might as well have done. It was certainly present in the tone.

Dio flinched. He was sure that Kal was blushing. He knew that he was. Phyllida beamed. He decided that it was best to depart swiftly before she dropped the subtle approach.

They said their goodnights and left. He glanced back as they went, and Phyllida made the traditional ribald gesture with her finger and fist. He stared in pure horror, and Dymas collapsed in a fit of laughter. Mercifully, Kal was walking across to the guest house and remained ignorant of the little cameo played out behind her back.

He caught up with her, and they continued across in silence. The stars vaulted the heavens with beauty, and the frost sparkled in the bright moonglow and crunched underfoot.

As they entered what they now regarded as home, he had the sudden urge just to reach out and hold her, but the iron hoops of habit and self-control stayed him.

Kal hung her shawl up. The fire was burning low, and he stacked some logs on. She sat down before it to warm her hands. He sat down opposite her.

She looked across and smiled, but her eyes seemed sad. 'I'm glad that you're back. I've missed you.'

He should have said that he had missed her too, but didn't. 'You're safe now. You can go where you wish.' It was the wrong thing to say, and he winced inwardly.

She gave him a despondent little smile. 'I don't know where I want to go. I might even stay here if Phyll will have me. I like the life. What are you going to do?' There seemed a slight sharpness to the question. 'Are you going to accept the emperor's offer of the polemarchy?'

He shook his head. This was going badly. Every time he tautened himself to say something, the moment just glided by. She was watching him, but when he looked at her, she turned away slightly to gaze into the fire. 'So, what are you going to do?' she repeated quietly.

'I really don't know.'

She sighed. It spoke of winter and the going down of the sun. 'I think I'll go to bed.' She stood. He could not bear for her to go. The dam finally broke before the relentless pressure. He closed his eyes for a moment and took a deep breath. He stepped forward and took her hands in his. She stared at him in wide-eyed surprise. If he was making an awful mistake, it was too late now.

'Kal,' he said awkwardly, and every word was a struggle. He could swear that he heard his own heart beating. 'Kal, before I went, you said that you needed something that was not available.'

She was rigid, her face expressionless, her eyes boring into his.

He looked down, unable to look into her eyes, where he might well read instant rejection. An extra heartbeat of hope might be all he had. 'If I'm wrong, I can only apologise… but…' He paused, then forced himself to continue. 'Did you mean that you wanted more from me, something more than friendship?' He looked at her white hands laid within his, convinced that she would pull them away.

But there was no movement. None. She appeared to have stopped breathing, and he was transfixed in the moment. A marble statue. Unchanging. Unmoving. Existing for eternity on the cusp between rejection and acceptance. Only the crackling of the logs marked some kind of time.

Then she said 'Yes.' Very quietly. She had said yes. Something leapt inside him like a salmon flashing high in the bright sunlight, and he looked up to meet her sad eyes. 'But,' she said, and the joy that had flared within him guttered and died. 'I know it's not in your nature.' She looked down in turn. 'I won't make you miserable, no matter what I would like.'

He was desperate. Now that he had spoken, the thought that she might go gored his mind. 'Kal, there would be no misery. There's nothing I could possibly want more. Nothing.'

Her gaze clutched at his again. 'Are you serious?' Her voice trembled slightly.

'I have never been more serious in my life. Or more frightened.'

She did not smile. Her gaze was unblinking, her nails digging firmly into the palms of his hands.

He collected his thoughts. 'I know I've fought against it, Herakla knows why. I'm sorry. I was stupid. But now I know what I feel. I love you.'

He had said it. It had been that easy after all. He wanted to keep on saying it, over and over again. It was like breaking surface for the first juddering breath after almost drowning.

She continued to stare into his eyes. Searching for something. 'You're not saying that out of pity? Because you think it's what I want to hear, what I need?'

He shook his head. 'I only know that it's what *I* want, what *I* need. But the question is you. Can you love me?' Even the logs on the fire stopped crackling.

She pulled her hands away, reached out and tenderly cupped his face. 'You silly, silly man. Of course I love you. I have for years. I suppose I could have written it in burning letters ten stadia high, but I thought I'd made it embarrassingly obvious. Though I did try not to.'

She was laughing, but there were tears in her eyes. He leaned forward and kissed her. Just a gentle and brief press of the lips.

'And about time too,' she murmured.

Then she wrapped her arms round him and hugged him more fiercely than he could ever have thought possible. Her hands went round the back of his head, pulled him into her, and she was kissing him, this time passionately, their lips tight and moulding themselves together and opening like flowers to the caress of the sun. He could feel the heat of her body against his, the taste of mint in her mouth, the smell of rosewater in her hair. There was a slight but relentless pull towards the bedroom door, and he was helpless in its power.

At the door of the hearth home, Dymas stood with his arm cupped round Phyllida's ample waist. They watched as glimmers of light rippled out round the window covers, but only at the end where Kal's bedroom lay. Phyllida smiled contentedly, and they turned and went inside.

SEVENTY-FIVE

THE HALF-LIGHT OF dawn seeped through the window, along with the early-morning noises of the city; the creak of wagons, the lowing of cattle being driven to market, the ebb and flow of conversation as people passed. Kal nestled closer, one arm lying across him, their legs entwined.

'I love you,' she suddenly said. She had the trick of saying it at unexpected times. It left him having to make the feeble response, 'And I love you too.' But it always made him feel good. He kissed her forehead, and she raised her face to kiss him properly.

'Mmmm,' she said as she snuggled down again. 'That was nice.' They lay there, in sleepy contentment. 'You are happy?' she asked suddenly.

'Of course,' he said. 'I couldn't be happier.'

'I'm happy too,' she said before he could even ask. 'It was lovely having Aglaia and little Pyrrhus there, and Antinous as well. I'm so proud of him. And the emperor was kind and nice. To have an emperor as my wedding father. Who would have thought it?'

'Hebe was most impressed,' he said solemnly.

Kal chuckled.

'But far more impressive was having Phyll as your bride friend,' he continued.

'Impressive, but not all that comfortable,' said Kal. 'I was just praying that she wouldn't turn round and tell the emperor off for something or other. Give him what Dymas calls an ear belting.'

'If she'd had cause, or thought she had, she would have. She's a law unto herself.'

'I think the emperor was rather taken with her.'

'That was the boiled goose egg she did for him. He has a thing about boiled eggs.'

'So, what is it like being a married man?'

'Something I never thought would happen, but now I wish it could have happened a long time ago.'

'Do you know?' murmured Kal, idly running a finger through the hairs on his chest. 'I feel guilty about it, but I wish Milt had seen fit to divorce me long before he did. We had grown apart anyway.'

'Perhaps we wouldn't have got together.'

'Yes, we would,' she declared definitively. 'Thais told me a long time ago, just after the divorce, that it was obvious that you adored me. Which begs the serious question; if she knew, how come that you didn't?'

'Well, you didn't either.'

'Don't change the subject,' she said severely, twisting one of his hairs round her finger and giving it a sharp tug.

'Ouch. Because I'm a man?'

'Of course. That would be it. That explains most of the nonsense in the world.' She suddenly giggled and propped herself up to look down on him. Her breasts brushed his chest. Her face was radiant. 'Did you know that Phyll told me once that, if I didn't get into your bed, she was going to carry me there?'

'I did, as a matter of fact, because she told me the same.'

'Ah,' said Kal, prodding him sternly, 'now we have it. That somewhat clumsy and inept declaration of love was brought on by sheer terror.'

'Well, what if it was? It's turned out more or less all right, hasn't it?'

'Beast,' she said and thumped him.

GLOSSARY

The references following place names are co-ordinates to be used in conjunction with the maps on harpalycus.com.

Achilleus : Gean semi-divine hero
Aggies : Nickname for Agrianians
agora : A marketplace
Agriania : Mountainous country of small tribes in the southeast of Gea. At this time, not under Troian control
Agrianian Mountains : The mountains dominating Agriania (8A3, 8B3, 8A4, 8B4)
Agrianian (s) : Inhabitant and language of Agriania
Akrochalcis : Fortress. One of the Five Fetters. Situated in Upper Phthia and dominating the Chalcis Pass to Eretria (1B2)
amphora (e) : Storage jar
Amyklai : Capital of Neritos's people in the Kodros Valley in Agriania (See Sea of Grass map)

Antenopolis : Troian naval base on the eastern coast of the Chalcidikian Peninsula (3B2)

Antimelos : A small village fifty stadia east of Gla

Aphroditea : The planet Venus, the Morning Star/Evening Star. Named for the Gean Goddess of Love

Aphrodites : Day of the week. Friday

Apollon : Gean God of light, poetry and prophecy. Symbol a sun disc

Apollonian red : Good wine from the region of the town of Apollonia in Greater Troia

Areos : Day of the week. Tuesday

Aresia : The planet Mars. Named for the Gean War God

Argenusae Islands : Troian province on two large islands north of Chalcidike

Argos : Capital of the Argolid (3B3)

Asopus : Lake in the Kodros Valley in Agriania (see Sea of Grass map)

aspis : Heavy round shield carried by a hoplite

Athen : Gean Goddess of Wisdom born by springing from the head of Dyaus. Symbol an owl

Athos : River running through Thrake and Leuctra to the Gulf of Scylla. The effective border between Gea and Thrake (8B1, 8B2, 8C2, 8C3)

Attica : Troian province north of Greater Troia

Attic Way : Main route north to the Attic Peninsula (2C1, 2C2, 2C3)

Basilides : An Attic aristocratic family claiming descent from Apollon

bell cuirass : A bronze, shaped cuirass, usually decorated with stylised muscles. Becoming obsolete in favour of lighter cuirasses made of layers of linen glued together

Black Guard : Charmides' bodyguard

bolt hole : Cleverly disguised hiding place in an isolated steading
bondsman : A household warrior sworn to an Agrianian king
Book of Truth : The holy writings of the Monotheites
boustria : Dried meat, jerky
bureau : The organisational offices of an authority

Caria : Capital of Lesser Troia (6C2)
Chalcidike : Gean province. Northeast of Greater Troia
Chalcis Pass : Strategic pass between Phthia and Eretria (1B3)
chariot crash : A complete disaster
chariot wheel, to break the spokes of : To ruin someone's plan
chiliarches : Commander of a thousand hoplites. Equivalent to a lieutenant colonel. Red sash of office and a silver boar on a laurel leaf wreath brooch
chiton : A draped dress, usually gathered at the waist
Ch'n : A people and land to the east of Thrake
Choraea : Town in the Vale of Tempe in the Thebeaid. West of Gla (7C1)
clint : The block in a limestone pavement
Confederacy : An alliance of Agrianian petty kingdoms, but with no real substance
coughing sickness : Tuberculosis
Cressid : Mythical character who betrayed her lover, Troilus
cuirass : Body armour made of bronze or, more commonly, layers of linen glued together
Cyzicus : Walled town in the south of Lesser Troia (6B3)

Debateable Lands : A buffer zone between Keltia and Gea. Bounded by the rivers Camlann and Granicus and the Acarnanian Forest
dekate : A tenth part of the night or day. Thus there are twenty dekates in a complete day. The actual length varies with the season

Delos : Town and army base in Thalassa (2B2)
deuteros : A second-in-command
didrachma (e) : Coin. A two-drachma piece
dilochagos : A double file leader, equivalent to a sergeant major
dilocho : Diminutive for dilochagos
Dionysian theatre : Drama and poetry competitions held in various major towns
discharge papers, to hand in : To die
don a plumed helmet : Get a reputation
donkey carrots : To feed someone donkey carrots is to make them believe nonsense
drachma (e) : Unit of money. Worth six obols
Dryop (s) : A member of the Dryopian people, noted for their fierceness
Dyaus (Pitar) : Chief God of the Geans. Symbol a keraunos or stylised thunderbolt
Dyme : Lake in the Kodros valley in Agriania (see Sea of Grass map)

earth : A prepared hiding place or secret cache
eilarches : Commander of a cavalry eile. Equivalent to a major. Dark green sash of office and bronze laurel leaf brooch
eile : Unit of 256 cavalry
ektatos (oi) : Lower ranking file commander, effectively equivalent to a non-commissioned officer
Eretria : Country to the west of northern Gea, connected by the wide Chalcis Pass. Inveterate enemies of the Geans
Eretrian (s) : Inhabitant and language of Eretria

Fetter : One of five strategic fortresses controlling Gea. See Five Fetters
feverfew : A medicinal herb supposed to lower fevers, reduce swelling and help with headaches
fire in the gut : Indigestion

Five Fetters : Five fortresses: Kerakos, Gla, Demetrius, Ithome and the Akrochalcis

Furies : Spirits of revenge that hunt to death a man guilty of murder, hubris or oath breaking

Gamelion : Second month. January 21 – February 19

Gea : Area of land on the south coast of the Pontis. Inhabited by a people with the same language and culture

Gean (s) : Inhabitant and language of Gea

Gla : Fortress, one of the Five Fetters. Set in the Vale of Tempe (8A1)

Glapolis : The civilian town surrounding Gla

Glaukon's Steading : Phyllida and Dymas's steading, named for Phyllida's grandfather (see Sea of Grass map)

god guard : Amulet worn as protection, made in the symbol of the chosen protective deity

Golden Gryphon : Mythological creature, proverbial for something unbelievable or something very special

graphotrapeza : Writing table with an angled top for easier writing

Great East Road : Highway from Ilios via Dardanos, Hekuba, Priamos, Kadmeia and Minyas to Leuctra (7A1, 7B1, 7C1, 8A1)

Greater Troia : Gean province. The largest, richest and most populous

Great Wakening : The awaited triumph of the Monotheite religion and the subsequent Reign of Peace

greave : Thin, shaped bronze armour that snaps round the leg to protect the shins

grip of Herakla : Heart attack

gryke : The gap in a limestone pavement

Hades : Gean God of the Dead. Symbol a skull. Also, the place of the dead

handle off the shield : Idiom for things going badly wrong

hay, which end of the horse eats the : Idiom for something so simple that only an idiot would not know it

hekate : Unit of time. The hundredth part of a dekate. Variable between half and one minute. Popularly regarded as a hundred heartbeats

hekatonarches : Officer in command of 256 light infantry. Equivalent to a major. Dark green sash of office and bronze laurel leaf wreath brooch

Hekatonbaion : Eighth month. July 25 – August 23

Heliou : Day of the week. Sunday

hemidekate : Half a hekate, i.e. approximately half an hour

Herakla : Queen of the Gean Gods. Her symbol is a pomegranate

holder : The designated official in command of a large town or fortress

hoplite : Gean heavy infantryman armed with stabbing spear and large shield

Household Guard : A subunit of the Imperial Guard who are the emperor's immediate bodyguard. Known as the White Cloaks

hyperetes : The equivalent of a company sergeant major

Ilios : Troian capital (3A4)

Imperial Guard : Elite unit tasked with the guarding of the emperor

Ithome : Fortress. One of the Five Fetters. Situated on Lake Tritonis in Makedonia (7A2)

Kadmeia : Capital and fortress of the Thebeaid (7C1)

Kalydonian : Pertaining to Kalydon, a town in the central plain of Phthia. A proverbial example of backwater provinciality (2A2)

Keltia : Country to the southwest of Gea

Keltos (oi) : Inhabitant of Keltia

Kerakos : Fortress in the Debateable Lands. One of the Five Fetters of Gea (6A2)

knucklebones : Primitive dice. Sheep or calf ankle bones that can come to rest with one of four different faces uppermost, with each given a value

Kodros Valley : Home of Neritos's people in Agriania (see Sea of Grass map)

kopis (oi) : A curved sword, broader and heavier near the point

Korinthia : Province in central Gea

Korinthian helmet : An enclosed helmet that affords good protection but poor vision

Krak : Diminutive of Kerakos

krater : Large bowl for mixing wine and water

kylix : Drinking vessel

Kyme : River in northern Agriania running through the Kodros Valley (see Sea of Grass map)

Lakadaemon : Gean province in south central Gea

Leda : Woman in Gean mythology who was raped by Dyaus, who had taken the form of a swan

Lesser Troia : Troian province in the south of Gea

Leuctra : Large port at the end of the Gulf of Scylla (4B3)

Maidean clan : A Thracian tribe

Makedonia : Gean province in the southeast

Megara : Town in the Argolid, famous for its rug manufacture, and the home of a prestigious military academy (3A4)

Monce : Derogatory term for Monotheite

Monist : Shortened term for Monotheite

Monos : God of the Monotheite religion

Monotheite : Member of the Monotheite religion, which accepts the existence of only one God

moontide : A month

mu : The letter m and the symbol of Monos
Mykerenos : Mountainous Gean province in the northeast

Naupraxis : An imaginary battle used as a code between Diomedes and Naukles
news from the agora : Something new and surprising, so 'not news from the agora' is idiom for being well known
Northers : Inhabitants of Northerlands, a country on the north coast of the Pontis
nous : Intelligence, intellect

obol : Small coin. Six obols to a drachma

Panormus Mountains : Range constituting the northern part of the Agrianian massif (8A2, 8B2)
Peiros : Tributary of the Aegospotomai, rising in the Panormus Mountains (8A1, 8A2)
Pegasus : Mythical winged horse. To 'pass Pegasus' is proverbial for speed
phalanx : A general expression for any formed unit of heavy infantrymen
Phthia : Gean province in the northwest, famed for its heavy cavalry
Phthian (s) : Inhabitant of Phthia, with a reputation for being slow witted
plag : Short for plagiophylax, a unit of 128 cavalry troopers
plagiophylakes : Commander of a plagiophylax. Equivalent to a captain. Light green sash of office and bronze crossed spears and helmet brooch
polemarchos : The supreme military leader in the Early Troian Empire. A term later replaced by the title of autarch
polemarchy : The position of being the polemarchos
Pot : Diminutive of Aegospotomai, a broad river that runs north

from the Dryopian Forest to the Pontis, effectively cutting off the eastern third of the Empire (3C3, 3C4, 3C5, 7B1, 7C1)

Poteidan : Gean God of the Sea. Earthquakes were ascribed to his anger

Pylos : Town in Lakadaemon (7A2)

rabbit watch : Overnight guard duty

read the liver : Work out what is going to happen. From the use of studying the liver of sacrificed animals for divination

Rhodian red : Fine wine produced around the town of Rhodos in southern Lesser Troia

Rhodope : Free town on the north coast of Thrake notorious for its pirates

Rhodopians : Mountain range to north of the Vale of Tempe, in Gean Thrake, noted for impressive thunderstorms (4B3, 4C3)

rhomphaia : A two-handed sickle-shaped weapon with a fearsome reputation

rove : Archery competition in which ad hoc targets are designated during a walk

salpinx (es) : Gean trumpet for conveying orders

satrap : Term for the holder of a province, used in the Early or First Troian Empire

satyr : Minor woodland deity, ithyphallic and with the legs and horns of a goat. Of a lustful and sexually depraved nature

scuttle : Slang for a rapid retreat or flight

scuttle bag : Prepacked blanket bag containing the necessities for a rapid escape

Scythian shot : A tactic developed by nomadic horse archers of firing over their shoulder as retreating. Used to describe a final decisive comment as leaving

Sea of Grass : See Vale of Tempe

Selenes : Day of the week. Monday

se'ennight : A week

sigil : A personal or unit symbol emblazoned on shields, pennants etc.

Sirenoi : Mythical creatures who entice their victims with sweet song

Skamandrian Gates (Skam) : Pass leading to the Kodros valley in Agriania (see Sea of Grass map)

Soli : Fortified town in Lesser Troia. So far from the sea that 'a codfish in Soli Market' is proverbial for being dead (6B2)

Southway : Track that connects Gla with the Great East Road (see See of Grass map)

spatha : A long, straight sword

sphairai : Strips of ox-hide bound round the fists of boxers

stade (ia) : A distance of approximately 1/10 mile

staked goat : A tethered prey animal to attract predators. Idiomatically, to use somebody else's behaviour to draw attention from one's own designs

steader : Inhabitant of a steading

steading : Isolated homestead, particularly in the Vale of Tempe

strategion : Headquarters

strategos (oi) : A general. White sash of office and gold eagle carrying a snake brooch

studded sandals : Worn by prostitutes. The studs spell out 'Follow me.'

Stymphalian Marsh : Large, almost impenetrable tract of marshland at the mouth of the Granicus and lying between Thessalia and the Debateable Lands (6A2)

Stymphalians : Indigenous people inhabiting the Stymphalian Marsh

Styx : The river that separates the Underworld from the Land of the Living

swordmaster : An expert swordsman who teaches others. Often used to train troops in general

symposium (ia) : A social gathering for food, wine and conversation

syntagmarches : Commander of a syntagma, a unit of 256 hoplites known as a tag Equivalent to a major. Dark green sash of office and bronze laurel leaf wreath brooch

tag roll : A citadel's record of entries and exits

talent : An standard ingot of silver or gold. A silver talent is 7,000 drachmae, a golden talent 15,000

Taranis : The Keltian War God

Tartarus : The place in Hades where the worst sinners are punished

taxiarches : Commander of a taxis. Equivalent to a captain. Light green sash of office and bronze crossed spears and helmet brooch

taxis : A unit of 128 hoplites

telarches : Commander of a telos of 512 hoplites. Equivalent to a colonel. Orange sash of office and silver bear on laurel leaves brooch

Tempe : See Vale of Tempe

tet : Short for a tetrarchia of 64 men

tetrarches : Commander of a tetrarchia. Equivalent to a lieutenant. Yellow sash of office and bronze crossed spears brooch

tetrarchia : Unit of 64 men. Known as a tet

Thalassa : Troian province in north central Gea. Strong maritime tradition

Thebeaid, the : Gean province in the east

Thera : A mountain in the far southeast of Gea. 'From here to Thera' – proverbial for a long way (5B2)

Thessalia : Province of Western Gea, noted for its light cavalry

Thracian (s) : Inhabitant of or pertaining to Thrake

Thracian wars : Three wars in all. The Second Thracian War, 486-9, effectively ended in stalemate

Thrak : Slang term for a Thracian

Thrakos (oi) : Alternative, and more correct, term for a Thracian

tilia : A game in which stones are moved around a board in accord with a knucklebone throw, knocking off the opposing stones by landing on the same square, until all are safely 'home' to win

tisane : An infusion of herbs in hot water

Toros : A mythical hero who owned a magical sword

trireme without a keel : Idiom for an idea that lacks any evidential basis, a fanciful notion

Troia : Largest province of Gea

Troian : Inhabitant of or belonging to Troia

Troilus : Mythical hero betrayed by Cressid

Tyrrhenian shuffle : Moving a shield line to its left but keeping the hoplites facing the front

Vale of Tempe : Eastern area of Thebeaid, often known as the Sea of Grass ((8A1, 8A2, 8B1, 8B2)

willow bark : Used to make a hot infusion or tisane to act as pain relief

World Serpent : A mythological serpent that encircles the earth in the beliefs of the Old Northers

MAJOR CHARACTERS

Adrastus : Miltiades' secretary.
Aglaia : Daughter of Kalliste and Miltiades
Antenor : Eilarches at Gla, married to Thais
Antinous : Son of Kalliste and Miltiades
Aristogeiton (Ari) : Emperor of Troia 494-499. Son of Idomeneus II

Charmides : Satrap of Lesser Troia

Dianthe : Kalliste's slave girl
Diomedes (Dio) : Swordmaster to Miltiades, the holder of Gla. The name means 'counselled by Dyaus'
Dymas : Steader. Married to Phyllida. Father to Gorgias and Xanthos

Eurybiades (Eury) : Major-domo at Gla

Gelon : Officer at Gla

Gorgias (Gogo) : Son of Phyllida and Dymas

Icarius : Hyperetes at Gla

Kalliste (Kal) : Wife of Miltiades. The name means 'the fair one'

Laomedon : Warden of the Debateable Lands

Miltiades (Milt) : Holder of Gla. Married to Kalliste

Neritos : Agrianian kinglet

Pandarus : Famous swordmaster. Mentor of Diomedes
Patroclus : Aide to Miltiades
Pheidon : Messenger between Miltiades and Raxamenes
Phyllida (Phyll) : Steader. Married to Dymas. Mother to Gorgias and Xanthos

Radamanthus (Rad) : Miltiades' deuteros

Theophanes (Theo) : Commander of the Skamandrian Gates fort
Troilus III : Troian emperor. Son of Idomeneus II. Succeeded his brother Aristogeiton

Xanthos (Xan) : Son of Phyllida and Dymas

Zeuxis : Imperial swordmaster

MINOR CHARACTERS

Aella : Officer's wife at Gla
Aeropus : Officer at Gla
Agetos : Taxiarches with Diomedes at Caria
Anaxis : Polemarchos of Troia
Anchises : Commander of the Imperial Guard
Antikles : Satrap of Mykerenos
Antisthenes : Early strategos 307-373
Apollophanes : Troian strategos
Apollos : Leader of the Troian Imperial Council, and the power behind Emperor Aristogeiton
Aristamos : A Theban officer who bravely died stopping an incursion of Thracians along the Great East Road in the First Thracian War of 479
Aristandros : Holder of Leuctra
Aristobulos : Thalassan philosopher c. 360-424
Aster : Neighbour to Phyllida and Dymas

Blackwing : Diomedes' horse
Bousaeus : Makedonian philosopher 453-516

Charopos : Imperial spymaster
Charos : Chief clerk at Gla
Chileos : Neritos's son
Chromius : Thessalian tragic dramatist 461-511
Cybele : Brothel madam in Glapolis

Diodoros : Satrap of Makedonia
Dmetor : Commander of a taxis at Caria
Dorian : Holder of Ilios
Doris : Hetaeros or high-class prostitute, at Cybele's
Dorithea : Officer's wife at Gla

Fat Delia : Tavern owner in Glapolis

Hebe : Gorgias's girlfriend
Helena : Officer's wife at Gla
Herodian : Neighbour of Phyllida and Dymas

Icarion : Officer at Gla
Idomeneus I : Troian emperor, ruled 471-476
Ilus : Officer at Gla
Inachos : Satrap of Lakadaemon
Iocaste : Officer's wife at Gla
Isodemos : Satrap of Thalassa

Kerberos : Kalliste's mastiff
Kymon : Troian philosopher 294-360

Leodes : Miltiades' bodyguard
Lethos : Satrap of Korinthia

Linus : Theophanes' deuteros at the Skamandrian Gates fort
Lycidas : Satrap of Thessalia

Maro : Officer of the Guard at the Imperial Palace
Melissa : Kalliste's slave woman
Menester : Hoplite in Gla
Merope : Daughter of an officer at Gla
Mikkos : Satrap of Phthia
Misenus : Stable owner in Glapolis
Monomachus : Eilarches with Diomedes at Caria
Mopsus : Name adopted by Adrastus when visiting Cybele's

Naukles : Friend of Diomedes in Leuctra
Nisos : Monotheist in the Imperial Guard

Paleius : Eretrian philosopher 461-502
Parmenio : Troian strategos
Peri : Groom at Gla
Perimedes : Diomedes' grandfather
Periphetes : Magistrate in Glapolis responsible for 'civilian' policing
Philomena : Officer's wife at Gla. Friend of Kalliste
Philon : Recruit at Gla
Podargos : Retired hyperetes running a wine shop in Ilios
Priam : Founder of Priamid line of early Troian Emperors. Ruled 451-471
Priskos : Officer of the Guard at Gla
Pyrrhus : Son of Aglaia and grandson of Kalliste

Raxamenes : Satrap of the Thebeaid

Sofia : Miltiades' intended bride
Stratios : Local thug in Glapolis

Tenebros : Hoplite at the Skamandrian Gates fort
Tereus : Powerful Thracian war chief in the Rhodopians
Thais : Antenor's wife at Gla. Friend of Kalliste.
Theagenes : Officer at Gla. A Monotheite
Theopompus : Owner of an eating establishment in Glapolis
Tiro : Junior officer at Gla
Tithonius : Officer at Gla

Xen : Clerk in the bureau at Gla
Xeno : Ektatos at Gla

Zagos : Thracian chieftain in Gean Thrake
Zagreus : A Thracian God
Zarzed : Agrianian kinglet

MEASUREMENT

Time:
Each night and each day are divided into ten dekates each, so there are twenty dekates in a day and they vary in length according to the seasons. They are roughly equivalent to hours. A hekate is theoretically the hundredth part of a dekate and therefore around three quarters of a minute. Practically, it is taken as a hundred heartbeats. A se'ennight is pretty obviously a week and a moontide a month.

Length:
Mostly intuitive, paces and finger lengths, but a stade (plural stadia) is about one tenth of a mile.

Money:
Seven obols to a drachma.
One hundred drachmae to a mina.
A silver talent is 7,000 drachmae.
A golden talent 15,000.

Days of the week:

Selenes	Monday
Areos	Tuesday
Hermou	Wednesday
Dios	Thursday
Aphrodites	Friday
Kronou	Saturday
Heliou	Sunday

Months of the year:

Poseidion	December 22 – January 20
Gamelion	January 21 – February 19
Anthesterion	February 20 – March 21
Elaphebolion	March 22 – April 20
Mounichion	April 21 – May 20
Thargelion	May 21 – June 19
Intercalary Days	June 20 – June 24
Skirophorion	June 25 – July 24
Hekatonbaion	July 25 – August 23
Metageitrion	August 24 – September 22
Boedromion	September 23 – October 22
Pyanopsion	October 23 – November 21
Maimakterion	November 22 – December 21

Ranks in the Gean Army

Men	Arm	Rank	Modern equivalent	Unit name	Modern equivalent
		Hegemones:	**Commissioned Officers:**		
	all	strategarch	field marshal	stratia	army
	all	strategos	general	keras	division/corps
	all	chiliarches	brigadier	meros	brigade
1024	infantry	phalangarches	colonel	phalanx	regiment
1024	cavalry	hipparches	colonel	hipparchia (hip)	regiment
512	all	telarches	lieutenant col	telos	battalion
256	infantry	syntagmarches	major	syntagma (tag)	battalion
256	cavalry	eilarches	major	eile	battalion
256	light infantry	hekatonarches	major	hekatonarchia (hekaton)	battalion
128	infantry	taxiarches	captain	taxis	company
128	cavalry	plagiophylakes	captain	plagiophylax (plag)	troop
64	all	tetrarches	lieutenant	tetrarchia (tet)	platoon
		Ektatoi:	**NCOs:**		
64	all	hyperetes	company sgt major	tetrarchia (tet)	platoon
32	all	dilochagos	sergeant major	dilochos	platoon
16	all	lochagos	sergeant	lochos	squad
8	all	hemilochagos	corporal	hemilochion	section

The commander of the armed forces was called the polemarchos in the Early Gean Army, but was later known as the autarch.

Commands in the navy:
Keulestes : Lighter ships such as biremes or cargo ships
Trierarches : Triremes
Kataphractarches : Heavier ships such as hexeres
Thalassarches : A squadron of vessels
Navarches : The equivalent of a strategos i.e. an admiral

Map of the Provinces of Gea.

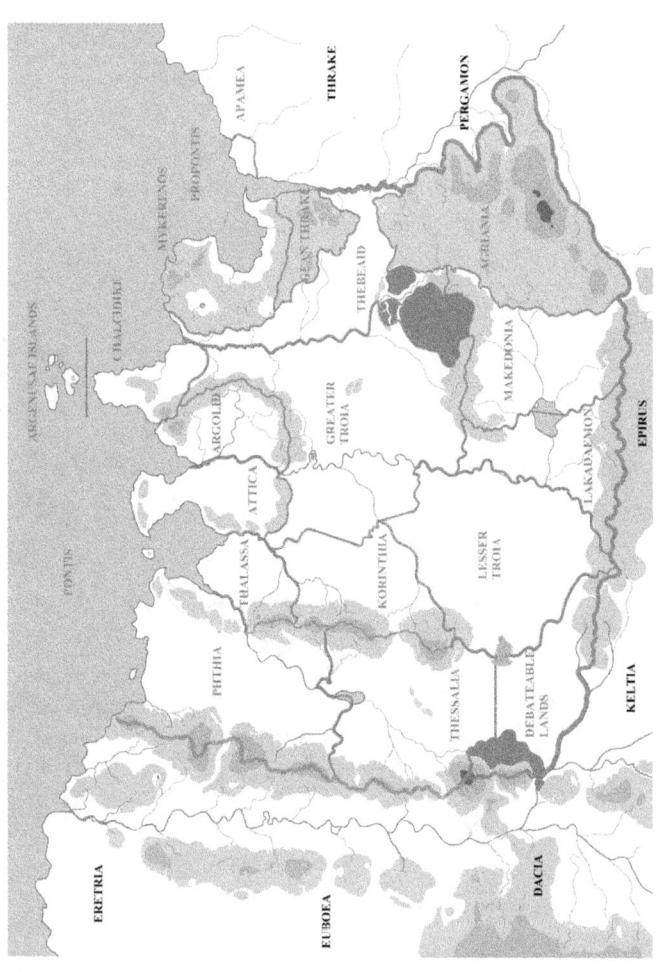

Map of the Sea of Grass.

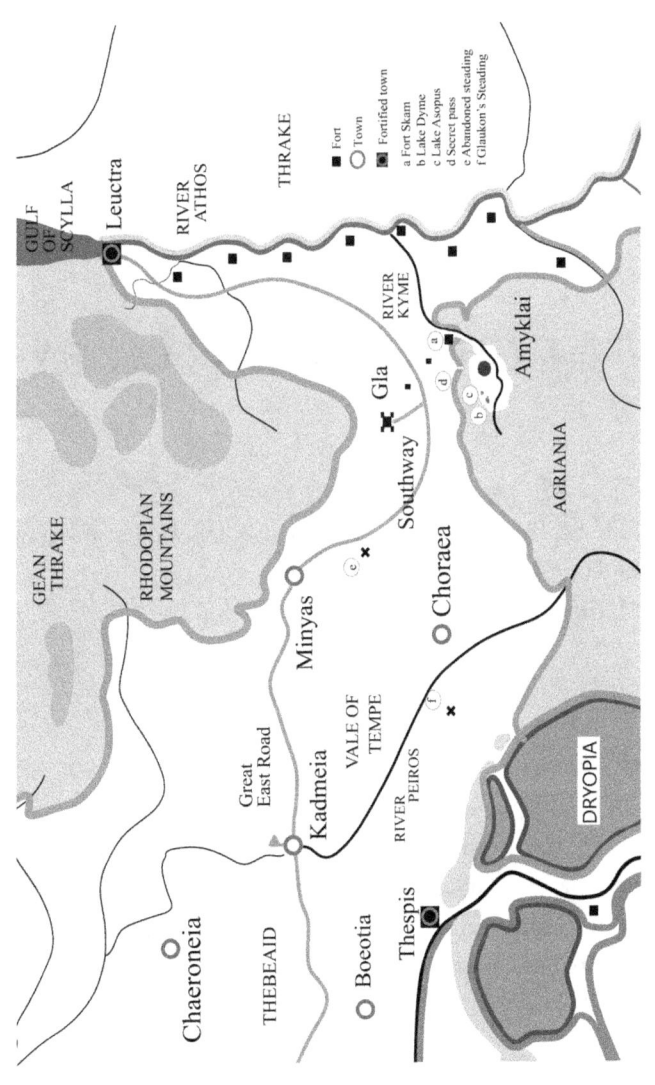

THE CHRONICLES OF GEA

None So Blind has been the first of a series of related but standalone novels in this setting.

The others, in chronological order will be:

What Dreams May Come.

Troilus, the grandson of Kal (None So Blind), sees his town razed to the ground and all the inhabitants slaughtered. He swears revenge and finds that the trauma has swept all pity and warmth from his makeup. He finds himself caught up in the turmoil of the rebellion that erupts after the massacre. It is a long way back.

When First We Practise.

Eugenia, the niece of the new, tyrannical Emperor observes a battle against the rebels. It does not turn out as foreseen. She decides to manipulate her captor, Telamon, to regain her freedom, but manipulation is a two-edged sword.

The Key.

The rebels' advance is stopped by the impregnable fortress of Gla. It needs to be unlocked. Perhaps Thallia, the daughter of its commander, might prove to be the key? Harpalycus, the Mykerenaean military commander (What Dreams May Come, When First We Practise) attempts to use her but unlocks far more than he planned. She is more important than is realised and becomes a helpless pawn in dangerous power plays.

The Initiate.

The fifth book is set in a subsequent civil war. Andro, the son of Xanthos (None So Blind, What Dreams May Come) is conscripted and his file members discover that he is a virgin. Regarding this as bad luck they take him to a high-class brothel. Here he is entranced by a young prostitute called Theodosia, but believes that she has humiliated him. In the subsequent battle his phalanx is broken and he runs away. He hides deep in the surrounding woodland, only to find a fleeing and desperate Theodosia with a deadly secret to conceal. To what extent are his feelings genuine? Or hers?

The White Prince.

In yet another struggle for hegemony in the tortured land of Gea, the sixth book finds the young Belisarius, an illegitimate member of a royal family, becoming the effective new emperor after his abduction of a princess and a subsequent forced marriage to create an alliance. Although Belisarius falls for the princess, Iphigenia, the great niece of Thallia (The Key), she does not respond, and he is faced with the deadly threat of the Dokari Horse Lords who are about to invade Gea.

Shadow Wolf.

A new emperor attempts to conquer the neighbouring land of Keltia. His chief of scouts, Hermolycus (son of Andro (The Initiate)), warns the inept commander of impending danger, but is not listened to. He is captured, but Kern, an old ally from the fight against the Dokarians, frees him on the agreement that he will protect his daughter, Branwen, against the threat of the insulted and humiliated king's son. But Branwen finds herself torn in two directions and Lycus has to face the ultimate test of his love for her.

Beholder's Eye.

The eighth book follows immediately after the seventh. Pyrrhus, the son of Troilus (What Dreams May Come), desperately defending Gea against a counter invasion following a massive defeat, arrives at a waystation run by a young woman whose face has been smashed by the Dokari. He becomes friendly and, after her waystation is destroyed, offers her the post of housemistress at his villa. There she is accused of embezzlement and murder, but Pyrrhus is determined to find the truth.

Huntress.

Bran (Shadow Wolf) becomes a bounty hunter. She takes on a mission to find the son of a previous king, Belisarius (The White Prince), now seen as a threat to the youthful, new emperor. A young trainee is taken along, and Bran and she are mutually attracted. Then they find Belisarius's son and Bran is faced with a dreadful decision for the second time.

The Epigoni.

The tenth and final novel is a sequel to Huntress. After escaping from Thrace, Bran (Huntress) and Kiza, the son of a previous emperor, Belisarius (The White Prince), are still being hunted by the Imperial Watch. Individuals linked to characters in all the earlier books come together to stop the increasingly out of control young Emperor, Lysander.

The opening sections of all these novels can be downloaded and read at harpalycus.com

www.ingramcontent.com/pod-product-compliance
Lightning Source LLC
LaVergne TN
LVHW011943060526
838201LV00061B/4193